THE DANISH KING'S ENEMY

THE EARLS OF MERCIA
BOOK TWO

MJ PORTER

MJ PUBLISHING

Cover design by M J Porter
Cover image by Photo 77474087 © Nejron - Dreamstime.com

ISBN: 9781914332012 (ebook)
ISBN: 9781072955818 (paperback)

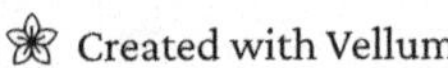

CONTENTS

For my history teachers and lecturers for their passion and for academic historians everywhere, who spend their lives producing a dry and dusty tome filled with knowledge that they hope someone, one day, will appreciate for its true value. Today might just be your lucky day! Special mention for Miss Dyson, history teacher, for her easy acceptance of my late burgeoning passion for all things Elizabethan, and for Dr Maund, history lecturer, for inspiring me with her passion for the Anglo-Saxons, the early Welsh kingdoms and the Vikings.

THE STORY SO FAR...

Leofwine is the ealdorman of the Hwicce (a part of Mercia) at the beginning of the eleventh-century in England. Wounded in an attack led by King Swein of Denmark in Shetland five years ago, Leofwine has no vision in his left eye, and uses a hound to guide his steps. Leofwine's wife, a prominent member of the Hwiccan nobility, gives legitimacy to his governance.

King Æthelred, initially sceptical of Leofwine's abilities, has come to rely on his ealdorman, and took his advice in waging war on the kingdom of Strathclyde in AD1000 as a step to preventing further Viking Raider attacks on England.

The Danish King's Enemy begins with Leofwine still in the north of England, the battle having occurred only the day before.

1

AD1000

Leofwine sat on his camp chair, feet propped on Hunter lying at his feet. Mud and grime still streaked his face and he'd not removed any of his fighting equipment apart from his helm, which lay discarded upside down on the floor.

Rain dripped incessantly outside, a steady torrent that pounded in his head in time to his over fast heartbeat. His eyes were shut as he reclined on the chair, paying negligible regard to its precarious position. On any other day, he might have cared that he was only a dog's favour from falling on his arse on the mud-splattered flooring. Not today.

But Leofwine didn't sleep, instead seeing every image of the recent battle before him, and every possible outcome of the future that had just been snatched from him. He knew he needed to face his king, inform him of the words of Swein of Denmark, and usually, he would have sprung smartly to attention.

Not now, though. His king didn't realise how personal the threat to Leofwine was. The words may well have been that Swein of Denmark was coming for England. However, the audience had been Leofwine, and that meant the threat was explicitly applied to him.

They'd stumbled back into camp, bone-weary and dripping wet from the heavy shower that had covered them only a short distance away. It had drenched them instantly, as it seemed could only happen in the mountainous region of the north of England.

Wulfstan had barely been sitting in his horse's saddle as he passed in and out of consciousness with the pain of his wound.

Leofwine felt sick, just watching Wulfstan. A cold fear had overcome him as he'd watched his friend and surrogate father fade from his typical hale colouring to a deathly pale blue as if the very life was seeping from him with each plodding step of the tired and similarly drenched horse.

Leofwine had insisted on Wulfstan being carried to his tent and stripped of his filthy, dirty clothing before being laid on his camp bed as soon as they'd stumbled into their previous day's camp. Those who'd not heard the stray horseman's message were jubilant and had joyfully skipped to their shelters, unheeding of the rain, muck and blood that stained them.

The healer had been waiting expectantly for them and had cleaned and bound the shoulder wound as Wulfstan had uttered faint protestations, only falling into deep unconsciousness when the pain had engulfed him.

Wulfstan's snores now filled the small space of the dubious shelter provided by the canvas above their heads, and rather than being annoyed at the monotonous drone, Leofwine was finding it comforting. Wulfstan's echoing snores coupled with the drumming rain made the tent feel noisy and lived in, and was a valiant effort to distract him from his unsettling thoughts regarding the battle, Swein of Denmark and his king.

The healer had spoken words of reassurance to Leofwine regarding Wulfstan's full recovery, but all the same, he'd had the camp priest come and perform rites for his friend.

It had made him ill to consider his commander was dying, but he knew he needed to face the possibility. The healer had looked at him in disbelief at the words of the priest and that more than anything else had made Leofwine think he might have overreacted, and his friend would be well after all.

Outside the tent, the camp had turned quiet and strangely subdued. His men had retired to their shared tents to sleep off the battle and mourn those they'd lost. There was little point in doing anything else. While the rain fell as heavily as it did anyone stepping outside was soaked instantaneously. It felt a little surreal: to go from the heat and intensity of battle to a rain-induced silence. He could hear nothing other than Wulfstan's heavy snores and his own slightly too-fast breathing.

Leofwine craved the calm of sleep but found it wouldn't come, even with the aid of a bit too much mead. He'd tried thinking of Æthelflæd, knowing that she usually brought peace to his mind, but that didn't do the trick either. If anything, it made it worse because it reminded him of his two young boys and his baby growing even now inside her.

He idly wondered if this one would be a boy or a girl. Not that it mattered, but he thought his wife would like a girl, someone to teach how to run a house and keep the men in check and someone to buy ribbons and dress in beautiful clothing.

Still, Leofwine's heart raced, and his head pounded with the falling rain. He knew what he needed to do. He needed to talk to someone and speak out loud the fears that were running through his head. Usually, he'd have turned to Wulfstan, but he was incapacitated and Horic, his next choice, was overseeing the men, allowing them to drown their sorrows or their triumph without getting out of hand.

Leofwine knew he should be with him, but Horic had insisted he stay and watch Wulfstan. Leofwine had a suspicion that his man knew how hard it would be to smile and join in the rejoicing or the grieving. He was grateful for his insight.

There was only one option available to him, and that was to seek the king. He hesitated, though. He didn't want to face his wrath just yet. Pulling the gifted wolf pelt nearer to his chin, Leofwine closed his eye and inhaled deeply of the slightly musty smell that being carried around in a travel pack had imbued the fur with. It was an almost pleasant smell, reminding him of his journey across the sea to the Shetlands, with a man now long since dead, who'd remembered him from across the waves.

Leofwine wondered whether that memory had been one of guilt or fondness. Had lord Olaf blamed himself for the injury inflicted by Swein on Leofwine? Or had Olaf given it no thought at all?

Leofwine decided that guilt must have guided lord Olaf's actions – why else send the scribe and the fur to a man he'd little known, and possibly, little regarded. Craving some warmth, Leofwine unwound the fur from its tight bundle, a loud clatter rattling through the tent. Leofwine looked down to the wet floor, amazement on his face.

Hunter eyed him with annoyance for his noise, but as he reached down to scoop up the item that had fallen there, he could hardly believe what he was seeing. How had Olaf of Norway even known the golden cross, with its rubies, had once belonged to him – and to his father before him?

Leofwine felt humbled once more by the friendship he'd not realised he'd shared with the man. His hand splayed over the cross, an attempt at comfort despite his fears, a stray moment of wellbeing to overlay his deep-seated worries.

The cross wasn't changed at all, if anything, shining brighter than it ever had done. Leofwine was amazed, staring at the intricate heavy gold and the rubies that marked its four arms. His eyes feasted on the glory of the workmanship and the pride his father had felt in his family's position and wealth.

A commotion at the door to his tent startled him and sent Hunter scurrying forward, upending him as he'd feared, on the floor, the chair a twisted tangle beneath him, the cross forgotten about as it once more clanged to the floor.

Hunter turned to look at him questioningly not fully understanding what had happened to make him fall on the ground. Leofwine shrugged and pulled himself to his feet, his upper arms and thighs tweaking in pain from the heavy usage they'd taken earlier.

Hunter slipped through the partially opened door outside into the rain and returned straight away, her short coat dripping with moisture. He didn't blame her. Leofwine strode a few paces forward and released more toggles on the inside of the door. He could vaguely make out voices and wondered who was there.

Swinging the fabric door wide, Leofwine caught a whiff in his nostrils of the goose grease rubbed into the canvas and gagged slightly. It might keep his tent dry, but the smell was overpowering, especially in the damp heat of the rainstorm.

The camp appeared quiet all around him, but then he realised, through the low-lying clouds and thick fog, that someone was standing there: the king's uncle, Ordulf.

He too still wore his battle equipment and bowed deeply to Leofwine, his greying hair dulled by the rain, and crushed from where he'd been wearing his helm.

"Lord Leofwine, I'm sorry to disturb you, but the king would like to see you ... if it's convenient?"

There was a question in the words, but too slight for the instructions not to instantly obeyed.

"Of course, of course, I'll come straight away. Let me just call for someone to watch over Wulfstan." Leofwine's voice was a little crackly from lack of use. He turned back into the tent to consider picking up the cross, returned to him after so many years, but he shrugged the thought aside; no one would find it where it lay hidden in the mud beneath the camp bed.

"Wulfstan? Your commander?" Ordulf queried, trying to peer over Leofwine's shoulder.

"Yes, he took a nasty injury, although the healer assures me it'll heal well and quickly," Leofwine replied, busily righting the upended stool.

"I'm pleased to hear it. He's a talented warrior."

"Yes – and a fine friend."

Ordulf didn't respond to his almost whispered reply, instead standing just inside the open doorway to keep out of the incessant downpour.

While Ordulf stood and waited, Leofwine walked to the nearest tent, splashing through the rapidly-forming puddles, and called Oscetel to him, explaining what was needed. The man looked as exhausted as Leofwine felt, but looking from the figure of the king's son to his own lord, he obeyed the request to sit with Wulfstan without question for which Leofwine was grateful.

Stamping through the escalating mud was less than pleasant as they made their way towards the king's section of the camp. Ordulf didn't speak, and Leofwine was grateful for Hunter at his side, as she skilfully manoeuvred them around tent posts and abandoned equipment, hidden from his partial sight by the gloom of the rain, and the low clouds.

Leofwine assumed the king wanted to know who the messenger was and what they'd wanted, but he wasn't sure. Perhaps he simply wanted him to pray with him, as he'd asked earlier. Ordulf gave nothing away with his body language, and Leofwine tasted sour bile in his mead-infused mouth. He didn't know if he should be eager to see his king, or reticent.

When the pair arrived at the king's tent, Leofwine could clearly make out the voice of the king's priest raised in prayer, and immediately found comfort in the words. It was a familiar and calming sound.

Ordulf ushered him inside the tent, and they both sank to their knees where a piece of stray tent material had been laid down to shield them and the king from the water pooling in every available dip of the uneven ground, trickling beneath the walls of the canvas.

The king didn't look up from his prayers, and neither did the priest. Leofwine listened to his gradually slowing heartbeat as the familiar words spoken by the priest swept over him.

He, his king and his king's uncle, stayed kneeling for the entire length of the Mass, as the priest praised their lord and offered long prayers of thanks for their victory. Leofwine was consoled by the words of the holy man and relaxed for the first time since he'd been met by Finn and heard the unwelcome news he carried.

The pounding of the rain eased into background noise, and when the words of the holy man finally died away, and Leofwine opened his eyes, he was surprised to see that a meal had been brought into the tent and laid out on the small camp table. Darkness had fallen too, meaning candles and lamps had been lit.

As soon as the soft voice of the priest faded away, Ordulf stood quickly, while a younger version of himself, no doubt his son, served them all in the position of a squire. Æthelred acknowledged the arrival of his uncle as he stood and then sat down on a camp stool close to where the food had been laid.

Æthelred gestured for his uncle and Leofwine to join him on the two other stools, and Leofwine hobbled a little painfully over towards the offered seat. He'd been kneeling for so long that his battle-weary muscles had stiffened, and he reached downwards for Hunter to steady himself on the uneven ground.

His king did him the courtesy of not noticing his stumbling as he waved the priest away to other duties and drank deeply from a small drinking horn. He passed it to his uncle, who then offered it to Leofwine. He took a small sip of the dark red liquid and tasted a wine from the southern vineries, delicately spiced and warmed a little to combat the chilly air.

The king sat with a smile on his face as he helped himself to the small selection of meats and loaves of bread. Leofwine assumed that they'd been provided by the reeve of Chester's cooks, as there was no way to roast the fine meats and cook the dark bread in the campfires.

Leofwine chose some finely sliced beef and a large piece of bread and ate quickly and with precise movements. He was suddenly starving but mindful of his host he curbed his hunger.

A small brazier burnt a little petulantly to the far side of the tent sending out tantalising fingers of warmth which only served to remind Leofwine of just how wet he was. He would have liked nothing better than to slink back to his tent, check on Wulfstan and change his clothes, but it was clear that the king had something on his mind, or he wouldn't have called only Leofwine to him, or sent his uncle away.

Leofwine feared he knew that somehow the king had learnt about his visitor and that he was sitting patiently, waiting for the confession. Leofwine felt uncomfortable with the knowledge and knew that he needed to speak first, even if it wasn't the way he wished this day to be remembered.

The king sat pensively. His clothes had long been changed, and he was clearly not suffering from the discomfort of wet and sticky clothing. He was well dressed in a vibrant tunic, finely embroidered around its edges in an interlocking curving design. The gold thread caught the light of the candles and dazzled Leofwine's tired and weary eye.

"My king, I fear ..." Leofwine finally uttered softly.

"I know of what you speak already. Don't worry my friend. The messenger carried a message for me as well, and I waylaid him before he could get to you. I assume you have seen to his needs." The king's tone was querying and held no trace of anger or annoyance. Leofwine was temporarily stumped, and it took him a moment longer than usual to process the words.

"Yes, yes, of course. Finn is with the men from my household troop. I think he thinks he's staying there as well." Leofwine spoke with a smile on his frozen face.

Finn had slunk inside the tent that housed Horic and his cronies, quickly finding the furthest spot from the tent opening to lie down his bag of possessions with a wary glance toward Leofwine that had almost dared him to tell him to move.

Leofwine had left him alone, too concerned with how Wulfstan was faring in his tent to worry about the rest of Olaf's message concerning the man. Perhaps he could find space for a scribe in his household after all.

"Did Finn inform you of Swein's words?" Leofwine asked hesitantly, wanting to be sure that his king knew everything.

"Regarding England? Yes, he did."

"Doesn't that concern you?"

The king looked at him searchingly now, and Leofwine felt suddenly exposed, as though his king could see all his fears etched plainly on his person.

"Well, it should, I know. However, before I left the South, I was approached by another, and I'm finding it difficult to reconcile what the two men are saying."

"Another, My lord King?" Leofwine was unaware of all the events that happened in Winchester, despite his close ties and influential position.

"Yes, I've been contacted by Pallig, Swein's brother by marriage through his sister. He's anxious to swear his allegiance to me, and I was going to offer him an ealdordom. Now, I'm unsure."

"An ealdordom, My Lord King? Why would you offer a man you barely know such a position?" Leofwine was astounded by the king's admission. Yes, England needed more ealdormen, but really it was high time that the king's oldest son was considered rather than other men, especially a Danish man. Especially a Danish man married to the Danish king's sister. The man who wanted Leofwine dead.

"I'd foolishly thought it would endear me to Swein of Denmark. He's a man I don't wish to entangle myself with, and I assumed this was an attempt at an alliance." Æthelred spoke forcefully, stressing his words, as though trying to make Leofwine believe what he said.

"He's a king and a warrior, and he knows his way around my lands almost as well as I do. It's a blow that he's killed lord Olaf. What little of good I can say about lord Olaf, he did at least give his word that he'd stay away and then do so. He has my respect for that, and for beginning the spread of Christianity amongst his people. All kings should further the spread of Christianity."

"What do you plan to do now?" Leofwine was intrigued and also dismayed. But, he couldn't deny that an alliance with Swein of Denmark might well be the peaceful solution that England and her king needed. Perhaps, after all, Finn's message was old, and Swein had since changed his intentions toward England.

"I've not yet reconsidered my plans, or given it the thought it deserves. Luckily, I've not given any overtures of friendship yet. And you, My Lord, what do you plan to do with the wolf still baying for your blood?"

Leofwine grimaced at the brutal voicing of his fears.

"I don't know either. I'll need to give it as much thought as you do regarding Pallig."

The king laughed at Leofwine's rueful tone.

"Indeed. I suggest we both give it some consideration and then discuss it again in a few days. I'd like you to know that for my part in your feud with the man, I'm sorry. I didn't consider that you'd cross the path of another warlord on the journey north, and certainly not the king of Denmark when I sent you away with Olaf all those years ago."

"Such a personal vendetta against you must be a constant worry. Swein may well hate me, but he hates me as a figurehead, not personally. It's a small consolation denied you."

"In the meantime, I still think we've accomplished something good and needed here. It feels right to have defeated the king of Strathclyde, Owain, even if we've not killed him. We must, however, press the advantage. We'll not be withdrawing yet."

"Are we to pursue the king back to Strathclyde?"

"No, we're to claim our land back and lay waste the border region. That should act as a deterrent to the bastard. Your men and my household troops will advance again tomorrow and carry out my orders. You and lord Ordulf will be the commanders."

"And you?"

"I'll stay here and consolidate the advantage. I've plans for my ship army when I can communicate with them in this awful weather, and I also intend to survey the land here."

"As you wish, I'll seek out Ordulf at first light."

"Excellent, and now I'll let you return to your men. I hope that Wulfstan recovers well, and please tell him that if he's able, I'll have a task for him while you're gone."

2

AD1000

Leofwine walked back to his tent with the rain still falling heavily. Soft tendrils of mist rose from the wet ground as the temperature climbed to an uncomfortably sticky level.

The burning cooking fires smoked incessantly, adding to the heat and the mist, and men called to each other as they stood in the rain, shields used to keep the water from their heads as they waited for food or cooked it. It was a haunting reminder of the use the shields had been put to earlier.

Leofwine ducked inside his tent and was instantly met by the less than gentle snores of Wulfstan, joined by Oscetel, who'd managed to fall asleep on the camp stool, his head resting on the taut canvas of the tent. Leofwine couldn't foresee the arrangement lasting too much longer.

Hunter quickly lay obediently beside the camp bed and looked at him reproachfully as if it were his fault she'd been forced outside in the downpour. He thanked her, and she closed her eyes and quickly fell asleep, her snores joining those of Wulfstan and Oscetel.

Leofwine checked Wulfstan and once assured that his friend slept naturally he collapsed back onto the campstool he'd been roused from by the king's call. It was still uncomfortable, worsened by his wet clothes unchanged from the battlefield. He now thought there was little point in changing as he was going back into battle the next day. He also doubted that his spare clothes were any drier than those he wore as they'd spent a day in a saddlebag and then been dragged inside his damp tent.

The canvas was doing an excellent job of keeping the rain from his head, but there was still water seeping in through some of the larger holes in the seams. He bent to retrieve his discarded golden cross and placed it amongst his possessions, ready for his departure the next day.

He was cold, wet and frustrated by the news Finn had brought him about Swein of Denmark, while at the same time elated to have his family cross back. He was also worried about his friend and far from home. He couldn't imagine that he'd possibly sleep, and yet somehow, no sooner had he sat and made himself as comfortable as possible than his snores joined those of Wulfstan, Oscetel and Hunter's. It was only when Wulfstan stirred in the night that Leofwine's rest was disturbed.

Wulfstan petulantly demanded to know why Leofwine was not in his bed, as soon as he woke, and why he was, and immediately started to berate him. Even colder and wetter than before, Leofwine snapped at Wulfstan, causing the older man to cease his moaning, see quickly to his need for water and return to sleep meek as a newborn baby.

Leofwine's head felt fuzzy and his eyes burnt with tiredness, but he noticed that Oscetel was gone from his place in the tent, and Leofwine hoped he found somewhere more comfortable to spend the night.

Dawn was far off, and Leofwine could barely see in the grey light that infected the tent. The brazier had long burnt low, and he was shivering uncontrollably. Knowing that sleep was a thing of the past, he quickly found his unworn clothes and peeled the clammy ones from his body.

Leofwine made so much noise in the confined space, bumping into every piece of furniture in the tent, that the sound of others stirring in the tent next to him could be heard. He felt grim satisfaction knowing that others would be as muddle-headed as he when they rode out to pursue the enemy later that day.

Hunter glared at him in the slight light from the feebly smoking brazier, and Leofwine remembered that he'd not fed her when he'd returned the night before. He wasn't surprised that she scowled at him.

From outside his tent, Leofwine heard men calling softly to themselves and smelt the aroma of pottage wafting on the damp air. As unappealing as camp rations were, his stomach rumbled, and Hunter cast him a look of barely veiled disbelief as she stalked from the tent. Leofwine followed behind, his intention to inform Horic of the plans for the day.

Leofwine squelched through the sticky mud mindful of where he placed his feet, pleased that the rain had finally ceased. Mist curled around the tents and the men, lending the early morning a spectral feel as thin tendrils of the sun's rays wove in and out of the temporary camp.

Within his tent, Horic was snoring loudly as a few of the men tumbled from their low camp beds, groaning and moaning at the noise coming from Horic's wide-open mouth. Leofwine stifled a smile of wry amusement and let Hunter do her work of waking the man by licking the side of his face. Hunter was, for an unknown reason, inordinately fond of the huge man.

With a swot of his large arm on the dog's nose that set his silver armbands jangling, Horic spluttered awake, a glare of outrage on his face. He wasn't quite as keen on Hunter when she woke him in such a manner. He abruptly stood when he saw that Leofwine accompanied the dog, and muttered an apology, grimacing as he stood on his own clearly aching legs.

"We've orders from the king to ride out again today with lord Ordulf and his men. Can you ready the men and ensure we have enough supplies for three days? The king is staying here, but we've some unfinished business in the north."

Horic's face lit with joy at the thought of felling more of his enemy, his years with lord Olaf as a Raider failing to fulfil his desire to kill. His movements quickly became more alert as he reached for his cloak that had been discarded on his bed.

"I look forward to it," Horic quipped, deigning to stroke the inquisitive head of Hunter who was looking at him expectantly. Leofwine grunted in agreement and stepped from the tent. He felt light-headed. He needed to eat.

By the time the sun had fully risen, Leofwine and his men were assembled and ready to move out. A messenger had sought out Leofwine and informed him that Ordulf and his men would be prepared with the light. They were taking no supply wagons with them and instead formed up as a highly mobile, mounted force, with spare mounts carrying what else was needed.

Leofwine had woken Wulfstan and informed him of what was happening. Wulfstan had protested feebly that he must accompany his lord. Only when Leofwine had mentioned that the king had a chore for him, had he subsided into silence.

Wulfstan looked far better than the night before, but Leofwine didn't like to leave him. He considered ordering Hunter to stay with Wulfstan but realised that then both would be miserable. In the end, Leofwine walked briskly away from Wulfstan, convincing himself that all would be well and ignoring the stabbing feeling of foreboding in his chest.

The king stepped from his tent. He looked a little the worse for wear after his day of battle yesterday, but Leofwine could see the glow of triumph that suffused him.

"Ride north," the king ordered his warriors. "For no more than a full day and a half. Hunt down the retreating enemy, and establish England as masters of these lands." The words were greeted with a roar of approval and Leofwine allowed a huge smile to grace his face, a mirror of the king's own, and the same on each and every face of the men who'd been ordered to continue the fight.

Just before the force road out, the king called to Leofwine. "Your man, he's well?"

Leofwine was taken aback that Æthelred had remembered before recalling that he'd mentioned he had a role for Wulfstan.

"He slept, my lord king, lucky sod. I'd say another day in bed, and he'll be well enough. I'd feared for him and sent for the priest, much to the disgust of the healer."

Æthelred smiled tightly at the words.

"It's always best to be prepared. I'll ensure the healer and the priest check on Wulfstan during your absence."

"With thanks, my lord king."

"It's only right that I ensure the man's health while you're away. Now, to the north, and happy hunting," Æthelred's face only twisted slightly at the words, an indication that he didn't relish the thought of the deaths of more men at his hands, although it was needed all the same.

3
AD1000

It took less time than Leofwine remembered to reach the site of the battle the day before. He noticed with satisfaction that the bodies had all been buried, only the mess of disturbed earth showing where a mass grave had been dug on the flatter land.

Sticky, red mud covered the sides of the rise he'd fought his way up during the battle, the only true testament to the slaughter that had taken place there, footprints easy to make out in the muck and filth.

Hunter stood stoically by his side, unhappy with the after-smells of the battle as Leofwine took a long moment to remember his friend who'd lost his life here.

Brithelm's death had not thoroughly punctured his consciousness, but on this spot, the reality hit him and anguish temporarily stole his speech. Around him, he noticed Horic and Oscetel also had their heads bowed in memory as they sat on their mounts.

Ordulf's men rode at the front of their force, acting as a scouting party, although Leofwine kept his eyes firmly fixed on the king's uncle. Abruptly, Leofwine noticed that all wasn't right with Ordulf's force and called for all his men to be ready to dismount and arm themselves if necessary.

Horic and Oscetel raced forward to determine the cause of the commotion, only to return quickly with reassuring grins on their faces, and Leofwine relaxed a little in his saddle and signaling for the rest of his men to be less alert.

"It's only Ealdorman Ælfhelm and his men. They've had the same thought as the king and are running a sweep of the area. Come; he and Ordulf are discussing tactics." Horic urged Leofwine forward, and he nudged his sturdy horse to where he could see a gathering of men.

Leofwine was too far away to make out their facial expressions but was quickly greeted by the joyful voices of Ordulf and Ælfhelm's men raised in a cacophony of loud laughter. To the side of them, Ælfhelm and Ordulf were in conference.

Ælfhelm's vast bulk looked as flushed with triumph as the king had earlier and he was enjoying having the ear of the king's uncle to himself. He turned and greeted Leofwine with a respectful nod of his bearded face, devoid of his helm, although not for long, as his hair was crushed close to his skull, as he continued to speak.

Leofwine didn't disrupt the flow of the conversation by talking, merely inclined his head respectfully to his fellow ealdorman. They'd reached an accord over the years they'd known each other. They too often shared similar concerns in the ancient Mercian lands to allow any potential disagreements to escalate, and of course, Ealdorman Ælfhelm's sons were much in favour with the queen dowager, and Leofwine was much in favour with the queen dowager.

Belatedly, Leofwine heard the discussion taking place between the men, realising they were discussing the integrity of Ealdorman Ælfhelm's northern borders and how they were to be maintained now that the enemy had been sent scurrying away.

"The king intends to meet his ship-army and order them to attack either the land of the kings across the sea or slightly closer to home if the weather stays so bad," Ordulf spoke easily of his nephew's plans.

"Perhaps the Isle of Manx – it's not far and often used as a staging post for those travelling between here and Dublin?" Ordulf nodded at Ælfhelm's words.

"Yes, the king's been informed that Manx would make a good target. Perhaps they'll even find some of the stragglers from yesterday. There's a feeling that the people of Strathclyde didn't act alone, but enough of the ship army." Ordulf shook his head as if to clear it. "What are your plans now?"

Ealdorman Ælfhelm didn't hesitate in responding, soothing his fractious horse as he spoke.

"I intend to go as far as the Old Wall and seek out any retreating enemy. I know they have their small horses and so are probably long gone, but for peace of mind, I want to check. I don't want to inform my people that the menace has been routed until I'm convinced myself."

Ordulf grunted his agreement. Leofwine wasn't surprised. It had taken years to get the king to this point. It felt good to be the aggressors for once.

"I suggest we take separate routes then; we'll cover more area that way. We've been ordered to travel for a day and a half toward the Old Wall before returning to Chester. We're going to track the coastline, but can go elsewhere if you wish that route for yourself."

Ælfhelm nodded in quick understanding.

"It's a good idea. Then if there are any stray ships either from Dublin or Strathclyde, you'll be able to repel them. I was going to travel via the coast myself, but instead, I'll backtrack and move along the borderland that's long been disputed."

"I'll inform the people we meet that they need to look to King Æthelred for protection. It might even be an opportunity to survey the state of the people, make sure they have what they need to bring in the harvest. I don't want the worry of attacks to be replaced by that of hungry people."

Ordulf accepted Ælfhelm's words with a sharp grunt of agreement and quickly bowed his head in farewell, returning to where his force was quietly milling around.

Ealdorman Ælfhelm watched him with narrowing eyes before turning to Leofwine.

"He's not at all like his nephew."

"No, he isn't. He's been fighting the Raiders for years."

"We'll see what the future holds," Ealdorman Ælfhelm offered, ominously.

Leofwine fixed him with a stern stare, confused by the intent implied in the words, but Ælfhelm didn't elucidate, turning towards his troops and shouting a goodbye over his shoulder. Leofwine sat for a moment, watching the older man issue commands to his men before he, too, turned on his way with another burden to add to those he already carried.

The weather improved with every step towards the Old Wall, and before long, bright sunshine was drying the damp land and the men and their steads. Leofwine watched the area around him with interest. On his journey home from the Outer Isles, he and his men had navigated along this coast in their ship, but he'd seen little or nothing of the land, too ill and too unused to his limited vision to take any enjoyment in the views.

Leofwine was astonished now by the sight of the hills rising steeply towards the land of Ælfhelm's ealdordom, festooned as they were with lush grasses until their rocky peaks. He could see why the king wasn't happy that the kingdom of Strathclyde had appropriated the area even though it appeared to have few inhabitants

The few people who crossed their path were well dressed and looked prosperous for all that they had more skill at conversing with Horic in the native tongue of his home, than in Leofwine's own.

Leofwine considered just how long the Raiders had been settling this land and how many of the small population were a holdover from the time before the first Raiders had arrived over two hundred years before, or so the Chronicles said.

Those he encountered were more akin to the people who dwelled on the borders of his lands near Deerhurst, with their patchwork of petty kingdoms, known collectively as the Welsh, to the English.

England had once been the same, before Alfred and his son had worked to defeat the Vikings and to unite the broken land.

By the time the sun was bleaching from the summer sky, late in the evening, they'd encountered no enemy, but had found a sandy cove to shelter near for the night.

"Horic, this land ... have we been here before?" Leofwine called to his warrior, recognition creeping over him as he gazed at the view out to sea, with his limited vision, turning to stare inland, scowling as he fought for the memory.

Horic glared at the stretch of beach and rough grass as though it had done something to offend. His eyes narrowed slightly, and his brow knit together in thought.

"I think not, My Lord, although it does look similar to places we've been."

Leofwine grunted in agreement, a hazy memory tugging in his mind of a time when he'd been barely healed from his eye wound and on his long journey home through the worst that late winter could bring a tired ship and her men.

They'd been forced to make many stops down this stretch of the coast before they'd fetched up at the court of the king far in the south. He assumed that many of the places must have looked similar.

"I think you might be right," piped Oscetel, "I remember a stretch of land such as this. And look over there ... I'm sure we pulled up on that piece of land that juts out towards the sea."

Leofwine followed where Oscetel pointed and felt a jolt of recognition. Horic looked too, and a memory flickered on his face.

"I think Oscetel may be right after all." Horic agreed, a shrug of his shoulders the entire apology Leofwine could expect, or even need. Leofwine felt some consolation in his memories. His limited sight wasn't always the curse it could be.

That night, they made a small camp just above the beach. Ordulf joined Leofwine for a meal of hardened bread dipped into a tasty pottage as conversation flowed smoothly between Leofwine and the king's uncle.

It was no secret that they'd been allies for many years now, since before the death of Leofwine's father. Nor that Leofwine was close to Ordulf's sister, the king's mother.

A handful of men kept vigilant high on several surrounding hills, primed to attack if any of their enemies should make an appearance, but none did. The sun finally dipped low, and eerie half darkness fell under the bright moon enabling men to sleep or stay awake as they were commanded.

Leofwine quickly dropped to sleep, the shortness of his previous night's rest enough to ensure he slept soundly and deeply. He dreamt all night of his reunion with his wife and woke disappointed to find himself on a bed of grass, wrapped in his cloak against the slight summer chill, as opposed to in the warm and inviting embrace of his wife. He supposed he should be pleased that, at least, it hadn't rained during the night.

Leofwine spared a thought for Wulfstan, hoping he was well again, and then a cry from the men on watch alerted him to a sighting of mounted horsemen.

Well practised, the contingents of both men were soon in pursuit. Leofwine cursed his limited eyesight that caused him to rely on a running commentary from Horic regarding the people they followed along the jagged coastline, rising ever higher the further north they travelled.

"I believe there are about thirty of them, My Lord. They're all mounted on sturdy, if short, horses, and are fleeing back the way they must have come. I can make out little of their clothing, or what weapons they carry, but the glint of iron from the sun assures me that they're armed."

"Let's just hope they're not leading us into an ambush."

Horic grunted in agreement. "We shall soon see, My Lord." Leofwine thought the words far from comforting.

Only they didn't see anything soon. Instead, the ragged band of men before them stayed at a steady distance away, no matter how often Leofwine and his men sped up or slowed down.

At regular intervals, Ordulf instructed a select group of his men to attempt to catch the fleeing men by shooting forwards as fast as their horses would allow, but those they pursued always outpaced them. Finally, as the sun reached its zenith, Ordulf drew back. He beckoned to Leofwine, who directed his horse to the side of the older man.

"I don't think we can catch them. I feared an ambush but the more we follow them, the more I believe they're just trying to escape with their lives."

The older man was sweat-streaked and the frustration of the morning's fruitless chase was evident on his animated face, as he puffed out his bright pink cheeks, his hair stuck to his head with the sweat of his endeavours.

"We've followed them beyond all signs of habitation. I think it'd be fair to say that they're gone for good," Leofwine responded. He'd been aware of the thinning of any form of settlement for some time. The land they passed no longer showed any signs of management – no wicker fences and even fewer herd beasts could be glimpsed on the gentler slopes of the hills. If anyone lived higher than that, Leofwine was unable to see.

He'd even begun to consider that they'd gone too far north and were close to entering the land of Strathclyde itself. Only the lack of a sighting of the Old Wall gave him comfort that they were still in the English king's land.

"Yes, perhaps. But I'd prefer to join battle with them just to reiterate our win against them two days ago." Ordulf sounded disgruntled not to have encountered the enemy while Leofwine chuckled in sympathy for the lost opportunity.

"Come, I think I saw a small settlement not far from where we slept last night. Let's go back that way and see if the inhabitants are prepared to offer us some insights into the lay of the land."

Grudgingly Ordulf agreed, although it was evident he'd rather disobey his king's orders and venture further towards the Old Wall. Leofwine knew that Ordulf often acted outside the king's parameters, mostly because the king was so sluggish to take action. On this occasion, he was relieved when Ordulf turned back toward the south.

THEY RODE BACK THE WAY THEY'D COME AT ONLY A SLIGHTLY LESS ROBUST speed. Behind them, he'd ordered Oscetel and some of the men to delay their return to ensure that the enemy they'd chased away didn't return. Oscetel had been pleased to oblige and Leofwine happy to command.

The building they came upon, close to the beach of the night before, was an isolated farm with neatly demarcated fields stretching far back towards the gently rising hills. Further out the walls were made of heaped stone; closer to the house they were more temporary and made from sheets of thinly threaded branches.

Sheep grazed peacefully in the grassy fields, and a sleepy boy watched the troop of men ride slowly by, just as he'd watched them race north when the sun had first been rising. Leofwine questioned how often the boy saw mounted men in shiny helms race past his home that the occurrence merited so little concern from him. If the area were truly as lawless as the king had implied, he would have expected a more worried response.

Horic rode at Leofwine's side.

"This looks like a fine farm. I'm confused by its prosperity. Surely if they're constantly under attack from the northmen and their allies in Strathclyde, it should appear ramshackle?"

Leofwine took a moment to consider his reply. Horic was correct, the farm was well tended and only had the smallest of defences around it, and his thoughts have been running the same as Horic's.

"I assume they're happy to please whoever claims this land as their own. Certainly, they're rich enough in animals and crops to keep themselves throughout the year, and they probably have some spare to buy Raiders off with. We all know how keen the Raiders are for silver coins." Leofwine teased Horic as he spoke; smiling while Horic tried his best to ignore the reference to his past with Lord Olaf, feared Viking warrior, and the King of Norway.

"I suppose it's possible. Still, I'd be happy if my home looked like this, and I live in an England that's peaceful, or so you'd have me believe."

Leofwine continued to smirk. "Are you saying I don't reward you well enough?"

Horic turned in shock at Leofwine's words, all traces of good humour gone from his face between one heartbeat and the next.

"My lord, not at all, not at all."

Leofwine laughed with delight at the horror his words had caused.

"I'm only jesting with you, Horic. I know what you mean. I think that we might learn some interesting facts from these people." As Leofwine spoke, he indicated the farm before them.

By now, the sound of the horsemen had caused someone to venture outside. A woman stood, silhouetted by the falling sun against the side of her home, one arm raised above her head so that she could see who approached. She showed no sign of concern and no men rushed to her defence from inside the building.

Ordulf and two of his men dismounted and strode towards her. Leofwine was too far away to hear what was said, but he could tell from the group's body language that it was not an easy conversation.

After some gesticulation from Ordulf, one of his two men stepped away and strode to where Leofwine and Horic stood beside their horses. He dipped his head respectfully, for all that he was one of the king's thegns, and began to speak, his voice encouraging despite his appearance of a seasoned traveller and dirt stained clothing.

"My lord Leofwine, and Horic, the lady didn't seem to understand all my lord Ordulf's words and hoped Horic might be able to assist us?"

Horic flushed slightly and rushed forwards.

"Of course, my lord ... is she from the north?" Horic called over his shoulder as he strode confidently through the few remaining muddy puddles from the storm of a few days ago.

"I'm unsure. Some of her words seem to be your own, and yet others are those I'm used to speaking. I wonder if she's been taught a mixture of both the language of the English and that of the Northmen."

Horic stopped abruptly as he considered the idea,

"I suppose it's possible, but it would be a little ... odd."

"See what you think when you speak to her."

And so Horic did. He looked travel-stained himself, and yet somehow he still stood tall and proud as he walked unarmed toward the well-maintained house with its rounded walls of finely woven sticks and densely layered fresh-looking daub.

Smoke puffed excitedly through two small holes in the roof, and Leofwine was struck with how warm the house looked, and also how similar it appeared to those he'd seen on the Outer Isles that had housed the people who'd sheltered him while he'd healed.

Horic greeted the woman calmly in his tongue, and immediately her face lit with recognition, and she began to gabble away to him. Leofwine joined Horic only to stand and watch the exchange patiently.

He knew that Horic would inform them soon enough of what she said. In the meantime, Leofwine looked at the woman with interest. She was handsome with long brown hair securely tied back from her face in an intricate pattern of braids.

Her clothing was simple but well made, and the brooches that adorned her dress were beautifully designed, flashing green and red with the slowly setting sun. Her eyes were bright green, and her face refreshing to watch as she animatedly spoke with Horic.

With a bellow of laughter, Horic turned to where Ordulf stood waiting a little impatiently at being excluded from the conversation.

"It would appear that by some complex arrangements that even I find difficult to fully comprehend, that Gita and I are somehow related, or at least we think we are. She's from near where I grew up." Horic grinned as he spoke.

"Her husband, who's away on a fishing trip, has lived here all his life, and his family dates back years and years. They aren't chieftains or lords or anything like that; they simply farm this land and keep on the right side of all who attempts to claim it."

"Will they give their allegiance to King Æthelred?" Ordulf interjected, impatient with Horic's reminiscing.

"I don't think she will be, My Lord," the smile fell a little from Horic's mobile face. "But I've not asked her. I think to pay allegiance to any specific person will harm them. She says Raiders from Dublin and the far northern lands often stop here when they see the smoke from their fires."

Ordulf nodded with grudging acceptance.

"Well, can we at least stay here tonight? I crave a bit of dry shelter from the elements."

"Oh yes, My Lord, apologies. She's offered us hospitality for the evening. She says there's also a barn a short distance away in the fields whereas many of the men as would be comfortable can spend the night. However, she can only feed a handful of us. I've assured her that we wouldn't expect her to feed us all."

"Indeed," Ordulf muttered, but when Horic returned to gossiping, he coughed loudly to remind Horic that he'd welcome being allowed inside the house.

"Sorry, My lord, step inside, only she's not quite as alone as we thought, so please be careful."

Ordulf froze mid-step and looked at Horic with some concern,

"Are they armed?"

"No, but I imagine that they're quite fierce. I've found that those who live for such a long time in virtual social isolation are." Horic inclined his head as he offered the warning.

Ordulf gestured for his two men to precede him inside the house and hovered slightly uncertainly on the periphery. Horic was deeply engrossed in conversation and, with a nod to Ordulf, Leofwine turned and went to inform the men of their respective forces that they were to spend the night.

Leofwine pointed out where he could faintly make out the roof of the barn a few fields over, and a frantic discussion ensued about who would take shelter there and who would camp between the house and the exposed beach. In the end, Leofwine's men won the honour of guard duty, and the small shepherd boy appeared to direct Ordulf's troops to the barn, even without sharing their speech.

Leofwine eyed the little lad with amusement. He was no higher than the waists of most of the men and was unfazed by the flash of iron and metal that must have caught his eye. A sleek hunting dog followed him, similar to Leofwine's own Hunter, but the dog stayed firmly at the lad's heels, barely even noticing where Hunter circled around Leofwine possessively.

The dog and the boy took in everything before them with appraising eyes that belonged to a man grown, not a young lad, and Leofwine wondered what horrors the boy had seen, for it seemed his calm exterior was a mask. He'd learned to be still and quiet as a way of keeping out of the attention of any would be Raiders.

"Come this way," he called, in a high boyish voice, surprising Leofwine when he spoke in English. "Mother has clearly allowed you to stay the night, so I'll show you where you can sleep."

The boy spoke with a lilt to his voice, but he understood and spoke their language, that much was evident. Leofwine speculated as to why his mother's words were such a mixture of the two languages when her son was evidently able to speak and understand English.

With Oscetel busy mustering and organising the fifty warriors within his warband, Leofwine and Hunter meandered back towards the house, where Horic and the woman were still loudly conversing. As Leofwine drew level, he realised that Horic was wiping tears from his eyes. Horic noted Leofwine's approach and turned to him, laughter lines etched onto his broad face.

"Gita here was just reminding me of a famous incident back home. It's an old, old story but she tells it well. Would you like to hear it?"

Leofwine smiled at the man's enjoyment. "Perhaps later, when we've eaten and rested a little, and seen what Ordulf is up to."

"Of course," Horic sobered immediately, remembering he served the king's uncle and indicated that Gita should walk inside first.

Leofwine was not sure what he'd been expecting, but it wasn't what he found when he walked through the sturdy wooden door. The display of brightly coloured ceramic pots on a wooden dresser and the neatly stacked pile of swords and shields just by the door indicated that the house was prosperous to a level similar to his home.

The doorway opened into a small space where thick-winter cloaks were stacked, some overflowing from a wooden chest. A small door then led into a larger room lined with benches surrounding a huge fire pit piled high with brightly burning logs and rolls of peat.

The heat was almost stifling, and he noticed with interest that the select group of inhabitants inside the room, from a wizened old man to the toddler running around naked, were people who were rich enough in resources that a fire on a warm summer's day was possible.

Ordulf was seated next to the old man who was chattering away to him. He laughed at the man's words and turned a beaming smile Leofwine's way.

"Leofwine, let me introduce you to Ragnor, he's regaling me with tales of his father's raids on the lands of our forefathers. I think he's trying to shock me, but he tells such a good story. I'm transfixed."

Leofwine stepped forwards and clasped the hand of the elderly man, whose hand shook with age but who had eyes bright with mischief.

"Have you asked him how he came to live here?"

"Not yet, but I will."

Leofwine left Ordulf and his two warriors to the old man's stories and continued to look around the house. Horic and Gita were busy tending to the fire, and pouring out a warmed aromatic wine for them all to enjoy, the scent rich in the superheated air.

The small child ran up to Gita and blathered something to her that made her smile. She shooed him away from the scorching heat and back towards a mat where several carved wooden toys were scattered around for him to play with as he pleased.

An older child, probably a girl because her hair was so long and trailing all the way down her back, held out her arms and called in a sing-song voice for the toddler. It had little effect, and with a huff of effort, she crawled to her feet and retrieved the boy from under Gita's feet.

"Here Leofwine, have something to drink. Dinner will be ready soon."

Leofwine took the offered wooden beaker from Horic and settled onto one of the benches, Hunter attentive at his side. She'd quickly explored the new house and had then guided him around so that he avoided falling over in the darkened interior. It was lit mainly by the fire and by a few small lamps smouldering near to the display of pottery.

The warmth of the fire stole over Leofwine, and he woke with a start when a wooden bowl of steaming meat was placed before him. He accepted it willingly and as he ate Horic finally relayed some of his conversation with Gita.

Every so often, the old man Ordulf was sat next to interjected with a comment, and Gita would raise her eyebrows in outrage at his words. Leofwine doubted that the couple was related in any way other than through married kin, and he could tell that they didn't get on well.

"The men who live here are away fishing for a few days. They've a large ship that they use to trade with, and occasionally they take it out into the deeper currents and fish for supplies for the winter months."

"Gita says that as almost all their visitors come from the sea, the men don't mind being away as they know they can chase back any would-be attackers. She says it's rare for men to come on horses. Her husband, Osbert, is Ragnor's son; Osbert married his mother, who'd lived here all her life, and then Osbert went to seek himself a fine northern woman to help him keep the farm here."

"He travelled to my home country and found Gita. She's happy here, although it can be quite isolated. You didn't see, My Lords, but she greeted us with her sword behind her back, and her shield hidden behind one of the small wicker walls. She's truly, a fine northern woman."

His voice was warm with approval as he spoke and Leofwine didn't miss the appreciative glance Horic levelled at the woman.

"Why Horic, I think you might be a little smitten," Leofwine teased him.

Horic didn't take offence, merely stated, "As you should be, My Lord."

Leofwine laughed, and Gita turned to Horic with a question on her face, which he quickly brushed aside.

They slept that night in the space near the merrily burning fire pit, wrapped up in their cloaks and safe in the knowledge that their men were watching for any would-be attackers outside.

Horic had eventually turned to the question of the battle, and the men of Strathclyde and Gita had shrugged her shoulders with disinterest. Horic explained to him and Ordulf that few men ever rode the path past their door.

They had no concerns that they'd be attacked without warning as they could see far out to sea and few men wanted to be lord or king over only one farm. Leofwine appreciated the easy acceptance of the situation but felt that he'd not have been quite so easy-going about the whole thing. He didn't think he'd leave his wife and small children with none but an old man to stand guard over them, even if Horic assured him that Gita was well able to protect them.

4
AD1000

Leofwine was woken early the next morning by a raucous noise from outside. He stumbled to his feet, Hunter immediately at his side, and rushed with Horic towards the closed door.

Stepping out into the bright early morning sunshine, they quickly realised the commotion was coming from the cove where a beautiful ship was being driven up the beach on the high tide.

It was high-sided, crowned with a great ship's head, and the wooden vessel gleamed in the early morning sunlight. Leofwine was instantly reminded of his own craft and wished, not for the first time, that he'd been allowed to sail north instead of ride.

Gita raced past the pair of them in the doorway and rushed to the beach as Leofwine's worry faded. He assumed it must be her husband returning from his sea voyage. He followed her hasty path along the rough grasses towards the ship and stopped on the high-tide mark waiting to greet the man whose home he'd found welcome shelter within.

Cries of welcome came from the ship, and Leofwine counted at least ten different men busily stowing items on board before jumping to shore.

With her arm draped around a well-built man who trailed several youths who must also be their sons, Gita walked towards where Leofwine and Ordulf stood. The man was eyeing them speculatively, but a huge grin split his face when he saw Horic. Leofwine turned a questioning look Horic's way, but he shrugged in confusion; Horic apparently didn't know the man by sight.

"Well met," the man said, reaching out to firmly clasp both Leofwine and Ordulf's arms.

"And you." The men then turned to Horic, "Don't panic for I've never met you, but I know you from your brother. Has he never told you about the time we spent together chasing girls? I'd recognise you as his brother anywhere."

Gita swatted him on the arm, understanding his words, but Horic stilled. Leofwine didn't even know that Horic had a brother.

"I'm afraid my brother died many years ago, off on a raiding trip with Harald of Denmark. I can only imagine that you saw him one more time than I did."

"Ah, my apologies; he was an exceptional warrior and even better with the women."

Horic smiled at the words.

"He certainly was good with the women. He taught me everything he knew. His fighting skills were clearly a little lacking, as he's no longer with us." Horic stepped forwards and clasped the man's forearm warmly.

"I'm Osbert. Lord of all you survey here. I hear you've had the honour – or the misfortune – to meet my father, whichever you think. I understand that he's also now met the king's uncle – something else for him to constantly remind us of."

Ordulf greeted the words with an incline of his head, "He's a fine old man and his stories of the old wars are informative."

"If you think so, then maybe you should take him with you!"

Ordulf chuckled at the suggestion. "Perhaps not, but I'd wondered if I could send a scribe this way and have him write down what he remembers. It would make a good history."

"If you wish; I'd have no problem with that, as long as it wasn't one of your priests sent to convert us in stealth."

"Well, he might be a priest, in all honesty, there are few others who have the skills to write and prepare the vellum, but I'd ask him to keep his faith to himself."

Osbert smiled at the honesty of the words, "We do look to the Christian God, but our religion is old here. The people of the north brought their Gods with them, but we already had our own God, and we're pleased to keep him."

"Well, that's interesting as well. Perhaps I actually will send the priest. And now, and with thanks for your wife's hospitality, we must be on our way. The king expects us home today, but be wary of the horsemen we chased away yesterday."

"And you, My Lord. There are many ships on the sea the last few days. I knew that something must have happened, but I'd caution you to watch your own back. The King of Dublin and the lord of Manx are clearly up to something."

With that, Leofwine and Ordulf returned to their horses, and with a final wave for the old man, Ragnar, who'd stumbled his way to the door, Ordulf led the troops back to Chester.

THE MOOD AS THE MEN MOUNTED TO RETURN TO THE KING'S CAMP WAS A mixture of disappointment and relief. They'd no great glory to regale their king with, but neither did they have any losses to speak of. They'd also gained valuable insight into the land between Chester and the Old Wall.

Ordulf was particularly pleased about his encounter with Gita and Osbert, or more specifically, the old man, and he spoke much of the way home about the stories the ancient warrior had regaled him with.

The weather remained fair, but as they drew closer and closer to the site of their camp, a growing sense of unease developed, and as they passed the location of the battle the outriders came racing back, shouting a warning. Every man looked to the skies where a plume of thick black smoke billowed in the lazy windless day.

Spurring their mounts, they galloped onwards, fearful that somehow they'd missed another advancing force from Strathclyde, or that the arrival of a ship army from the king in Dublin, and their king was even then engaged in battle.

What they finally found was a small force of the king, led by a pained-looking Wulfstan, still in agony although he sat mounted on his horse. They were setting fire to a significant swathe of the countryside, or rather watching fires that they'd already established.

The smoke blew fiercely away from them, taking with it the smell of the fire. Leofwine frowned at the wanton destruction while at the same time understanding the significance of the king's actions. It was imperative that the Raiders understood England was not open for the taking; destroying the good land close to the coastal regions would act as an immediate deterrent to any who wished to take advantage of the potential crossing to Northumbria.

"I see the king's role for you was not particularly to your liking," Leofwine muttered up to his friend, having dismounted from his horse so they could speak in some privacy.

"No, it's not. It's a waste of time and energy that's gone into seeding these fields. The king at least gave the men some time to harvest what they could, but it's too early in the year. The yields would've been higher had he resisted the urge."

"I agree, Wulfstan. But how do you fare? You look uncomfortable."

Wulfstan shrugged off the question with annoyance, "It's nothing – a minor wound. It'll heal and leave me with a scar to scare your lads with, nothing more. Now stop fussing. I let the king send me off with this lot because I was fed up of the healer fussing, and the king fussing and Finn fussing and just about everyone else who could."

Leofwine laughed at the frustration in Wulfstan's voice. It was evident he was healing, even if it didn't look like it just yet.

"Okay," he replied, holding his hand up as if to ward off blows, "I won't mention it again. The king, he's well?"

"Yes, he's fine. Enjoying himself like a child with his toys. He's managed to make contact with his ship-army and has sent them onwards to Manx. And you, how did you manage?"

"Nothing of real importance; we did see a band of warriors, but they stayed out of reach as we chased them ever northwards. Other than that, we met some natives of and also Ealdorman Ælfhelm. He was on a similar route to check that the lands were clear of any retreating warriors."

"I don't know where they all went, but they've melted away as quickly as they appeared. They've clearly learnt much from the Raiders. Lord Ordulf thinks we should as well, but that's a story for another day. Come, I need to return to camp. Are you coming?"

"Yes, I can stomach no more of this today." The troop of Leofwine's men had already intermingled with the returning party, and in a rowdy crowd, they returned to camp.

As Wulfstan had said, the king was full of enthusiasm for tackling his enemy and highlighting the might of England. Ealdorman Leofsige was high in the king's favour as well, and Leofwine felt his old annoyance with the man surface immediately. Why did the king tolerate him when he did little but make excuses for his failures and grow ever fatter?

5
AD1000

THE FIRST COLOURS OF WINTER WERE STARTING TO TURN THE LEAVES GOLDEN by the time Leofwine rode through the wooden enclosure of his principal residence. It wasn't yet cold enough for any of the men to be complaining, but Leofwine was looking forward to a warm fire and a warmer bed, devoid of wildlife or pieces of grass irritating his nose as he slept.

He'd dispersed the men who'd comprised his fighting force and travelled only with a handful of his household troop. Horic had departed to check on his family and Wulfstan was a grumpy presence hunched over his saddle. His wound had festered slightly after his abrupt return to duties at the king's request.

Leofwine damned the man's stupidity for not telling the king while accepting that he wouldn't have done so either. He cursed them equally loudly for fools.

The king's relaxed demeanour had lasted throughout the military operation, which should have made Leofwine happy, only it had been marred, for the king had extended it to all of his ealdormen, even Ælfric and Leofsige.

Leofsige's incompetence had been forgiven far too quickly and with little or no repercussions. In fact, Leofwine had returned from his three-day foray into the north to find Leofsige and the king closeted inside the king's tent, feasting and thinking no more of the campaign.

Leofwine supposed he should be pleased that the king had directed his ship army towards the Isle of Manx. They'd heard some rumours regarding unrest amongst the Dublin kings.

Leofwine had wondered if the attack against Strathclyde had been so easy to accomplish because many of the Dublin Raiders were involved in a war on their home territory. He wasn't sure, though.

Rumour also had it that Manx was under the control of the once-met Jarl of Orkney, and Leofwine considered whether he was working for or against Swein of Denmark. He couldn't imagine that Sigurd would welcome the influence of Swein, but perhaps he'd had no choice. He was undoubtedly a force to be reckoned with and the Northmen he'd met so far didn't seem keen to keep to alliances that were no longer favourable to them.

Leofwine had tried to discuss the situation with the king, but Æthelred appeared to have changed his opinion about Swein and the threat he did, or did not, present to the kingdom of England.

The king had decided, on Leofsige's advice, that he'd welcome Pallig into his kingdom. The decision had been made to gift him with an ealdordom in the Western provinces. Æthelmaer, old Æthelweard's son, had made his view of the situation clear to his king and to Leofwine, outraged that Æthelred had overlooked him in favour of a man he'd never met and knew nothing about.

Pallig of Denmark was to be informed of the king's decision and would be formally introduced to the witan in the coming weeks. He'd then be escorted by the king's troops to the property that had been settled upon him as part of his new position.

Æthelmaer wasn't the only member of the witan in uproar at the advancement of the man; he was simply the most vocal. Leofwine had himself chosen silence on the matter. The king didn't like to be thwarted, as had been proved by his past experience, and so he'd determined, unwillingly, to let events play out.

His unease was profound. England was more than ever surrounded by enemies, and his king had by all accounts not quite learnt the lessons he'd hoped he would. His king was not a fool as such, but he was foolish to think that a victory in one battle would drive the concerted efforts of the Raiders to look elsewhere.

His relief at being home, if only for a short time, was profound. Word had reached him that his wife had safely delivered a girl in the early days of high summer, and he was excited to have a new baby to be delighted by. His wife was well, or so she said, and he hoped she might even appreciate some attention from him if the babe was not too demanding.

A handful of his men whom he'd left to guard his wife and children greeted him cheerfully when he dismounted in the neat and tidy forecourt outside his front door. A whirlwind of activity around his unsteady feet alerted him to the presence of his small sons, and as he picked them both up and turned to walk inside his home, his wife appeared in the doorway, her daughter safely cocooned in a sling strapped to her chest.

A bright smile graced Æthelflæd's, and Leofwine rushed forwards to envelop everyone in his arms, hampered by Hunter who managed to tangle amongst his legs.

His sons screamed with laughter as he embraced them all. Once deposited back on the ground, Northman and Leofric were besieged by an over-excited Hunter who sniffed them and licked them from head to toe, as if to ensure that they were still who she thought they were.

Æthelflæd was occupied with both showing off her daughter and checking on Wulfstan, who laboured behind Leofwine to dismount from his horse. Leofwine heard her gasp with shock and he shushed her gently, his breath hot against her neck where he was gazing down at his new child and simultaneously kissing her in welcome.

The baby girl was a pretty little thing, although he could discern no noticeable difference between her and his sons at the same age. Covering his hasty conversation with his actions, he muttered, "He's a stubborn old goat. We'll need to nurse him as best we can, but he doesn't need to realise that we're doing so. He was injured in the battle and didn't take enough time to heal before returning to his duties. Try not to act too concerned."

More loudly, he continued, "She's a beauty. Have you named her?"

A wicked gleam entered Æthelflæd's eye. "I might have done my lord, but I'll let you get to know her a bit before I tell you her name. Now, here, hold her and get acquainted. I wish to go and see how obstinate Wulfstan is."

Still wearing all his travelling clothing, including his cloak, Leofwine found himself juggling a sleeping baby as well as his two sons. Æthelflæd swished past him in an enticing aroma of summer herbs and new baby, and he watched her with amusement. She'd apparently not be taking his advice about Wulfstan.

Thinking it best to leave her be, he walked inside his home, enjoying the comfort and noise of his busy household. He was amazed by how much both boys had grown while he'd been away. Leofric was chattering away quietly to Hunter. Northman was standing proudly with his small sword, desperate to show his new skills to his father.

Leofwine sank gratefully onto the wooden bench nearest the fire as he was handed a welcome horn of mead with his spare hand, and Northman began showing him his skills with the assistance of one of the other small boys who seemed to run riot around his home. He wondered to whom the boy belonged; it was sometimes difficult to keep track.

The doorway darkened as Æthelflæd led Wulfstan inside the room. He was trying in vain to convince her that he was fine. Sadly his actions were belying his words as he shuffled in, his back hunched against the pain and his face a little green from the effort.

Æthelflæd called to her maids, who ran to do her bidding, and in only moments, Wulfstan was sat deeply ensconced in Leofwine's favourite wooden-backed chair in front of the fire, furs piled high around him and a bowl of broth in his hands. He turned tortured eyes towards Leofwine, but Leofwine shrugged helplessly, hiding his amusement. He felt relieved for Wulfstan; the old man would now get the much-needed rest and care he needed to ensure he recovered fully.

While Wulfstan slept, Æthelflæd left his side, her face still concerned.

"Why did you let him ride with his wound so infected?" Her voice was an angry hiss. He'd been expecting a loving tone now that the evening had slowly wound its way down, with his children sent to bed and his daughter fed and calmed in the maid's arms.

"You know I've no control over what he does?" His response was sharper than he'd meant, but he'd been thrown by the vitriol in her voice.

"Well, I suggest you teach him to take commands, or you'll lose him. Remember, he's the same age your father would have been. Your father would have been almost akin with Æthelweard, and he was deemed an old man at his death, for all that he'd kept his wits about him."

"Æthelflæd, what would you have me do?"

"I'd have you look after the man who treats you more like a son than he does his children. If he dies, you'll be without your main advisor. Horic and the other men have their life experiences, but it's Wulfstan that you turn to whenever life becomes a little too involved, and you need options." Her tone was matter-of-fact for all that it was heated as she spoke.

"Look, the healer assured me he would be well. I called upon the priest, and the healer grew angry with me. I didn't let him travel to the Old Wall with me. It was the king who commanded him when he should have been abed, not me." Leofwine spoke defensively, his words falling quickly into their debate.

"The king should have known better, and you should have known that leaving him behind would not ensure that he rested. Honestly, Leofwine, for a man in your position you on occasion display the common sense of a child. Now come – bed for you! Wulfstan will be easy throughout the night, and the maid is on hand if he needs help."

Her tone had not softened as she spoke, but as her tirade continued, he'd realised that it was fear and exasperation that coloured her mood and her words. He reached out to pull her to him, and with a sigh, she relented and tumbled into his lap. He held her there, whispering nothings into her hair, as the fire burnt low and finally after she'd again fed the daughter whose name he still did not know, he guided her towards their bedchamber.

He was reminded of the night of their reunion after his disastrous trip to the Outer Isles, only this time they were both a little older and a bit better versed in how to please each other.

Still, she'd not long birthed their daughter, and that knowledge inhibited him as he gently caressed her full breasts and rounded stomach. He was inclined to comment on how well she'd kept her figure, for all that she'd birthed him three children, but he knew better. Horic had sat him down one day and explained that woman didn't like to be told about any changes to their lithe bodies brought about by childbirth. He'd remembered the lesson well. Better to enjoy the slight variations without comment than have them denied him.

Now he steadfastly bit back any remark, preferring instead to enjoy the touch of his woman for the first time since the early summer. He kissed her tenderly on her lips, thanking her for his daughter, while she giggled away his compliments and tried to act severely against his intentions.

Her resolve was dissolved quickly though as he trailed kisses all along her naked back before straddling her so that he could carry out the same attention to her breasts and stomach. Her gasps of pleasure at his touch mirrored his own as she turned the tables, and began caressing his battle-hardened chest and arms.

It was good to be home, he thought, as finally sated, his wife slept safely within his arms. He only hoped that the peace won on the battlefield would hold for many years to come.

6

AD1000

His time at home flew in a riotous disharmony of screaming babies, raucous boys and noisy dogs. Wulfstan allowed himself to wallow in his injury. Leofwine felt he worked hard at restoring the order that his absence and those of the men of the fyrd had temporarily caused. He hoped the ending of the year would be a relaxed affair, with a good harvest and a joy to the darkening days that called him to his bed early and allowed him to linger there throughout long lazy mornings.

Æthelflæd had relented after a week of him being home and told him his daughter's name was Ealdgyth, a beautiful name meaning 'old battle'. He'd laughed along with Æthelflæd at her fortuitous naming of all their children and had not shared with her the fears he harboured that the barely 'old' battle of the year would not be the last.

He wondered if perhaps Leofric – his 'dear power' – would prove to be short-lived too. Maybe, after all, it was Northman who had the right of it, with his name and his mother's vow of retaliation against the men who'd wounded his father.

Finn, Olaf's one-time scribe, had insinuated himself into the household in a not entirely unwelcome way. His stories amused the two small boys and all the other children as well and occasionally, when none of the children realised, Finn even managed to teach them a little too.

Finn was versed in the old Gods of the north and the Christian God too, and he could weave tales sophisticated enough that somehow the Christian God always won but only with the aid of the old Gods. Leofwine wondered for how long he'd been telling the same stories, and if the easy assimilation of the two religions was why he'd found such favour with Olaf.

Finn might have arrived road-weary and dishevelled, but he'd cleaned up quickly and looked every part the lordly scribe. When he'd grown comfortable in his new position, and come to realise that Leofwine had every intention of allowing him to stay, he'd even relaxed enough to fill them in on Olaf's exploits since they'd last met.

He regaled them with the stories of the wooden church Olaf had built in his capital, Trondheim, dedicated with an enormous golden cross, festooned with bright rubies.

He also told them of Olaf's attempts to find a new wife and of the escalation in the dispute between Swein of Denmark and Olaf which had come to a bloody end when Olaf had tried to marry Swein's sister against her brother's wishes.

Horic had roared with laughter when he'd learned of Olaf's incendiary activities, muttering on about how he always liked to tempt his fate. He'd sobered when he'd realised that Olaf had finally met his match and his end in just such a way.

But all was not well for the king, and Leofwine learned with shock of the death of Æthelred's wife in childbirth, not long after their return from the north.

Rumour had it that the king was drinking heavily and was inconsolable, the only brightness, that the new girl child had survived.

Leofwine hoped that this might just make the king pause in his decision to make an ally of Pallig of Denmark, but equally, it might merely drive him to abide by his rash decision.

• • •

WULFSTAN WAS WELL ENOUGH TO ESCORT LEOFWINE ON A JOURNEY through the crisping morning when it was time to attend the king's witan not long after the funeral of the king's wife.

Oscetel was in attendance as well. Horic, he'd ordered to guard his wife and family, and that man had brought his wife along with him. Agata was the only woman Leofwine knew who was allowed to order his young wife around, and he thought that after three births in five years, years that had not been the most peaceful, she needed a bit of being told what to do so that her health didn't suffer. What had happened to the king's wife concerned Leofwine. After all, she'd birthed nine live children in fifteen years, only to then meet her death.

The king had called them together at Bath, the old Roman town, because it was close to the land that Pallig was being gifted with. Leofwine also hoped that it was because Bath had seen the consecration of past kings and had a rich heritage that would highlight to Pallig the longevity of the English kings.

Indeed, the king's own father and his mother had been crowned, for a second occasion at a grand ceremony in Bath in 973. There was a rich heritage there.

Leofwine expected the witan to pass quickly; he didn't wish to spend any more time away from his home. As such, he'd chosen to make the journey in a single day. It was rough going on them all, leaving in the dark tendrils of dawn and arriving long after the low winter sun had set, but at least it meant less time with his fellow ealdormen before the real business of the witan began.

Leofwine wanted to spend as little time as possible anywhere near Ealdorman Leofsige and the more than likely equally noxious Pallig. Neither did he wish to encounter the king in anything other than a formal setting. Leofwine was unsure what sort of state the king would be in following his wife's death, but he had heard that the king had taken the news badly.

Initially, the king had even refused to travel to York for her funeral, and now many said that the king was rarely sober.

Leofwine had some sympathy for the king. His triumph against the kingdom of Strathclyde had been repaid with the loss of his wife, birthing the king's ninth child. Even to Leofwine, it seems a harsh price to pay, as Leofwine's thoughts turned to the king's children, and Lady Elfrida, his ally at the king's court.

That night, Leofwine and his men found shelter in Bath with an acquaintance of his father's. He woke early the next day, ready to face his king and the unknown stranger from the Northern lands, kin, through marriage, to the man who'd vowed to kill him, Swein of Denmark.

It was not an appetising thought, and Leofwine ate little before leaving for the monastery where the king was staying with those of his family and entourage he'd brought with him.

A deep frost had fallen during the night, and Leofwine shivered through his thick winter cloak in the early morning light, his horse delicately picking its way along the roadway to avoid the frequent deep puddles of icy water.

Wulfstan had spoken little on the journey yesterday but appeared to be well. He's not fallen from his saddle when they'd arrived in Bath as he had when they'd returned from the north. Leofwine was wise enough not to offer any comment that might set his friend either complaining about his continued concern or moaning that he was still in pain.

Meanwhile, Oscetel was gawping in shock, as he finally saw Bath in the daylight. Leofwine was amused by his apparent interest in the place and vowed that they would find time to explore the ancient ruins of the city at some point during the next few days.

The voices of the monks raised in prayer greeted his small party as they approached the monastery and one of the monks, accompanied by two of the king's men, directed them inside.

By the time they'd walked through the gates of the monastery, they'd already passed twenty members of the king's household troop monitoring the comings and goings of the king's men.

Their appearance raised a lukewarm greeting from young Athelstan as he too made his way inside. Leofwine was concerned to note the worry lines that already graced the young man's face. He was seemingly a child no more, following the untimely death of his mother, and the current state of the grief-stricken king, as even Athelstan walked with a renewed confidence.

Once inside the austere monastic church, Leofwine, devoid of all weaponry, made a point of noting who was in attendance. He wasn't surprised to notice that all the current ealdormen were there, curious no doubt to see what this Pallig had that he'd been offered a position they'd spent years and years vying for, and which other English men were keen to hold.

Æthelmaer, the previous ealdorman's son of the Western Provinces, was also in attendance and not just because his main home was close to Bath. Æthelmær wore a frown of thought that he often directed towards a knot of men and women standing close to the front of the church, where the choir stalls were screened from view, and from where soft voices rose and fell in melodious prayer.

Leofwine shivered. The monastery was known for its stringent adherence to the Benedictine rule and clearly providing warmth for any guests to the church was not of high importance. In places, the smallest braziers Leofwine had ever seen had been placed, and it was around these that the men of the witan clustered, speaking quietly, their breath misting before them as though they were still outside, and not inside the stone walls.

The king wasn't yet amongst his councillors, and neither were the churchmen who would begin the day's events with, no doubt, a long and detailed sermon on something they felt the king and his men should give more thought to. Leofwine didn't dislike Ælfric of Canterbury, the man who he'd been informed was to lead them that day. In fact, he held Ælfric in revered awe.

Ælfric's strict observance of his principles had allowed the monastery to be held up as a pinnacle of how those within the monastic community should act and behave. That his hermit-like activities had been rewarded by the bestowal of the archbishopric of Canterbury brought a small smile to Leofwine's face. He wondered if the man would rather have remained a hermit.

Ælfric had an almost personal tie to Leofwine as well. His training had begun at Deerhurst, and Leofwine's own abbot often spoke of the man who he held in high esteem and attempted to emulate. Thankfully, Leofwine's abbot was more generous with heat than Ælfric was.

Leofwine noticed that the prayer was slowing imperceptibly, and he hastened to find a seat where he was close enough to some source of warmth that he'd not fidget uncontrollably throughout what would be a long day.

The king entered the church in a swish of luxurious fabric and spices, his face white with grief, and his eyes red-rimmed. Leofwine thought he'd never seen the king looking quite so ill.

Four of his sons followed the king, all fair-haired, and with matching sombre expressions. At the rear of the small procession walked Lady Elfrida, the king's mother, Athelstan by her side, there to help should her steps fail her, as she stumbled along, back erect, but a walking stick gripped in a white hand.

Lady Elfrida's eyes were bright, although she seemed hunched now, perhaps worn down by the constant grief of the year. Leofwine was aware that one of her allies, the Abbess Wulfthryth, had died soon after the king's wife. He pitied Lady Elfrida the loss of so many close to her. He imagined that few yet remained who had known her when she was the king's wife.

The king and his family quickly took their seats near the front of the church just as the churchmen began their slow procession from behind the closed-off stalls. Ælfric was richly attired in the clothes of an archbishop, and while his face looked severe, he smiled in welcome to his king and the witan.

Leofwine smiled back when he caught his appraising eyes on

him. It was always best to respect the churchmen for they held much power in their own way.

The service and sermon were far shorter than Leofwine expected, the archbishop offering a small sermon on the bounty of the Harvest in his lilting tones before stepping away and allowing his king to take centre stage. It was clear he wasn't intent on sermonising to men who'd come to talk business, not God's words, and perhaps aware that the king and his family had suffered greatly of late.

Æthelred stood.

"My lords, and of course, ladies," here he cast a swift glance toward his mother. "I would thank you for attending my witan during such a bleak time of year." His voice was sombre, seeming to hitch on some of the words, as though laced with more meaning than he might have realised. There was also a nervous excitement in the king's movements, and the way he kept twisting his hands, one inside the other.

"As many of you know, I've been approached by Pallig of Denmark, to bring about an agreement between our two great nations, and bring about an end to the constant raiding we've endured in recent years. This, I've decided to agree to. It is better to make allies than war."

As he continued to speak, Æthelred's gaze swept over the faces of his other ealdormen, as though looking for confirmation of his words. Leofwine kept his face neutral. It was apparent that the king would genuinely rather make an agreement with the devil himself than go back to war again.

Leofwine imagined that there was a twisted logic to his words. But still, he wasn't convinced that Pallig's intentions were genuinely to strike a peace.

"Today, Pallig will become Ealdorman Pallig of the Western Provinces, an English ealdorman, to help keep England secure, and his family will shortly join him from Denmark."

The king looked pleased with his announcement, although there was an undercurrent of unease amongst the assembled witan.

Leofwine felt it in the shifting looks and stiffening of shoulders, rather than hearing it. All the same, Leofwine couldn't help thinking that the king was unnecessarily exposing England to a threat, rather than solving it.

Archbishop Ælfric, at a beckoning from his king, stepped forward then, in his arms, he held an intricately decorated wooden box containing the king's favoured saint's relics, a slither of Christ's Cross collected by King Athelstan, his great-uncle.

Over these relics, Pallig would make his oath to the king, and yet Leofwine already doubted it. Was Pallig even a Christian or did he still hold to their Old Gods?

Just for a moment, Leofwine glanced at Lady Elfrida. Her expression was as guarded as his. That worried him. The king had never been known to listen to all of his mother's advice before, but if she, who'd once struck a deal with lord Olaf, the man responsible for the Battle of Maldon where his father had killed, was uneasy about making an alliance with Pallig, then Leofwine knew he was also right to be fearful.

Pallig's voice was loud, his accent clear to hear as he spoke the words of commendation, his hand on the relics the archbishop held out to him.

"By the lord and these holy relics, I pledge to be loyal and true to Æthelred, and love all that he loves, and hate all that he hates, in accordance with God's rights and my noble obligations; and."

Leofwine was unsure whether the man understood all of the words he spoke. Lordship amongst the English was very different from that between the northmen. Yes, oaths, and gift giving bound it, but it was also more. The honour involved in the mutual agreement was just an essential aspect of the relationship, and it couldn't be easily revoked. Pallig's gleaming eyes made Leofwine fear that this vital element of the arrangement was incidental to him.

As if Leofwine's worries hadn't already been great, he then heard the heavy accent of Pallig trip over the oath of a commanded man, mangling the words, running them together, as though he barely spoke all of them.

"Never, willingly and intentionally, in word or deed, do anything that is hateful to him; on condition that he keep me as was our agreement, when I subjected myself to him and chose his service."

The king then welcomed Pallig, a firm grasp of each other's forearm, and Pallig was beckoned to join the row of ealdormen, a smirk on his face. Pallig had accomplished what he wanted.

But Leofwine tasted bile in his mouth. All his hard work and persuasions to ensure the king was perceived as a powerful force that Swein of Denmark and other Raiders who eyed England with covetous eyes would fear, would now be jeopardised.

Once the formality of inducting Pallig to his ealdordom was done, the meeting immediately dispersed as the other ealdormen vied to be introduced to Pallig.

Leofwine sat still through the hubbub of conversation, his gaze on the box of relics that the archbishop had left on the table at the front of the church.

Only a touch on his arm and a whine from Hunter alerted him that he wasn't alone. Looking up, Leofwine met the gaze of Lady Elfrida.

He stood abruptly, trying to bow at the same time, as a low chuckle rumbled from her throat.

"Ealdorman Leofwine, it's always good to see a friendly face." Her voice was tired, her words laboured, for all her smile was genuine.

"What game is he playing now?" She asked, and Leofwine knew there was no need to ask who she spoke about.

"My Lady, I do not like this," Leofwine complained, as she nodded her head.

"Neither do I, or the king's sons. But, he is riddled by grief and simply looking for an easy way out. We must, as ever remain vigilant." The caution in her voice, soothed Leofwine's worries a little, but also sparked them even more. Once more, it seemed, he must be more alert than the king to enemies.

"Then I will do all that I can," Leofwine confirmed, as Lady Elfrida smiled sadly, a look of respect on her tired face.

"Then I will thank you, on behalf of my son, and his sons, and bid you a good day. I am tired beyond all imaginings." Again, Leofwine bowed, and when he looked up, Lady Elfrida was making her way out of the building surprisingly quickly, her walking stick the loudest noise in the room.

He suppressed a smirk and a judder, as all eyes followed the king's mother.

Only then did he exhale loudly, and stand to mingle with the other ealdormen. It seemed he had work to do, even if he didn't want to.

Leofwine plotted a course toward Pallig, Hunter at his side, and as he did so, he studied the new ealdorman carefully.

Pallig was a well-built man, with long light brown hair falling down his shoulders and overflowing onto his luxurious white fur cloak. His cloak was clasped shut with a bright jewel that glinted in the candles of the church and made Leofwine's eye tear if he looked too keenly.

Pallig wore his clothing easily and moved with confidence that Leofwine envied. However, when he fixed his cold ice blue eyes on Leofwine, he knew that the man had explicitly been searching the church for him and him alone.

Momentarily Pallig paused, eyeing Leofwine with interest but no emotion. Pallig didn't even flinch at the ruin of Leofwine's face, although he stared at it with no apology.

Leofwine returned his stare in equal force, taking in the man's long shaggy beard and the tight line of a mouth. His face showed no laughter lines and Leofwine doubted that the man ever smiled. His face appeared to be carved from the finest marble.

Pallig abruptly turned around, to approach the king, who even now drank heavily from a goblet that never seemed to run dry, a servant on constant attendance to ensure the king was never left wanting.

Leofwine watched Pallig with interest, as he sought to ingratiate himself even further with the king.

Leofwine had a good understanding of Pallig's intentions at the court of his king, and he wondered how the man had managed to convince the king that he'd be honourable when Lady Elfrida disagreed. Was it the king's mourning that caused such a catastrophic misjudgment?

Pallig's expensive clothing, his relaxed confidence and his piercing eyes were undoubtedly just a ruse by Swein of Denmark to infiltrate England from the inside out, as opposed to from the outside in.

As Pallig clasped the hand of first the sly Ealdorman Leofsige and then the traitorous Ealdorman Ælfric, Leofwine knew that Swein of Denmark would make a move soon, and he'd be on his guard against any such actions.

As he always had been where the Danish were concerned.

7
SUMMER AD1001

LEOFWINE ANSWERED AN INSISTENT SUMMONS TO ATTEND ON THE KING AT Oxford, not for a witan, but for something far more urgent. Arriving mud-splattered, cold and hungry, despite it being summer, a contingent of twenty men with him, including Wulfstan and Oscetel, Leofwine was surprised by the utter sense of calm that initially greeted him. Only when he sought out the king in person did Leofwine find any source of confusion or panic.

The king was angry and frustrated, his face bright red, and not from drinking too much mead or wine, as he listened to the advice that a multitude of men was offering him about the rumours of yet more attacks in the lands of Ælfric to the south-east.

The king was attempting to seek clarification on where the alleged Raiders were and how many they numbered, but with each new report from a different messenger, the picture became more and more confused.

Leofwine well understood the king's anger within a few moments of being inside the hall. According to the messengers, there could be anything from ten to a thousand men, in either one or ten different places.

Leofwine announced himself to the king as soon as the opportunity presented itself, and a look of relief covered the king's lined face, flushed and seemingly terrified in equal measure.

Hastily Æthelred drew Leofwine to one side, unheeding of the hungry eyes of the other ealdormen who followed Leofwine's every move, no doubt concerned as to what the king was about to gift a man they disrespected. Leofwine ignored those eyes, focusing only on the king. He felt a premonition of foreboding even before Æthelred spoke.

"I'm sorry to ask this of you Ealdorman Leofwine, but the reports have me greatly worried, and not just for Hampshire and Kent, but for my mother and the children, in Dean. I know it's in Wessex, but the settlement lies too close to where I'm led to believe these Raiders are."

Leofwine immediately comprehended the king's problem.

"I'll take my men, ride with all haste, and have them taken to Winchester."

At the words, Æthelred's worry lines eased, although his blue eyes still gleamed with confidentiality.

"It's difficult, I'm sure you must understand, to be seen riding to protect my family, when the whole of England might be in peril."

Leofwine bowed his head at the remark, rare for his king to appreciate the difficulties his decisions could cause.

"That might be, My Lord, but your mother, and the children are England's future. There's little point in doing anything to combat the Raiders if your own dynasty is threatened." Leofwine infused his voice with understanding, even though he was desperate to be gone, and riding south even now. The news had unsettled him more than he liked to admit.

Lady Elfrida, the king's mother, was one of his longest-held allies, a hold-over from when his father had yet lived, and in Athelstan, Leofwine knew the future of England rested.

"I knew you'd understand. None of the others would. All the same, lord Leofwine, I'd advise caution in whatever happens. You can, of course, take command of the Wessex forces if it proves necessary. They ride for my kingdom and my country, and the lords and reeves there will be keen to win favour from me."

As the king spoke, he reached out, gripping Leofwine's forearm firmly, his own hand shaking. Leofwine read far more into that gesture than the king's words had provided. The king was frightened for his family. His wife dead the year before, and now his children were in peril. Leofwine understood far too well the terror of a man who was a father, as well as a king.

"Do this for me, and I'll make you ealdorman of all of Mercia." While Leofwine knew the prize should have pleased him, he merely felt shocked that the king thought he needed to bribe him. Had the king still not realised just being the ealdorman of the Hwicce was enough of an accolade for him.

"My lord King, I'd do this for you and your mother regardless. I don't need enticements to ensure I act honourably."

A flicker crossed the king's face at Leofwine's words. What it meant, Leofwine didn't know, until the king smiled sharply.

"My mother has always been a good judge of character," the king confirmed, before striding away, a steadier gait to his steps now that he'd taken steps to protect his mother and children.

Leofwine paused only for a breath, before heading for the door, and his men, who waited beyond, saddled and ready, prepared for whatever disaster had befallen the king now.

Wulfstan met his gaze evenly. "What is it?" he demanded to know.

While Leofwine explained, his voice low so as not to be overheard by any who lingered in the yard, resolve settled over Wulfstan's face.

"We'll rescue the king's mother, and his children, and then no matter what you say, and what your honour demands, you'll accept the ealdordom of Mercia. It should have been yours all along. The queen dowager would agree with me. But first, we rescue an old woman and babies from the clutches of the bastard northmen."

Leofwine grunted his agreement, mounting his horse, and calling Hunter to his side. The animal obeyed immediately, and Leofwine gave no consideration to whether she would keep up with the horses or not. He knew that she would.

Aware that Ealdormen Leofsige and Ælfric observed his every move, Leofwine cautioned all of the men to silence, a directive passed from one to another, with an assurance that an explanation would be given as soon as it was safe to do so.

Leofwine knew his men would trust him enough to accept such a terse command.

The men rode even faster than they'd raced to Oxford, but all the same, Leofwine worried that they'd simply not reach Dean in time. The settlement lay far to the south, in hindsight, not far enough away from the coast for comfort, but it had been the home of the royal children for many years. That, perhaps, had not been the wisest decision the king had ever made. Not with the Raiders so insistent on attacking England.

It was probably more through luck than planning that Dean had not been attacked before.

Leofwine urged the men onwards, concerned looks trying to determine how long it would be until darkness obscured the road they travelled, but they all seemed as keen as he was to reach Dean, as soon as they realised the peril the king's children could be in.

With consternation, Leofwine watched the sun sink ever lower on the western horizon. He wished to accomplish the journey in one day but knew it would be challenging to ride in the dark, and keep their movements concealed.

As the day turned almost to full darkness, Leofwine called Wulfstan to his side.

"We should stop. To ride on would be foolish."

"I can't agree, My Lord," Wulfstan's voice was rich with foreboding and then Leofwine smelt it too.

"Damn," the oath was wrenched from deep inside Leofwine's gut. The smell of burning was abruptly ripe in the air, the stench of burning flesh and wood, as the sky suddenly flared before them with lightning, only to be followed by a rippling crescendo of thunder, and a sudden downpour easily capable of drenching them all between one heartbeat and another.

"I thought it was always bloody warm in the south," Oscetel complained loudly over the dying echoes of the thunder, while Leofwine hunched into his cloak, suddenly needing it to try and keep some small part of him dry.

"Look," Wulfstan pointed into the darkness, and while Leofwine squinted with his one eye to see what his commander had spotted, the view before them unexpectedly lit with the glow of a fire.

"Where are we?" Leofwine said, his ordinarily staid horse dancing beneath him, unsettled by the storm they'd ridden into, while Hunter's ears pulled backwards, an unhappy whine escaping her mouth. The animals could sense the danger as well.

"North of Dean," Wulfstan informed him. Leofwine grunted.

"How close are we to Dean?"

"At least ten miles yet, and down that road, there," while Wulfstan pointed in a vague direction, Leofwine looked at his commander instead. He couldn't see as well as Wulfstan.

"Apologies, My lord, the road to Dean is filled with Raiders. I can make out smoking fires, and swarming men, even from here."

"The way is blocked then?"

"Only the easier way is blocked. We can find an alternative. But it'll take longer. Or we can fight our way through here."

Leofwine peered into the gloom but could see little beyond the driving rain, and the swirling, smoky fog that accompanied it.

"It's impossible," Leofwine complained. "I can see nothing."

"No, My lord, but that does mean that the Raiders won't be able to see us either."

"A fair point," Leofwine conceded, still torn as to what to do, aware he needed to make a decision fast before he was entirely drenched by the summer storm.

"It would be better to reach Dean sooner rather than later, but we're only a small force. I'm sure that the Raiders vastly outnumber us."

"From what I can see, at least five to one," Wulfstan confirmed, the answer hardly reassuring, for all that it was an estimation based only on what was visible in the shadows of the fire and the flickering lightning.

"Then we should make our way around the Raiders. Our priority is Dean, although I don't enjoy the thought of leaving so many people here to face the ravages of an attack."

"I believe we would be too late to help the majority of them," Wulfstan confirmed, his voice firm, as though he had too much experience of making such difficult decisions.

"Then we go round. Get to Dean, protect the queen dowager and her grandsons, and earn an ealdordom in the process."

A ghost of a smile played around Wulfstan's lips, as he nodded his assent in time to yet another chord of echoing thunder, the settlement before them suddenly cast into a light brighter than day. Leofwine winced at what little he could make out, in that flare of light, and resolutely turned his horse to follow Wulfstan.

If they could see the Raiders, it was possible they could also see Leofwine's small force. They needed to move on quickly.

Hastily, all of the men rushed to follow Leofwine and Wulfstan, using the glow of the after image of the lightning to guide their animals into woodlands that lay away from the settlement under attack.

It was difficult going, especially for Leofwine in the murky conditions. Every so often, lightning split the sky, to be followed by the clamour of rumbling thunder. Relying almost entirely on his memories of those brief moments of illumination, and Hunter, pacing along at his side, Leofwine was able to keep pace with the rest of his warriors.

Only when they'd made their way both into the forest and then some distance through it, did Leofwine even think of calling a halt. By that time, they were covered by heavy branches above their heads, blocking out even the flicker of the storm, and Leofwine called for brands to be lit. He was drenched. Being able to see would go some way to alleviating his discomfort.

As sparks of orange flame took hold, he looked to Wulfstan. It was evident that Wulfstan didn't feel they'd made enough progress to stop, already trying to ride on, but the remainder of the men were drooping in their saddles and would put up little resistance should they be forced to face the Raiders.

"We should rest, at least until dawn," Leofwine instructed, riding to where Wulfstan waited impatiently.

"Yes, we should, although I'd sooner not. But, here's as good as any other." That was an admission from Wulfstan that Leofwine quickly agreed with.

"Half can rest, and half can stand a guard," Leofwine called softly, the sound muffled by the richness of the ground beneath their feet. "One fire, and then the brands can be doused. We ride at daybreak, or sooner if we need to." Grunts and groans greeted his words, as the men argued good-naturedly back and forth over who would have which dubious honour, while Leofwine slid from his horse and secured him to a low hanging branch.

The animal was tired, Leofwine could tell just from looking, but all the same, the animal pawed at the ground while Leofwine removed the saddle, and brushed the sweaty back down with some leaves from a nearby branch.

Leofwine felt himself sway a little with exhaustion. It had been a long day of riding, from Deerhurst to Oxford, and then on, toward Dean, and he knew that worse was to come.

As the campfire sprang to life, quickly kindled using the brands, he turned to Wulfstan, his mouth opening to speak, only for Wulfstan to interrupt him.

"You sleep. You have the second watch," the older man commanded, with no room for argument, so Leofwine snapped his mouth shut. Long experience had taught him the futility of arguing with Wulfstan.

Closer to the fire, Leofwine hunkered down, wrapping his cloak around him, while Hunter settled at his side. A deep swig of water from his water bottle, and he lay down, resolutely closing his eyes, although he feared sleep would never come, not with the storm overhead and his heart thundering so loudly in his chest.

A hand on his shoulder woke Leofwine and blinking abruptly, he almost head-butted Wulfstan as he jumped to his feet.

"No need to fear. It's time for me to sleep," Wulfstan grunted, already wrapping himself in his own cloak. Around the campsite, Leofwine could see others waking their partners, and ordering the same.

With Hunter at his side, a far better guard than he could ever be, Leofwine found himself a comfortable pile of leaves to settle on and gazed out into the thick embrace of the forest. Everything was a subdued black, and in time he could make out the shapes of the tree trunks, if little else, as lighter shadows against the darker ones where nothing filled the space.

Leofwine was reasonably content that he'd see any skulking figures that threatened his small force, and certainly, Hunter would sense them long before he did.

Alone with his thoughts, Leofwine allowed his mind to drift, settling on the half-seen and half-imagined scenes of destruction that they'd encountered earlier. Leofwine grimaced. For all he'd respected lord Olaf when they'd travelled north together, Leofwine couldn't deny that the Raiders preferred means of funding themselves were not to his taste. Not at all.

When the gloom of the forest began to lessen with the coming daylight, Leofwine instructed all of the men to be woken. He was unsure if the division of the night had been fair, but felt it was time to move on. If not, he worried that he'd be too late to save the king's mother. It had taken all of his patience to wait as long as he had.

As the men readied themselves, voices soft in the morning air, Leofwine sniffed, and then inhaled even deeper. Shaking his head, he turned to Wulfstan.

"Can you smell it?" Leofwine demanded. Wulfstan paused in arranging his supplies over his animal's back.

"Smell what?"

But now Leofwine wasn't the only one abruptly alert. More and more of his men's heads popped up from whatever task they'd been doing with settling their beasts.

"Smoke," Leofwine answered, but there was really little need. Wulfstan had detected the stench as well.

"God knows how much is on fire for the smell to reach us even here," Wulfstan's words were spoken quietly, and held no hint of assurance about them, as his hand indicated the interior of the woodland.

"Come on, men," Leofwine called, aware of uneasy looks, and dark moods descending quickly. "We make our way to Dean. Any Raiders we encounter on the way, if they're alone, or in small groupings, we try and capture for information, and if impossible, we kill them. But the priority, as terrible as it might sound, is to reach the king's mother and her children. Leave the area for Wessex lords to patrol. They should be here soon, if not already."

Resolved, Leofwine had Oscetel lead them onwards. Even though he'd never been to this area before, Oscetel had an accurate sense of direction, even in the blackest of nights, and without the aid of any brands to light the way.

A silence fell over the group, broken occasionally by the crack of dry leaves and twigs underfoot, and the hurrying sounds of birds and animals in the undergrowth as the scent of approaching fire intensified.

Leofwine was unsurprised to find those animals that did cross their path, even the occasional deer, were heading in the opposite direction to them. The men left the animals to their own destiny. They didn't need to be hampered by hares or deer carcasses as they picked their way carefully south.

More than once, hands strayed to weapons, handy on weapons belts, at unexpected noises, but none of the Raiders joined them, only ever small animals dashing away. Leofwine looked up, hopeful of at least seeing the sky through the thick canopy of leaves and branches above his head, but there was never any break, only the occasional shower as raindrops fell, either from the sky above, or the treetops, Leofwine was unsure.

He felt hemmed in by the damp earth beneath his horse's hooves, and the damp leaves above his head, and while grey and brown light had infiltrated the forest with the advance of the day, Leofwine still struggled to see well in the dim glow. He had no idea of how the day progressed, but the fear that they were already too late was potent.

More than once, Leofwine bit down a demand to move more quickly, to argue for returning to the edge of the forest, to do anything but what they were doing.

Whenever the urge became too strong, he turned to Wulfstan, noting his calm assurance, and easy seat in the saddle, and urged his body to relax. All the same, Leofwine knew he was losing his internal battle, and that it wouldn't be long before he ordered a new tactic to be deployed.

Before that happened, Leofwine became aware that the stench of smoke had grown almost overpowering, and with it, the tightness of the trees had reduced. There were the odd patches of sky overhead, and what he saw disturbed him.

The clouds hung grey, menacing with rain and yet it was warm as well. The earthy tang of mulch reached his nostrils, conflicting with the stench of death, and he called his men together urgently.

"Oscetel, scout to the front. We need to know what's out there before we stumble into it."

Oscetel slid quickly from his horse, handing the reins to Leofgar who took them immediately, settling the animal beside his own, while Oscetel slipped quietly through the trees.

Leofwine could feel the pressure of what lay beyond his view, could almost taste it mixed with the ash and stray sparks that permeated so deeply into the forest.

Oscetel returned quickly, his eyebrows furrowed, a glance behind his back an indication that he didn't wish to be followed. Leofwine knew without asking that the news would be difficult to hear.

"It's been raised to the ground. Where the people have gone, I don't know, but there are only the Raiders out there now, checking for what they can find, which is clearly little. There are no more than thirty of them, but I can't see how they could have caused so much devastation alone. There must be more somewhere."

The news was hardly reassuring, but thirty enemies was a better number to face than three hundred if it became necessary.

"Can we get to Dean without crossing their path?" Leofwine asked, turning to Wulfstan who knew the area better than anyone.

Wulfstan's forehead was furrowed in thought, his eyes far away, as though seeing something other than the forest-scape before them.

"The swathe of trees goes further south yet, but of course, it'll be slow going."

Leofwine grunted in frustration but knew it was the right course of action.

"Then we carry on as we are." Oscetel was mounting his horse as Leofwine spoke.

"The trees will keep us safe, if not the king's mother," Wulfstan confirmed unhappily, while Leofwine gazed longingly at the open space opening up before them, where he could make out the tendrils of damp smoke curling deeper into the forest.

"The directive remains the same, reach Dean, and rescue the royal family. We can't do that if we're dead, as much as we might wish we could slay the bastards out there." Resolutely, Leofwine turned his horse away from the enticing view and hunkered down back into the low hanging trees.

The day was far from over.

8

AD1001

THAT NIGHT THEY AGAIN SLEPT UNDER THE BLANKET OF TREE COVER ABOVE their heads, the sound of distant rain falling, a steady counterpart to hearts that raced with the sound of each and every stray movement.

All day they'd ridden ever south, making a careful path through long and straggling tree limbs, routinely sending someone to scout the area beyond the forest. At no point had any of the men returned with the news that the Raiders were out of sight.

It was as though the Raiders had raced inland, caused as much havoc as possible, and then slowly withdrawn, leaving a shipload of Raiders in each and every settlement they'd encountered. Leofwine felt his unease increase. There was something decidedly planned about these seemingly random events.

Leofwine could detect a giant hand at work here, someone who was not just opportunistic. He couldn't help thinking that the only enemy England had capable of such planning was Swein of Denmark, and his allies, who Leofwine was sure included Ealdorman Pallig. The thought made sleep difficult, no matter his exhaustion after two days in the saddle.

His alertness served him well.

Over the snoring of his tired men, the sound that reached his ears was distant, and yet also immediate. It was impossible to tell how close, or far away, anything was in the deep forest bed beneath them. He held his breath fearfully, and only when he was assured that he heard the hooves of horses coming toward them, did he stand, and alert all of his men.

Almost immediately, every one of his warriors was standing, vigilant, weapons in hand, all idea of sleep banished. Whispers rang out, quieter than breathing, and Leofwine's men arrayed themselves in a loose semi-circle, ready for whatever erupted out of the forest before them.

Wulfstan hovered at Leofwine's side no matter the command he step aside, and in the end, Leofwine submitted with ill grace. Wulfstan was right. His sight was severely limited in the gloom.

The soft nicker of one horse to another, ever closer, had Leofwine clutching his seax in one hand, his war axe in the other, Hunter growling at his side, white teeth showing over black gums. Leofwine held both weapons in one hand, as he rubbed his hand over her nose, attempting to quiet and comfort in equal measure.

Two horses emerged from the murkiness; figures slumped on their backs. Leofwine started at the sight, unable to determine whether they were enemy or ally.

"Fleeing the Raiders," Wulfstan muttered, and Leofwine was all for agreeing, but there was just something about the stance of one of the slumped figures that had his thoughts scattering elsewhere.

Without realising he did so, Leofwine walked forward, Hunter beneath his hand, his war axe discarded back on his weapons belt, while his seax stayed true in his left hand. He'd be able to stab if he needed to. But he didn't think it would be necessary.

Wulfstan's hand on his arm tried to pull him back, until, with a soft sigh, he simply followed his lord forward.

"Athelstan?" Leofwine said the word softly, fear almost paralysing him, and the sound little more than a whisper.

"Athelstan," reaching out, Leofwine ran his free hand over the slumped head, disturbing a mass of dirty blond hair, while Hunter sniffed the horse, her own examination of this strange sight.

No cloak covered the body, and indeed, Leofwine gasped as he lifted the hair away, to see the shadow of bruises at the rider's throat. What had befallen the rider?

A gasp of rattling air and Leofwine stepped back, his hand reaching for his seax, only for a young voice to fill the air.

"Lord Leofwine, is that you?"

"Young Edmund, what are you doing here?" Leofwine demanded, his eye peering into the bright blue eyes of the king's third oldest son, both as shocked as the other at meeting in such a strange location.

"They tried to strangle Athelstan. Is he still alive?" Edmund was already reaching for his brother now that he was awake again, but Leofwine rushed forward, grabbing the figure as it slid from the saddleless horse, where it would have dropped to the floor had Leofwine, Wulfstan and Hunter not arrested the worst of the fall.

"They captured him and tried to strangle him before Dean. I rescued him," Edmund sounded both pleased with himself, and also a little terrified as he recounted what had brought them here.

"Does he live?"

Wulfstan already had his ear pressed to Athelstan's chest, a hand raised for silence before he nodded.

"He lives, and he will live. He's just weak. Come, we should settle him before the fire."

"There's no time for that, lord Leofwine," there was a harsh tone to Edward's voice. "We need to find the lords of Wessex and their warriors, and we need to relieve Dean. My grandmother and the rest of my brothers and sisters are inside. Thorkell the Tall and Erik mean to attack come the morning, I'm sure of it."

Leofwine, almost unable to tear his eyes away from the ligature marks around Athelstan's neck, nodded, although he didn't know what to order first. Not right then. It was, luckily still night, but where would he find the Wessex lords, and make it to Dean before daylight struck?

Only then did Edmund pause.

"Why are you in Wessex?"

"Your father sent us to save you."

"And the Wessex lords?"

"The king says they're mine to command if we can find them."

"How many men do you have?"

A wry smile cracked Leofwine's strained face, as he listened to the king's son. He asked all the right questions. He shouldn't have expected anything different from Athelstan's brother.

"Oscetel, Leofgar, make your way out of the forest. One of you rides north, one of you west, find the Wessex lords if you can, and bring them to Dean. If you don't find them, ride to Dean all the same. We must be in position before daybreak."

That left them with little time, or so Leofwine feared. All the same, he didn't think they could take on two of Swein's famed commanders alone, for Thorkell the Tall and Jarl Erik were not new names to Leofwine. No, Horic had often spoken of the two men, enemies of lord Olaf, with the same reverence he'd reserved for king Swein himself.

"I've twenty men. We'll do what we can. How did you escape?"

"They underestimated me," Edmund smirked, a line of soot on his face, his hair matted and heavy with ash where it had dried from the dampness of the air.

"They underestimated my grandmother as well," Edmund added, his blue eyes peering out from his dirty face. He watched Leofwine's men make ready to ride out from their temporary camp, dried meat thrust into his hands, which he chewed as he spoke, and a water bottle as well, which he swigged from when the chewy texture of the meat strips became too much.

Athelstan stayed non-sensible, but Leofwine dribbled water into his mouth, and once assured that the bruises and swelling around the neck looked terrible, but weren't impeding his ability to breath, he ordered that Athelstan ride in front of Wulfstan, who could hold him upright.

Edmund too was placed before Leofwine, the boys' two horses too far gone to take any weight other than their own.

"We could leave them here, but then we'd need to remember where they were. Better to take them with us, at least to open ground," Leofwine ordered, and the two animals were tied to the saddles of Lyfing and Wulfsige, both animals head's downcast.

"If they slow you down, cut them loose, and we'll hope they make it to water and food," Leofwine instructed harshly. For now, he had two of the king's sons, but to save the rest of the family, and the king's mother, he had no choice but to take them both back toward Dean with him. He only hoped it wouldn't bring about their deaths when they'd already escaped once.

Still keen to travel under cover of the low clouds, heavy with ash and rain, Leofwine made the decision that the group should move to the edge of the forest. If they were undetected, then they could travel faster around the edge of the forest rather than through it.

The moon was hidden when they emerged, the light only a little brighter than under the forest canopy, and yet the horses were better able to pick their own path, avoiding hazards on the ground.

While every man there rode alert, Edmund whispered to Leofwine of all that had happened in Dean in the last few days. Leofwine was amazed to hear it all.

The Raiders had struck fast, kidnapped Athelstan, seemingly on the order of King Swein, tried to ransom him instead for a massive sum of money, threatened the king's mother, demanded payment, refused the amount offered by Lady Elfrida, and then tried to kill Athelstan all the same.

They'd taken captive some of Lady Elfrida's men who'd ridden out to assist in the attack on the areas, and, or so it seemed, Lady Elfrida had frustrated all of the Raiders attempts to steal a prince or be paid to leave, and then Edmund had stolen away their prize from under their noses.

Leofwine could only imagine how desperate the Raiders were to accomplish something now. The news that Swein of Denmark wanted one of the king's sons was beyond worrying. It seemed his threats toward England were greater than Æthelred had comprehended. Far greater, and no doubt with the connivance of Ealdorman Pallig, who would have been ideally placed to let Swein know where the king's children were being raised, away from the king's court.

Wulfstan listened carefully, asking sharp questions, determining all that had happened to the settlement around Dean, and only when Edmund slumped in sleep, did Wulfstan lapse into silence.

"We use the forest," Leofwine commented.

"Yes, we do, to cover us, and hope that the Wessex lords and their warrior arrive in good time."

Before Wulfstan, Athelstan abruptly stirred, sitting upright so suddenly he almost broke Wulfstan's nose with his head.

"What," the voice was strangled, filled with confusion.

"Your brother found us," Leofwine commented quickly before Athelstan could reach for one of Wulfstan's weapons and fight his way to freedom.

"Your father sent us to rescue your grandmother and you."

Only at those words did Athelstan relax, and only then for a few breaths, before the rattle of harness again filled the air.

Leofwine was about to call his men to a halt, ready to face whatever was coming at them, when Oscetel raced into his line of sight.

"We found them, My Lord, some of the Wessex lords and their warriors. I have them with me.

Leofwine gasped in shock, turning to meet the eyes of the men on horseback and in command of their own warriors from Wessex.

"My lords, it's good to see you," Leofwine could see many brands raised high, it was evident the men had dashed to intercept Leofwine's small force, choosing speed over stealth.

"Come, we have the king's family to rescue, and then we'll chase these damn bastards from our country, killing as many as we can in the process." The words were greeted with a muffled cheer from those who could hear them, the sound muted in the damp conditions.

For all that Leofwine knew the men were keen to fight. Wessex was the king's own estate. Most here would owe ultimate loyalty, and their commendatory oath either directly to the king, his mother, or one of the young æthelings. He couldn't imagine any of them would stint in trying to ensure the long life of those they owed their oath to.

Certainly, he hoped that the Wessex men were as loyal to the crown as he was.

9
AD1001

Racing through the night, brands lighting their way because speed was more important than surprise now that their force was so much more extensive, Leofwine and the Wessex warriors only slipped back into the safety of the on-going forest when Edmund began to recognise where they were. Athelstan still drowsed for much of the time, although he was quick to reassure everyone that he was well.

Calling his men, and the commanders of the fyrd together, Leofwine quickly explained what would happen as soon as the sun began to rise, and his idea met with no complaints, and only respectful nods of agreement.

"We make them believe there are more of us than there are. That'll worry them, have them half running away even before the sun has wholly lit the sky."

Leofwine had thought of the correct tactic to employ throughout their journey south. Using the forest to cover their number was a given. With his own men, numbering twenty, and those of the mounted warriors of the Wessex lords, and with some foot soldiers as well, hiding in the forest just in case, he was sure that they would have enough to overpower the Raiders, even if those men were commanded by Thorkell the Tall and Jarl Erik.

Leofwine knew of them both by reputation. Horic often spoke of them. It was always with a grin of appreciation for their violent natures, and also their innovative battle strategies. Leofwine knew he faced men of considerable cunning. He'd have to be just as clever to ensure they left England without one of Æthelred's sons or any of her gold and silver.

As they snaked their way ever closer to Dean, the forest once more grew thick and almost impassable in places, as they slipped back into its cover. Leofwine could see how the two youths had used the thick growth to hide them from any who might have thought to pursue them, but it made difficult work for his warriors, even those who merely walked.

Before they'd entered the forest once more, Leofwine had gazed upwards, unsurprised to see thick cloud obscuring the moon, mingled with the smoke from fires that still flared occasionally to the east of their route.

While they aimed for Dean, Leofwine was sure that there must be Raiders all around them. Somehow, they were all managing to avoid each other, and it was far more by chance than planning.

Hunter led his horse ever onwards. Her paws padded softly over the ground, her ears alert for all signs of danger, and it was she who sniffed out the remains of not one, but five different fires, still smoking gently, and clearly not long abandoned in the thickness of the trees.

All of the men were called to arm themselves, Leofwine's command being passed by word of mouth, rather than hollered in the stagnant air. Sound travelled strangely, and Leofwine worried that for all their stealth, it might be for nothing. The enemy might have been aware of their approach all night long, just waiting, when they finally arrived, to engage them in bloody battle.

It was Edmund who announced they were close to Dean, and

Oscetel who once more slipped through the thinning trees to determine what was happening at the royal settlement.

Oscetel returned quickly, his mouth in a tight smile.

"They are oblivious to us. A thick fog coats the area. None could see us, and certainly, there's no one watching the forest for signs of reinforcement. They think themselves safe."

"And Dean itself?"

"Impossible to tell the state of the walls. The settlement before it is in ruins. But the walls hold, and I believe there are guards on duty. Certainly, I saw the flicker of flame. It either burns, or men guard it. I couldn't risk getting any closer."

"Well done, Oscetel," Leofwine gripped his forearm in thanks. Oscetel was one of his oldest friends. He didn't like to put him in danger, but neither would Oscetel have thanked him for holding him back.

"Ensure everyone has a brand," Leofwine instructed, while Athelstan slid free from beside him, alert now that the journey was coming to an end.

"I would have my own horse, and weapons," the young prince wobbled, and Leofwine nodded, for all it made him feel uneasy. He'd have Oscetel ride close to the prince, Leofgar as well, ensure that both boys wouldn't need to fight alone. Leofwine knew that Athelstan prided himself on being a warrior, unlike his father, but right now, Leofwine would have been far happier if the prince had simply asked to wait until the fighting was over.

Hasty rearrangements took place, the original horses, rested from being without a rider throughout the rest of the night, were returned to Edmund and Athelstan, suitable weapons and arms found from amongst Leofwine's household warriors.

None of them ever rode to battle with just one of everything. Not if they could fit more in their saddlebags, or along weapons belts.

When all was ready, everything so still that none would think over a hundred men sheltered within the overhanging trees, dripping now and again with the aftermath of the terrible rainstorms that have fallen for days, Leofwine gave the command.

His brand flared to light first, and then he lit the one to his left, and then the one to his right, the action being repeated by his warriors, and by the lords who led the Wessex forces as well.

Leofwine gazed to his left and right, as the circle of fire expanded outwards, the harsh pitch filling his nostrils, and trying to blind his good eye with the acrid smoke.

And still, they waited and then waited some more. There was the light to see by, but the damp mist and smoky ash hung heavily. And Leofwine appreciated that they needed to wait for the light of the day and certainly for as long as they possibly could. They couldn't attack in the dark.

As Leofwine's arm began to ache from holding the brand aloft, Oscetel assured him that there was movement on the walkway of Dean itself. Edmund joined Oscetel in agreeing. It appeared that the inhabitants of Dean still lived, and Leofwine and his force still needed to fight the enemy to gain their freedom.

Only then Oscetel barked an instruction that the Raiders must have spotted the force, as they try to slink away, and Leofwine finally gives the order to attack.

The horses raced across the expanse of burnt land, bursting from the cover of the forest, with Hunter in front, her ears alert to all sound. Dawn was finally more than a shade of bruised purple on the eastern horizon, and while shadows still plagued Leofwine's limited vision, he was content that he could see well enough.

Leofwine rode from shadow to daylight, and beneath the hooves of his horse, the wet ground was churned up, while the surprised Raiders attempted to escape the mass of horsemen suddenly amongst them.

The Raiders rushed from Leofwine's household troop evidently not ready to face an attack. Leofwine watched them go hungrily, pleased that few would meet their death that day, and yet the king's mother, and the king's children would be rescued all the same.

With no opposition at all, the gates of Dean cracked open as a loud voice called the command. Leofwine's horse and hound rode inside, accompanied by the royal grandchildren.

At Leofwine's command, Wulfstan rode on, content to chase down the Raiders, or ensure they made it back to their ships and off English land. In the wake of the mounted warrior, the Wessex foot soldiers examined each and every burnt out building, ensuring none of the Raiders had decided on the dubious shelter offered there, rather than fighting for their lives.

Leofwine jumped from his horse, Hunter in front, and showing him the way by leading him up the steep stairs to the interior of the walls surrounding Dean. There, Leofwine exhaled with relief, pleased to find Lady Elfrida watching him with her keen eyes. She looked both overjoyed, and so very, very weak.

10

AD1001

The return to Winchester was not undertaken immediately. Instead, Leofwine and his household troop ensured the Raiders were chased back to their ships, and a full assessment carried out as to who had lost their lives in the Battle of Dean, as it was already being named by those who'd lived through it.

Leofwine learned then that the Raiders had not gone unopposed in Wessex, even before he and the Wessex lords had arrived. When he and his men finally made the journey to the site of the largest battle in daylight, to the north of Dean, no doubt the one they'd first come upon, he could tell that there'd been a great slaughter on both sides.

For the English, he had the names of those killed written down and sent on to the king. The king's high reeve of Hampshire, Æthelweard was dead; Leofric of Whitchurch was dead; high reeve Leofwine, his own namesake, was dead. And the church had suffered as well: Godwine of Worthy, the son of Bishop Ælfsige, was dead and so was his thegn, Wulfhere.

The most worrying of all was that those five named were only those thought most worthy of mentioning. Many, many more had been killed, children, women, men, the old and the young, it sickened Leofwine to see such carnage.

The survivors of the local settlements were busy at work, retrieving their dead, and burying those unclaimed by anyone.

It was a brutal business, yet Leofwine was surprised when Wulfstan excused himself from the duty.

"One mass burial is enough in any man's life," Wulfstan muttered, ambling his horse away from the grisly sight and smell of the carnage of battle. Leofwine allowed his man to go without calling him back.

Did Wulfstan think of the Battle of Maldon as he surveyed the ruin of so much life? If so, Leofwine was surprised. Wulfstan never spoke of the battle. Leofwine had thought it was merely because it was not worth talking about, now he wasn't so convinced.

Not for the first time, Leofwine wondered what the truth was regarding his father's death of the Battle of Maldon, and Wulfstan's survival.

THE JOURNEY TO WINCHESTER TOOK TIME, AND THROUGH NONE OF IT DID Leofwine allow any of his household troops to relax. If anything, the royal party was in more danger than when it had been safely behind the walls of Dean.

It was a relief to finally arrive in Winchester, although, a quick glance at Lady Elfrida's tired and drained face and Leofwine couldn't help thinking that she didn't share his opinion.

The king and his mother shared a problematic relationship, blame so often part of their cycle of being friendly or antagonistic and Leofwine, clearly more protective of Lady Elfrida than her own son could ever be, and mindful of the eyes of the king's children on him, felt pressed into intervening during their reunion.

For all that, the king surprised Leofwine that evening, calling him to his side in the great hall of Winchester.

"I'd like you to extend your authority to all of the old Mercian lands, as I promised. It should have been done some time ago. You've performed your duties well concerning the Hwiccan kingdom, and I need a man of your experience and steadfastness to hold all the old Mercian lands together, apart from to the east, where Leofsige will still command."

"The Mercians have borders with many of our foes and are open to easy attack in too many places. I'd meant to gift you with the added duties last year, but the arrival of Ealdorman Pallig drove the idea from my mind." There was almost the hint of an apology in the king's voice. Leofwine wasn't used to his king admitting to his mistakes.

"I'll write to my reeves and inform them of my decision. There might be some resentment, but I imagine that when they're faced with a shipload of Raiders, they may be more receptive to you and your men. And perhaps you could offer some advice on how they can best defend their lands. The burhs are most effective but might benefit from some repair work being carried out. The area has been without an ealdorman for some time. Please act as you see fit."

"With thanks, My Lord King," Leofwine managed to mutter, shocked that after all, he'd not had to remind the king of his promises, as Wulfstan had been badgering him to do throughout the journey to Winchester

"Don't thank me yet, Leofwine. You might well wish I'd not given you the title and the lands."

Before he rode back to Deerhurst, Leofwine took the time to speak with Lady Elfrida. The king had announced to his children that the royal household was to be broken up, the older sons given their own houses and household warriors to command, Lady Elfrida to finally relinquish her hands on the future of the Royal House of Wessex.

Leofwine expected to find her saddened and bereft, but was unsurprised to discover her in close conversation with Wulfstan, the hint of a smile playing around her old lips as they spoke softly to each other.

She eyed Leofwine with delight when he bowed before her, an apology for interrupting what had clearly been a private meeting between his commander and the king's mother.

"I would thank you," she began, "for rescuing us all, and for refusing to notice how old and useless I've become."

Leofwine's mouth dropped open in shock, all words fled at her admission. This served only to make Wulfstan and her smile even more.

"Ah, when they're young, they never believe they'll be old, and realise it as well." Her tone was jovial, and yet Leofwine was aware of sadness in her too bright eyes.

Wulfstan bowed low, perhaps his final obeisance for a woman Leofwine knew had counted him as a friend, and ally.

"Sit with me," the rich voice commanded, no waver in the words, although Leofwine had heard it enough times in recent days to know it normally reflected her weakness.

Leofwine settled quickly, on the chair beside her own, in front of the hearth in the king's hall. He didn't know what to say to Lady Elfrida, and yet had sought her out anyway, feeling as though he couldn't leave without speaking to the woman who'd done so much for him once more. He feared this would be their last meeting.

"My son will soon truly rule alone," she said, a lilt to her voice, perhaps of relief that she'd witness no more of her son's reign. Leofwine opened his mouth to deny her, but she continued speaking, waving her frail hand once to dismiss his concerns for her harsh words.

"He has many sycophants around him, and few who tell him the truth. You're worth far more to him than he believes. I know you're now ealdorman of Mercia, but my son is always a contrary beast. He seeks friends and finds only adversaries. Remember your worth, even when he doesn't." The words were surprisingly hard to hear and yet also a relief. Leofwine had few illusions about the nature of his king's personality, but to hear another say them, especially the king's mother assured him that he was correct in his summation of the king.

Again, Leofwine made to open his mouth.

"And his children, he doesn't see who they truly are either. I would ask you, for the sake of them, to stand firm, no matter what happens." Leofwine felt a sudden lump in his throat. It seemed this really was to be the final meeting between them, and it saddened him, more than he'd thought it would.

"May I?" before he could say anything, his eye caught a flicker of movement, and he bowed his head low. Strange, after all these years, that she wished to touch his scar.

"I've often imagined what it would feel like," Lady Elfrida said, her lined finger light on his too-tight cheek.

"Then you should have asked before," he chided softly, as her touch left his face.

"It's little different to the rest of you," she said, some amazement in her voice.

"It's become a part of me, and who I am," he agreed. "It taught me much. Gave more than it took away."

"It gave you your wisdom," Lady Elfrida confirmed, her voice tight with emotion. "Use it," she urged him. "Use it for my son, and my grandsons, and if they all fail me, then use it for England."

The words rang like iron, as Leofwine stood, and bowed once more, Hunter at his side.

"I'll do as you command." The words did not slide from his mouth easily but were instead wrenched from him. He meant them with every part of his being.

11
AD1001

Leofwine left Winchester with a heavy heart, but also a renewed purpose. He was clear in his mind that the old lands of the Mercians needed to be monitored closely. Mercia, now reunited with the lands of the Danelaw, the Five Boroughs clawed back from them by his king's grandfather and his brothers, could fall easy prey to the Raiders. The people there shared just as much heritage with the Raiders as they did the English.

Æthelflæd, Wulfstan, Horic and Oscetel held a lengthy discussion that first night back at Deerhurst as they considered the actions that needed to be taken. The king had gifted Leofwine with property and land to fulfil his role as the Hwiccan ealdorman, but Leofwine had chosen early on to spend most of his time in his father's house. That position, on the periphery of the Mercian lands, made remaining there unsound. Leofwine quickly realised that he'd need to spend more of his time in the central lands.

In the end, the decision was made that they'd set out for Lichfield, in the heart of Mercia, and then having assessed the situation, they could stay or move on to another house.

Æthelflæd was a flurry of activity as she tried to organise the household she was leaving while preparing for a house she'd not yet seen. Finn was quickly pressed into service by her as she made lists of things she needed and the things she wanted. His scribing skills had been more than helpful, and Æthelflæd used them as often as she could. She'd even convinced him that he could help Northman learn his letters.

Finn had been severely shaken when he'd first arrived following the death of Olaf of Norway. Like Wulfstan, after the Battle of Strathclyde, he'd needed to be handled with care. Finn's traumatised state of mind had been born with patience, and he was now an active member of Leofwine's ever-growing household.

Leofwine knew that all he needed was a priest and his household would be as elaborate as the king's own.

The king had, in gifting Leofwine the governance of all the Mercian people, increased the dues he owed to the royal household. It meant that as a matter of some urgency Leofwine needed to increase the numbers in his household troop. His men had some ideas as to which youngsters their lord could advance. Some of the youngsters would make good warriors, and so would some of the more adolescent boys who routinely joined in the training that his troop endured each day.

Leofwine preferred to have a direct say in any arrangements, but for once he deputised to Wulfstan and Horic. The men knew his mind well, and as they'd be responsible for training and would be dependent upon the warrior skills of the men they chose, he thought it best they have the final say.

It was also decided that Horic and his wife would stay behind to run his house near Deerhurst. Horic was also tasked with keeping Leofwine informed of events he heard about, just in case messages directly from the king to Leofwine were disrupted.

As they discovered the state of affairs within Mercia, Leofwine would act accordingly, possibly leaving others of his men in charge of swathes of areas so that he could attempt to keep abreast of the situation.

As darkness began to fall on his last day at the home of his birth, Leofwine felt himself grow melancholy. The king had both honoured him and given him an almost impossible task.

It had been nearly twenty years since Mercia had had an ealdorman to her name. He was more than aware that in the intervening years, pockets of influential individuals had risen to prominence. Ealdorman Ælfhelm's sons were Mercians, and so was their Uncle, and those were men who were not indifferent to Leofwine. How others would greet him was impossible to determine.

Both an advancement and a burden. All rolled into one.

Leofwine didn't think the coming months would be easy ones.

Lichfield was a distance of two days of slow and steady travel, allowing for his servants and his family to keep pace together, the trail of horses and carts stringing out over the roadway north.

They spent the night away from home sleeping within the walls of the monastery at Coventry and then hastened on early the next day when the early morning activities of the monks disturbed the children from their exhausted slumbers.

Tired and grumpy, the entire party set out on a blustery day, pulling their cloaks tight about them. Leofwine rode with Leofric wedged between him and his saddle, a memory of doing the same with Athelstan so recently reminding Leofwine that the smaller the child, the more comfortable it was. Northman sometimes rode alone on a small, sturdy horse, and at other times shared with Wulfstan.

The joy of the journey had soon turned sour for both young boys, and they'd lapsed into a sulky silence until allowed to run havoc around Coventry monastery the previous day. Not even the stern looks of the monks had flattened their energy.

Leofwine took in the view of the Mercian countryside as he travelled, and on occasion stopped to speak to the men and women who worked the fields. Often they were greeted with initial hostility – none of the hard-working farmers wished to see a small, armed troop marching through their land at harvest time – but once Leofwine or one of his men had made introductions, the reception was far more positive.

The people of the fertile farmlands were pleased to know that they'd not been forgotten by the king who in recent years had been more likely to send a reeve to see to his business than one of the ealdormen.

Indeed, not since the banishment of Ealdorman Ælfric Cild had Mercia had her own ealdorman. Leofwine knew it had been a bad decision on the part of the king, and that he'd have to work hard to earn the trust of men and women who'd become used to ruling themselves, and keeping their own farms and steadings safe from Raiders attacks.

They reached Lichfield during the early evening and were quickly able to find the ancient church, high on a hill and beside it a neat and tidy house where smoke billowed invitingly through the small roof slits for ventilation.

A petite woman, finely dressed, stepped through the doorway and closed it tightly behind her, an attempt at a smile of welcome on her face, as Leofwine slipped from his horse, pulling Leofric down as well. The little lad, relieved to be free from the horse, ran around excitedly until his mother caught him up in her arms as she too dismounted.

The woman stayed where she was, looking back a little uncertainly behind her as Leofwine moved forward to greet her. She didn't flinch at his lopsided face, but she stared openly and jumped back in shock when Hunter, at his side, stepped forward to examine her and sniffed her open hand.

"Well met, my lord Leofwine. I'm Brunhild, wife of the reeve. I'm afraid that he's away on business," her voice wavered as she spoke, her attention divided between the gigantic hound who terrified her and the well-armoured man who stood before her with all the menace contained in the story of his damaged face.

It was evident from the way that she spoke that she wasn't

sorry for her husband's absence, but it was difficult to tell whether she meant it from a personal perspective or whether it was intended as a slur against Leofwine. Leofwine smiled blandly at her, nodding once to acknowledge her words. She didn't welcome him inside.

"But you were clearly informed that we would be arriving? Otherwise, how else would you know my name?"

Leofwine watched her face process an assortment of emotions.

"Well, yes, My Lord, but only yesterday, and I'm afraid my husband was already away. Even if we'd not been informed, I'd know who you were anyway. Few men carry their disfigurement quite so openly as you," her eyes darted uncertainly to where she could see the members of his household troop dismounting behind him as her voice trailed away, perhaps in embarrassment, although he doubted it.

"It's no matter. Wherever he is, he'll have been informed of my arrival, and I must apologise if you've been in any way inconvenienced by making room available for us within."

She flinched at his words and looked a little helpless. Leofwine was left thinking that his king might well have spoken too honestly when he said not to thank him for the honour yet. It seemed that Leofwine couldn't even talk his way passed this woman to gain entry into the king's house.

Seeing that Brunhild wasn't going to welcome them inside, Leofwine merely stepped around Brunhild to glance inside the building. A searing heat greeted him, not unwelcome in the late evening air, but a shock all the same.

The room was not unlike his home at Deerhurst, only slightly smaller and more sparsely decorated. There was a massive roaring fire in the fire pit, and a handful of men and servants were happily eating from a table laden with meats and bread.

He moved his gaze back to Brunhild.

"I see that at least you've prepared a welcome feast for us?"

"My lord Leofwine," she swallowed nervously, "the feast hasn't been prepared for you, but of course, you're welcome to partake. I'm not sure if we've enough for all of your party, though."

"Who is the feast for? There are few of you here, and yet the eating has already begun."

Again, she looked about uncertainly. Leofwine had already decided he didn't like the nervous-looking woman. Whatever was going on here, his arrival was unwelcome and unlooked for, and that annoyed him. He'd come to do little but the king's bidding. He'd have expected to be at least hailed before the reeve began trying to see him off his area of responsibility; this cold shoulder at the door was totally unacceptable.

Behind him, Æthelflæd appeared with the children, the baby fussing to be fed. He felt uncertain, though, and before letting her enter, gestured for Oscetel to precede them inside. He was still fully armed from his time on the road. He'd heard most of the conversation between Leofwine and the woman, and inclined his head to her as he stepped into the building, his manners impeccable, even if hers were not.

Leofwine could hear him clomping around inside, and a few harsh words were spoken, and then the noise of something scraping over the wooden floorboards reached his ears. Oscetel returned with a beaming smile and bowed at the waist in welcome to his lord. Leofwine suppressed his mirth at the play-acting of the man. He'd taken an intuitive grasp of the situation and was now acting the part of the host better than the actual host.

Leofwine held out his hand for Æthelflæd, who glanced between the two men questioningly before stepping inside the house. Leofwine winked at her and then turned aside as his two boys and Hunter shot inside the house, almost knocking him from his feet.

Brunhild held back her shock at events and allowed herself to be led inside by Oscetel. Once inside, Leofwine noted that the scuffling noise had been Oscetel forcibly removing the table of food to a more central location, close to the fire pit so that all who entered would find a spot to sit and a bite to eat.

He sought out his man and found him having a powerfully polite conversation with two men, Brunhild's housetroops he supposed, who objected to Leofwine's unexpected arrival and who'd enjoyed too much mead.

Æthelflæd was seated close to the fire feeding a fussy Ealdgyth, while his boys tumbled on the floor climbing over and around Hunter who took it all with good grace as she licked at a massive bone that someone had thought to give her.

Leofwine's men were slowly trailing in behind him, Wulfstan having given instructions on who could eat and who could stand guard. Leofwine hadn't expected to need to guard himself within his own future home; he'd need to exert his influence here and earn the respect of the Mercian people.

The thought was a mar on his journey, which he'd faced with excitement instead of his constant dread of meeting new people and enduring their silent questions and open stares. Surely everyone in England knew of his story by now, as Brunhild's cold reception of him had shown. He realised he faced different difficulties. His face was no longer the only issue: what he stood for as an ealdorman was.

The reeve of Lichfield did not deign to show his face for nearly a week after Leofwine arrived. By the time he did appear with his small guard, his wife had been relegated to one of the well-maintained houses near their previous home, set aside for visiting officials of the king.

It was a lovely little space, but Brunhild didn't appreciate being displaced and was as unhelpful as possible. The only good to come from her removal from the house was that the servants who lived and served her refused to go, choosing instead to stay and serve the ealdorman and his kind if stern, wife.

In a matter of two days, Æthelflæd had instilled order and respect amongst the handful of tired-looking servants, and they ran to do her bidding, cleaning and tidying as they went, and Leofwine slept a little easier in his bed fearing an infestation of lice less and less.

Leofwine also quickly discovered that where Brunhild had been ineffectual, her husband clearly had not been, and when the man arrived he was full of apologies and contrition for not having been there when they'd arrived. He'd missed the king's messages as he'd been conducting a brief survey of the lands he was responsible for, having heard of the disturbances in the south.

The reeve was a fiercely energetic man, skinny to the point of boyhood, although his head was almost bald. He rode a horse almost as long in the tooth as he was. Evidently, the man loved his horse perhaps more than his younger wife, who he routinely shot disapproving looks at as she sat about her house doing nothing to maintain its comfort or his own, merely issuing commands to a select handful of servants who hated her. Leofwine quickly decided that he liked Eadred far more than he had at first thought he would.

While Æthelflæd settled to life in Lichfield, Leofwine and the majority of his men travelled and surveyed the significant towns of Mercia. First, they went to the ancient settlement of Tamworth where it was believed Penda, the great Mercian king, had housed his capital.

Then they travelled to the old border with the Danelaw, beyond Repton and Breedon as far as Nottingham. The journey of over two weeks, at a leisurely pace, allowed Leofwine to meet the royal officials the king had utilised to run the lands since the banishment of the last ealdorman.

They were a varied and vivid selection, from surly fat gentlemen, grown rotund on the goodwill of the king, to men who were keen to see the land governed well for the king and who were pleased to see an ealdorman who had military experience.

Oscetel was a constant companion on the journey, as was Finn, who made notes and wrote down details as Leofwine desired. There was so much to remember that he realised early on that he needed to have the details in writing, and he wanted someone else to remember annoying details for him.

Finn proved to be more than able, although Northman and Leofric missed him, as they made clear when he returned on a cool evening and found himself harangued for stories and games. Finn took it all in good stead, enjoying being the centre of attention.

Leofwine was pleased to send a report to the king which detailed how prepared the area was if there was to be another incursion.

Leofwine, like his people, prepared for an attack that now seemed inevitable. He trained each day, often all morning or all afternoon, watching with amusement as Northman tried to join in, making a passable attempt at much of the training regime.

Leofric was still far too young to be instructed with the men and yet he had a fierce desire to be just as old as his brother. Leofric worked just as hard and for just as long, carrying out his own interpretation of the sword strokes, and weight training, his father and brother, did.

All three often collapsed at the end of their respective days exhausted. Æthelflæd hid her own fears for her boys well and laughed along with them when they recounted in great detail their various feats, childish voices high and determined.

Wulfstan was the young boys' most virulent defender. He was convinced that the two were somehow prodigies who would make excellent warriors in only a few years. He spoke at even greater lengths of their instinctive fighting techniques, and as Wulfstan's beard turned ever whiter, Leofwine couldn't help but feel remorse that his own father was not here to play grandfather to the boys. At the same time, he was overjoyed to know that they had Wulfstan; his father would have approved of his oldest friend and comrade teaching his grandsons.

He was sent regular reports from Horic at Deerhurst, often by Horic's own sons, four of them now old enough to act in their father's name. Unease coloured Horic's messages. He thought it was too calm, too quiet and the longer it took for any significant attack to happen away from the far southern lands, the worse he felt it would be.

Taking heed of Horic's unease, Leofwine moved his family from Lichfield to the more defendable Tamworth, gifting Eadred back his home. Eadred declined to take it, much to his wife's disgust. He'd taken to living a less complicated life in his smaller house and had decided that he needed to be in constant attendance on Leofwine. Luckily he made it clear to his wife that she wasn't involved in his relocation plans.

12
AD1001

Leofwine was roughly shaken from his sleep by small urgent hands. He shooed whichever son it was away from him, but still, the little hands shook him, and in the semi-dark, he opened his eyes to be greeted by a white-faced Northman. The boy's eyes were bright in the dark, and his lower lip trembled. Leofwine held his arms out to his son, thinking he must have experienced a bad dream, but the lad backed away, out of reach of his father's grasp.

"You must come," Northman lisped, his voice trying to be quiet but sounding incredibly loud in the early morning silence. Only, Leofwine noted, it was not quite as silent as it should be.

From outside, he could hear the angry shouts of men, and he thrust himself free of his wolf pelt to follow his son. He stopped briefly to grab his cloak and threw it quickly around his shoulders. Noting that his son was wearing little but his bedclothes, Leofwine picked him up and pulled him inside his cloak. His son's rigid body relaxed at his father's touch. Hunter, instantly alert, wound her way carefully in front of her master and his son.

Once inside the common room, where the snores of the maids

and the cook and the men of the household troop were loud enough to mask conversation, Leofwine grilled his son gently.

"What's the matter?"

"There are men at the gate. Oscetel is speaking to them but they sound angry, and Oscetel worried, and when he saw me wandering around, he told me to come and get you."

"Good lad," Leofwine said reassuringly to his son. "Do you want to come and see the men, or do you want to stay here and go back to bed?" Even with his urgent need to see what all the noise was about, he thought to question his son. The lad was brave beyond his years, but this had frightened him.

Northman considered for a while and then nodded solemnly, "I'll come."

Outside, in the rain infused fresh morning air, there was a swathe of lit brands near the closed enclosure of the king's property in Tamworth. The brands made it difficult for him to see who stood at the gate, seeking admission. However, the angry voices of whomever Oscetel were keeping at bay were easy to hear.

Oscetel turned to his lord with relief when Leofwine appeared, and hastily introduced the stranger.

"The king has sent his high reeve to inform you of a raid on the south-western coast. He demands admittance but, my lord, I don't know the man and he speaks with a Danish accent."

Leofwine immediately understood Oscetel's dilemma when the man on the huge dark horse before them began speaking. His accent was far thicker than even Horic's, and Leofwine didn't recognise him either, cursing his limited sight. Behind the stranger was a small mass of mounted men, muttering quietly to themselves, but not one of them used Leofwine's language.

"How long have you been the king's reeve?"

"I carry a letter with his seal on if that's any help." The man curtly ignored Leofwine's question as he thrust a piece of vellum forwards in his gloved hand.

Oscetel sighed in annoyance, "Why didn't you show me that?"

"The king said it was for the ealdorman, and you, clearly, are not the ealdorman." The stranger's tone was smugly irritating where it cut through his accent.

"Well, no, I'm not, but it would have saved time and arguments."

"It's good to test the resolve of the household troops, Ealdorman Leofwine," and the man turned towards where Leofwine was attempting to read his message from the king in the faint glow of one of the lanterns.

"You're to be commended for the loyalty and vigilance of your men. The king would do well to surround himself with such as you have." Leofwine noted the man's words with a wry smile as he saw Oscetel relax at the praise.

"Indeed reeve? Sorry, I don't think you mentioned your name?"

"I'm Ragnor from Denmark. I've served the king for many years but in the far south. I don't often come to the witan. I prefer to guard my king's ship army and his lands with my own eyes, rather than trusting them to the less than watchful men who call themselves his reeves elsewhere."

"There's treachery. Even now Ealdorman Pallig, if the rumours are to be believed, attacks the king's forces. Now I must be gone."

"With thanks," Leofwine called to the rapidly departing back of the small troop of men the messenger rode with. No doubt, he carried messengers for other lords, and if not, then Leofwine imagined that they rode to counter Pallig's threat.

Leofwine turned back to enter his house. His steps felt heavy as he called Oscetel to him. This was not the sort of news he expected to be woken with, even if he had been anticipating Pallig's betrayal since last year and more Raider attacks since he'd rescued the king's mother and his children from Dean.

In a hive of activity Leofwine had Oscetel arrange those men who would accompany him south, and those who would stay behind. He then began the less than pleasant task of telling the rest of the household. The servants and his men were waking slowly to what was assumed to be a typical day. In a few short words, Leofwine had the entire household bustling around, readying the men and the settlement for whatever may come.

Æthelflæd and the maid quickly took charge of Northman but not before Leofwine had thanked his small son and bid him be brave in his absence. Northman seemed to have understood most of what the reeve had told them, and as Leofwine readied himself to leave, still well before the sun rose, the boy's high voice reached his ears.

"Mother, when the Raiders come here, will I be allowed to fight them?"

Leofwine grimaced at the words pouring from his child's mouth. He didn't want the boy to be thinking so, and yet at the same time, he felt relieved that his son was ready to defend his family.

Æthelflæd responded to his innocent question with only a slight tremble in her voice. "Only if the other men have all fallen, and it's to be hoped by God's grace that doesn't happen."

Northman seemed content with the answer and walked away to play with his younger brother. Leofwine caught Æthelflæd's sad eyes as she gazed after her oldest child, so keen to be a warrior at such a tender age.

"Did you not wish to have a sword and fight at his age?" he teased to calm her melancholy.

She glared at him and then her face softened, "I suppose so, but still, it's hard to see your own child so hell-bent on following his father's path."

"Come now. I only fight when I must. I don't seek it out."

"I suppose not," she sighed. "Travel carefully, and I'll see you soon. Send word if it'll be long, or I'll worry."

"Of course," Leofwine replied, "but you'll worry regardless." He stepped closer to his slight wife and gathered her in his arms, kissing her passionately, and trying to ignore his flaring desire for her.

"I'll see you soon."

13
AD1001

THE KING HAD ARRANGED FOR WATCH FIRES TO BE SET ALONG THE COASTAL areas, and it was in the Western Provinces that they burnt first. The fyrd of the Western Provinces, under the command of their old ealdorman's son, Æthelmaer, was beleaguered, or so Leofwine determined when he rode into the area and unexpectedly came upon them.

Æthelmaer had been pleased with the trust the king had placed in him but all of a sudden it seemed to be an impossible proposition, or so he told Leofwine in his first sentence to him.

In Exeter, the lands of the king's uncle, Ordulf, the Raiders had made landfall first. Turning their attention to the outlying religious houses of the area, they'd burnt as they'd travelled inland, leaving a trail of destruction until they met the fyrd, led by Æthelmaer with the assistance of the king's reeves, at Pinhoe. The battle that day had been bloody and by the end of it, two of the king's reeves, Kola and Eadsige, lay dead, and the Raiders were claiming another victory.

Only then had Ealdorman Pallig joined with the Raiders and taken his household troops with him. They'd raided and burnt and stolen as they'd travelled along the west and southern coast.

Leofwine was incensed. Lady Elfrida had suspected Pallig and Leofwine had never trusted him. It seemed they'd been correct to doubt him.

With Thorkell the Tall and Jarl Erik trying to kidnap one of the king's sons, and Pallig turning traitor, Leofwine couldn't help but wish the king had more trustworthy ealdorman to assist him.

At the witan, held earlier in the year before the attack on Dean but when there had been Raiders in Kent, there'd been evident unease amongst the ealdormen and the king.

The king had called his ealdormen swiftly to order. Ælfric of Hampshire had begged his king to consider paying off the Raiders in Kent as they'd done before, but Æthelred had been deaf to the idea.

Ealdorman Pallig had agreed with Ælfric, warning the king in dark tones that the Raiders would not leave of their own accord. He'd argued that they needed to be driven from the land, or bought off. Pallig had decided that paying them to leave was the better option.

Leofsige had also cautioned against further military actions. He'd said his fyrd were not well armed and the men of the household troops unused to sustained attacks. Æthelred had visibly bristled at the intended slights to his management of the country's military might, reminding everyone of the successes of the Battle of Strathclyde, almost despite Leofsige's involvement.

Of the ealdormen, only Leofwine and Ælfhelm of Northumbria had not joined the call for a purchased peace. Many of the churchmen hadn't wanted a peace either, saying that until there was a named and known force behind the attacks, it would be unproductive to offer a payment to the Raiders.

They'd cautioned that they were such a disparate lot that there was no guarantee that the payment would work. If the English raised a massive sum of money to pay the Raiders to go away only to have another group arrive expecting the same treatment, had worried the churchmen and women, as it had Leofwine.

Lady Elfrida's accord with lord Olaf, then King Olaf, had shown just how many northmen were intent on attacking England.

The king had listened attentively to all the suggestions and debates, and Leofwine had wondered how he could stand to hear such useless ideas from his ealdormen. It was evident that a further military offensive was needed, and it was self-evident that the fyrd and the king's ship army needed to be involved.

"My lord King, I must speak," Leofwine had interjected into a long-winded speech from Leofsige on the perils of attacking. Leofsige had cast him a look of annoyance, but the king had turned to Leofwine with evident relief on his face,

"Yes, my lord Leofwine, go ahead. I'd like to hear something of substance." The king's words had caused Leofsige to pale.

Leofwine had nodded to acknowledge the invitation. "We can't stand by and offer no further attack against these … these thieves and Raiders. They take what's not theirs, and they terrify our people and our religious houses. I know our losses have been significant. I mourn those men who've given their lives freely and those who didn't, and we must not allow their deaths to be for nothing."

In the background, Leofwine had heard a few murmurs of assent, and the king had smiled slightly. Leofwine had continued, spurred on by the tacit agreement within the room.

"We need to build on these sparks of victory, and we need to drive them from our shores. Our forebears were able to hold them at bay, and that was before they had the might of the combined force of England at their beck and call. The people of the Hwiccan lands don't long for a fight, but they do strive to protect what's theirs, as I'm sure the men of the other old kingdoms do."

Leofwine had seen the king's sons and his mother nodding along as he'd spoken. Calls from other members of the king's witan had also been heard raised in agreement. The king had let the men talk amongst themselves for some time before he'd restored order.

"I think lord Leofwine has the right of it. We know that the men who attack us are based in the far south. We must call out the fyrds of Hampshire and those of the western lands. We must plan patrols and monitor the Raiders every movement. We must have the ship army trail them and see where they go, and seek out the commanders who direct their endeavours, and we must have an efficient way to communicate with each other."

At the king's words, there'd been those who'd cheered so loudly and for so long that Hunter had skulked away in terror and had only returned to Leofwine's side when the king's hall had fallen quiet. As he'd tried to tempt his errant hound back to him Leofwine had laughed, giddy with the knowledge that he'd stirred the king to voice desires that the majority of the men agreed with.

Only ealdorman Pallig had looked decidedly uncomfortable at the thought of leading English men against his former countrymen.

The men of the witan had broken off into small groups to discuss the situation at greater length. A large swathe of the men had clustered around Leofwine, shouting out their ideas and passing different suggestions back and forth. As the conversation had swirled around him, Leofwine had glimpsed where Ælfric, Leofsige and Pallig had stood huddled together, surrounded by their own small group of followers. They'd cast anxious glances at their king and his sons, who like Leofwine, had had a large group of supporters around them.

Indicating to Wulfstan that he was to listen to the men who supported the decision to take military action, Leofwine had walked purposefully towards the three dissident voices. Pallig had watched him with mild interest, whereas Leofsige had openly glared, his fury at the turn of events marking his face with angry red splotches. He'd never been the most attractive of men, and now he looked positively ugly.

"My lords," Leofwine had begun respectfully, with an inclination of his head.

"My lord, half-blinded with power, Leofwine," Leofsige had retorted, spitting his words in his anger.

Leofwine had raised his eyebrow at Leofsige's childish retort.

"I'm sorry you so blatantly don't agree with the ruminations of the witan and the king. But, I must ask what else can we do?"

"We can pay the greedy buggers, and they'll sod off!" Leofsige's response had been instantaneous, and Ælfric had nodded emphatically in agreement.

"You've not watched them ravage your land, rape the women and the church and burn your crops. If you'd seen them in action, then you'd not want to face them in battle. They're lethal."

Leofwine had barely hidden his disgust at the man's cowardice.

"Obviously, My lord, I've never encountered them ravaging my lands, but I've faced them in battle, and my blindness, which you so kindly alluded to, was provided at the hands of one of the northmen. I'm not a swaddled babe to call for something that I don't understand."

"Of course not, Leofwine, you're an honourable man who's seen battle, faced death and lived to see another day." Again, Leofsige had spat in disgust as sarcasm marred his words.

"It's a great pity that none of the other ealdormen is quite as honourable, and stupid, as you, My Lord. You blindly ..." he'd barked a laugh at his unintended pun, "... follow your king and act as he asks. Do you not know how little he trusted you when you returned from the expedition with Olaf of Norway, how much he wanted to replace you? For God's sake, man, he cast your pregnant wife from the comfort of his protection when you were reported as being dead. The king has no love for you. He sees you as a tool, nothing more."

Leofsige's words hadn't angered Leofwine. Instead, he'd felt curious,

"Are we not the king's servants, to be commanded as he pleases?"

"No, we're our own men, and as such, we must guard our own interests if they run counter to the king's own."

"That sounds more than a little treasonous, and I wonder if you're still able to differentiate those lands that are yours alone and those that were gifted to you by the king only as ealdorman of Essex."

Hatred had glittered in Leofsige's eyes.

"The lands are mine, gifted by the king or not. I've held them and maintained them, and I'll gift them to my family after my death if there's anything left by the time we pay these Raiders off." He'd growled his retort, his voice dangerously low.

"Then I think, My Lord, you don't understand the commitment you made to your king, and I think that's why your heart is never wholly devoted to the king's cause. I suggest you reconsider your options, or you risk losing everything, Raiders or not. The king will not tolerate such disloyalty."

Again, Leofsige had barked a short laugh, "Well, what do you think Ælfric has been doing for the past twenty years?"

Ælfric had jumped at the mention of his name and turned to glare at the glowering form of Leofsige.

Leofwine had felt his anger rising, a situation made worse by the cool looks Pallig had cast his way. He hadn't trusted the huge man and cursed Leofsige for speaking so openly in front of him.

If Pallig had been working for Swein of Denmark, it would be a source of amusement to the Danish king to know that discontent ran through the select handful of men who allegedly supported the English king. Pallig had been shown the weaknesses in the king's court.

"I think your king's councillors are as riven with strife as those in the northern lands," Pallig had said, his words carefully chosen. He'd smiled slightly to ease the sharpened edge from their intent, but Leofwine had scowled at him. He hadn't trusted a word he'd said. The barb had been pointed and meant to wound.

"Ælfric has been the king's councilor for many more years than you. His position is ingrained. Yours I fear, like my own ..." Leofsige's grimace at the casual reminder of the words that he'd just flung in Leofwine's face was instant, "can be taken away whenever and wherever. I'd suggest you do the king the courtesy of supporting him." Leofwine had spoken honestly, trying to win some understanding from Leofsige.

"Why, what have you heard? Does he plan to replace me?" There had been panic in Leofsige's voice, and his total change of tact had shocked Leofwine. A moment ago he'd been bragging about his land and the king's land being indistinguishable, and now it appeared as though he did fear to lose them.

"I'm merely the king's servant, as you so rightly point out. I don't know the innermost workings of his heart and what he has planned for you. I do know that you disappointed him in the battle last year, and I don't suppose you've the sort of easy, forgiving relationship that Ælfric has with him." Ælfric had remained silent until this point but had visibly jumped at being mentioned in the conversation once more.

"Give it some thought, my lord – and you, lord Pallig. My man Horic has regaled me with tales of your youth and your relationship with Swein of Denmark. If you intend to double-cross the king, I assure you I'll pledge my intention to seek you out and kill you just as your brother in law has done to me."

Pallig's laughter had been loud at Leofwine's darkly muttered threat, as he'd smacked him heartily on the back.

"I'd wish you well with that. I've the use of my eyes and see much that you don't. However, I assure you, I plan no double-cross against your people or the king. Rest assured."

Leofwine had not been confident in the words that Pallig had so blithely spoken. The humour he'd exhibited only went so far, and as Leofwine had turned away, he'd realised that the laughter, smiles and words Pallig spoke had never been mirrored in his cold eyes.

Only malice had shone from Pallig's face as he constantly watched everything around him. Pallig's protracted silences before he'd spoken were not a result of him trying to find the right words in the English language to voice his thoughts; no, he'd been taking the time to decide how best to play every angle. Pallig had been devious, and his king had fallen for it. Leofwine had cursed the king's naivety.

His back had burned as he'd walked along the wooden, rush-strewn floor to where Wulfstan had been officiating over a rowdy discussion. Reaching for Hunter for support, where she mirrored his steps, he'd turned and swept the three men a meaningful look. They'd been watching him intently, muttering to each other. Leofwine had cracked a smile and offered a little wave of goodbye.

Now Leofwine joined his household warriors to the group, searching for Pallig. The trail of destruction had been easy to follow, and yet, they only ever arrived after Pallig, and his men had left. Always.

Eventually, Leofwine and Æthelmær received a summons from the king at Woodstock. Not wishing to leave the Western Provinces unprotected, Leofwine had committed to travel to Woodstock with only a small force, what he found there angered him more than anything else, and saddened him in equal measure.

Ensconced with the king and deep in his confidences was none other than Pallig himself.

Leofwine was forced to speak with the king and the treasonous ealdorman while curbing all of his frustration at the king's gullibility.

Pallig was full of himself, excusing his actions as those of a man doing his king's duty by infiltrating the Raiders, a ploy that Æthelred seemed to heartily approve of without questioning what the man had done in his endeavours. Æthelred didn't consider the men who'd died, the monasteries and houses that had been burnt, and the people who'd been forced to flee, and had lost their livelihoods.

Angrier than he'd ever been, Leofwine left the king as early as he could; weighed down with the unwelcome news of the king mother's advancing ill-health, now bed bound and unable to leave her nunnery at Wherwell.

It was not only clear that the king wouldn't listen to him, but there was also no longer a resource to the king's mother either.

Leofwine resolved that where his king might fail, he would not. He'd guard the land and the people entrusted to him, and he'd do it well. The king could play his foolish games; Leofwine didn't have to be a party to them.

Leofwine returned to the Western Provinces, informing

Æthelmær and Ordulf of what had happened. With no peace terms agreed, the Raiders had withdrawn all the same. No doubt, Leofwine surmised, it was some new trickery of Pallig's. Not that he could convince the king of that.

When he arrived home to a riot of excited children and animals, his anger got the better of him, and he marched sulkily inside his home, speaking to no one as he went. He shrugged out of his sweaty, muddy clothing and returning outside, upended a bucket of cold water over himself.

The children squealed with delight at the game, and he received an appraising look from Æthelflæd for flaunting his nakedness so openly. He shot her a challenging look as he walked back inside where his men were laughing at his exploits, a welcome relief from the stresses of the last few days.

Inside his bedchamber he lay fully stretched on his bed, trying to breathe the frustration from his body in calm, even breaths. But there was too much noise, and he was about to dress again when Æthelflæd entered the room, shooing Hunter outside.

Belatedly Leofwine realised that he'd not greeted his wife as he should, and he made a move to stand, which she stopped by coming to stand over him.

"My lord, is there something the matter?" she said, her tone playfully acidic. He didn't immediately respond, and into the pointed silence she spoke again, her face almost a stern grin, "Is there, perhaps, something I could do to help, My Lord?"

Leofwine growled low in his throat as she undid the workday apron that covered her elegant dress and dropped it to the floor, before concentrating on undoing the shimmering buckles that held her dress in place.

"Well, I might have an idea or two," Leofwine dryly muttered, as her overdress hit the wooden floor and she tugged her underdress over her head to stand naked before him, her body enticing.

"Indeed, My lord, as do I. Shall we see if you can at the least find some pleasure in your own household?"

He smiled at her choice of words and watched with mounting enjoyment as she stepped forward and straddled his naked body. Her hair was tied back in a complex array of plaits that she hastily released as their skin touched. He gasped in pleasure, and she winked at him.

"Perhaps, My lord could be a little quieter and a little less keen," she grinned, fixing her eye on his obvious need for her.

"Perhaps he could," Leofwine said, pulling her to him so that her body lay pressed against his own, her warmth covering his own body, still cold from the bucket of cold water. Their lips touched, and he whispered, "Or perhaps he could be quite quick and then take his time in a bit." She giggled around his open mouth and kissed him, passionately on his lips.

"Perhaps, he could just shut up and enjoy whatever he's got coming to him," Æthelflæd muttered before it became impossible to speak because they were too busy becoming reacquainted.

Her kisses became more and more fervent as he ran his hands up and down her naked sides, desperate to touch her breasts that lay between them, but unable to because she was effectively glued to him. In frustration, he wrapped his arms around her and rolled over her, so that he now lay atop her, but her legs wound so tightly around him that still, he was restricted to what parts of her pliant body he could reach.

A further growl of frustration, and a delighted giggle from her, and he realised that no, not even in his home, could he be master. He relinquished himself to her needs, and found, at last, a release for the pent-up frustration for the impossible situation the king had placed the entire country in.

14
AD1001

News of the death of the king's mother arrived with the worst of the winter weather.

From Tamworth, Leofwine knew it would be almost impossible to reach Wherwell Abbey in time for the funeral, but all the same, he was determined to attempt it. He felt he owed Lady Elfrida, and her grandchildren the respect of being there, and cursed the weather.

It had done little but rain for near enough two weeks, but overnight, the ground had frozen, and Leofwine had woken to find a crisp layer of snow settling over the ground.

It might, he reasoned, actually make travel easier, as he eyed the outside world with a jaundiced eye.

Æthelflæd joined him at the open doorway.

"It will be a terrible journey," she complained, so contradictory to his own thoughts that he laughed softly, only to earn himself a questioning look.

"I was thinking the opposite," he explained, and now she smiled.

"You always see the best in everything," there was only a slight complaint on her lips, as she turned, shivering, and made her way back to the hearth.

Closing the door, Leofwine almost collided with Wulfstan. Wulfstan had taken the news poorly, and his face was downcast. Leofwine bowed his head low, holding the door wide for him to escape into what daylight there was. It was clear his commander wished to be alone with his thoughts.

"I don't always see the best in everything," Leofwine complained, settling beside his wife, even though his leg was jiggling with an urge to be gone. He'd asked the five men who'd accompany him to be ready after their first meal of the day, but now he wished the departure time had been set closer.

"I act with the honour due to all. Lady Elfrida was a woman of immense influence, and she often used it to assist me, even when I didn't ask her to."

"Lady Elfrida was always too sure of herself," Æthelflæd complained, shocking Leofwine, while she smirked at him as though taunting him to continue the argument.

"If it hadn't been for Lady Elfrida, we would never have married, and I would never have been an ealdorman."

Æthelflæd arched an eyebrow at him.

"And would that have been such a terrible thing?" Leofwine laughed then, gathering his wife into his arms.

"Perhaps not the task of being an ealdorman, but certainly I would have missed being your husband." He planted a kiss on her smiling face, only to be summoned away.

"The men are ready, My Lord." Oscetel's voice was overly loud and meant to jar. Leofwine grimaced at him, while Oscetel smirked.

"Then I'm ready as well," Leofwine retorted, reminded of the unpleasant task at the end of what could be a terrible journey, and turned to kiss his wife in farewell.

"Keep warm," Leofwine urged her, his eyes seeking out his sons so that he could offer them an admonishment to behave in his absence, but as always, they were off with the other young boys of the household, no doubt causing havoc somewhere.

"And keep an eye on your children," he called. "They can be a real handful."

Æthelflæd grinned at his words but returned to her sewing task without concern. There was always someone with half an eye on their lord's sons, while her daughter was settled and sleeping in a crib beside her. So far, neither of the boys had fallen into great harm. Leofwine hoped it long continued.

Pulling the door open, Leofwine was assaulted by the tang of fresh snow, and he shuddered. Perhaps Æthelflæd had been correct after all, and it would be a terrible journey.

Hunter shot through his legs, keen to be outside as they both heard the high-pitched shrieks of the children, playing somewhere to the rear of the great hall. Leofwine took his steps far more carefully than his hound or his children.

It might well have started to snow, and the sky might well hang threaded with grey, the threat of more snow clear to see, but it was too bright for his one eye, and he needed to take the time to adjust his vision.

Squinting, Leofwine made his way carefully to his horse, hunkering deep into his cloak before he settled himself in the saddle.

"Come, men," he called when all were ready. "Let us try and enjoy this journey, and see if we can outrun the snowstorm."

The words were greeted with an assortment of grunts and complaints, none of them seeming to be keen to ride south, whereas Wulfstan was silent at his side.

Leofwine paused, considering the task ahead, and whether his integrity truly dictated he attend Lady Elfrida's funeral, only to sigh. It did. And he had no choice in the matter.

IT TOOK FOUR DAYS OF CONSTANT TRAVEL TO REACH WHERWELL. AND THE journey was far from pleasant. Whereas Mercia was sheeted in snow, by the time they reached Wessex, only rain fell from the sky, bitterly cold, but churning the pitted roads to mud.

Not for the first time on their journey, Leofwine cursed the king's mother for not dying during the summer, only to feel genuinely remorseful for his thoughts, and beg his God for forgiveness.

The mood of the men was sombre, only a few sparks of mirth showing when they sought shelter each night in the home of a local reeve or sheriff. The men and women they encountered were unaware of the death of the king's mother. While some offered respectful words, others seemed confused as to who Lady Elfrida even was.

Leofwine kept a close eye on Wulfstan during these exchanges. It seemed he was overly sensitive to any slight to the influential woman, and few had kind words for her, despite all she'd done for their king and the future of England.

Arriving in Wherwell, Leofwine felt only relief at having finally completed the task he'd assigned himself. The nunnery, Lady Elfrida's own establishment, was not far to the north of Winchester, and Leofwine was sure that the king and his children would be in attendance. Yet, when he strode into the great hall, he was surprised to find only the sisters and their abbess.

"Have I arrived too late?" Leofwine asked, apology rich in his voice, as it echoed far too loudly in the confined space.

"No, My lord Leofwine, the funeral, will take place tomorrow. The king and his children will attend only for the day." The abbess spoke well, but Leofwine detected very little sorrow in her voice. Perhaps the woman had not appreciated her founder either. Leofwine considered how Lady Elfrida could have come to be so little regarded, and so quickly. It upset him, almost as much as it did Wulfstan.

"Then could I seek shelter for the night for my men and me, there are six of us in total?"

"Of course, lord Leofwine. I take it you will need the use of the stables as well?"

"We will yes, and will my hound be allowed to stay with me? She serves as my eyes."

Leofwine felt wrong-footed by the mundane conversation. He'd expected to find the nunnery in deep mourning, the king sorrowing for his mother as well. But that was not the case.

"She's welcome, provided you keep her close. I'd not have her worrying the children and the other sisters." The reproach in the voice startled Leofwine, but he bowed his thanks all the same.

"Ætheling Athelstan is in the church, praying for his grandmother if you'd like to join him." So dismissed, but pleased to know he was not alone in his desire to respect the great lady, he quickly saw his men settled, and then, taking Wulfstan and Hunter with him made his way to the church the abbess had directed him to.

Under a shower of rain, he dashed into the church, only stopping to throw back the hood on his cloak once he was inside.

The church was almost silent, although he could see the coffin of Lady Elfrida before the altar, soft candles illuminating the fresh flowers that covered its length, over a cloth that showed the Wessex dragon depicted in shimmering threads.

Wulfstan strode silently from his side, to join the small party of those already praying, a number of the sisters amongst them, whereas Leofwine lingered a little longer, just staring at the interior of the church.

Leofwine hadn't been to Wherwell before. It was remarkably similar to his father's foundation at Deerhurst, and he wondered if Lady Elfrida had ever been there.

He felt a gust of wind around his ankles and turned to find the door opening behind him. Hastily, Leofwine stepped aside, allow the new person admittance. As they too thrust back their cloak, Leofwine recognized the man.

"My lord Ordulf," Leofwine bowed low. "My sorrow on your loss." The older man started at being greeted as such, barely with his foot in the door, but his face quickly settled into a grim smile.

"My lord Leofwine, you honour my sister with your presence, and I would thank you for making all haste to be here. It seems few others have bothered," a hint of outrage filled Ordulf's strained voice, and Leofwine wisely held his tongue.

Behind Ordulf, more people entered the church, and Leofwine quickly realized this was Ordulf's family, and he made to move away to allow them more privacy and space only for Ordulf to call him back.

"I know this is not the time to talk of politics, but I must thank you for rescuing my sister and her grandchildren from Dean. I would never have forgiven myself had the worst happened."

"It was my honour to serve your sister, always. Although it was the king, who sent me south."

"It might have been, I concur, but there was no other he could have trusted. My nephew is lucky to have you as his ealdorman, even if he doesn't realize as much."

With those words said, Leofwine felt a swell of pride but bowed his head to hide his flush.

"And now, we'll mourn her as she should be mourned. The first queen of England deserves more than this," Ordulf's voice was filled with disgust, a catch in his throat, revealing his deep sorrow, as his hand indicated the interior of the church.

Leofwine had no time to respond, for Ordulf led his family to pray before the coffin, drawn faces showing their sorrow, as an older woman, a handful of adult sons, and a collection of smaller grandchildren made their way around Leofwine. He watched them, only now realizing how mean the funeral for the king's mother would be.

Lord Ordulf was correct. A state funeral should have been arranged for Lady Elfrida, despite the terrible weather. All of the ealdormen and holy men and women should have been summoned, and not just her family, and those most closely connected to her.

The door opened once more, while Leofwine was lost in thought, and a man far older than him entered, his eyes glittering with unshed tears.

"My lord," Leofwine again bowed low, as though he'd become the official welcoming people into the church at Wherwell.

"My lord Leofwine," the response was muted, Leofwine was surprised that the man knew who he was, although he was sure they'd never met.

The other must have noticed his confusion.

"The scar, My Lord, I fear it marks who you are. I'm also called Leofwine, Lady Elfrida's step-son, son of Ealdorman Æthelwald, her first husband, and his first wife."

Understanding flickered over Leofwine's face.

"It's a pleasure to meet you, although I wish it were under better circumstances," Leofwine offered a firm arm clasp as they spoke.

"She would have been pleased to see you here," Leofwine replied, his eyes flickering time and again to the coffin.

"Please, go ahead. I was simply admiring the church before I went to pray myself. It's similar to my establishment at Deerhurst," Leofwine found himself speaking and offering overly long explanations. The older Leofwine smiled wryly.

"Funerals are always uncomfortable affairs, especially for a woman such as Lady Elfrida. I would have hoped she'd have had a state funeral, be buried beside king Edgar or even within the Old or New Minster, but it seems not."

"Lord Ordulf has just said the same. Perhaps this was her wish," Leofwine tried to console.

"Perhaps, but I doubt it," the older man bowed as he walked beyond Leofwine, and still Leofwine found himself unable to move. But, not wanting to be in the way, or have to speak to any more disgruntled relatives, he took himself to the rear of the church, settling on a bench there, Hunter at his side.

Looking upward Leofwine gazed at the church roof once more, noting the construction of the roof, and how the building was half made from stone, and half from wood. Like so many churches, it seemed the intention had always been to make it even more magnificent than it was.

Leofwine thought that Lady Elfrida had no doubt simply run out of time to complete her project. He somehow doubted that the king would continue the work, although it was possible that her grandchildren and brother might do so.

So lost in thought was Leofwine, he gave a slight gasp when another settled beside him. Athelstan.

The ætheling's face was white with sorrow, his blond hair hanging lank, and his clothes rumpled and clearly far from fresh.

"I blame myself," Athelstan began morosely. "If I'd not demanded to join the warriors when the Raiders attacked Dean, she'd not have sat in the rain for three straight days."

Unable to help himself, Leofwine snorted with laughter at the words, only to be greeted with an outraged look from the younger man, and an angry 'shush' from someone at the front of the church.

"Do you genuinely believe that your grandmother would have done anything she didn't wish to? If she waited for you, in the rain, then that was what she wanted to do. It's not your fault. That was many months ago. Lady Elfrida, as indomitable as she was, could not live forever, no matter how much we might have wished she could."

A sullen silence filled the space, Athelstan lost in the memories of his grandmother, while Leofwine sat silently beside him, Hunter settled on the floor, snoring softly. She was never one to appreciate the solemnity of any occasion.

"I will miss her," Athelstan's words were filled with regret. "She was the only person who could stand up to my father," he continued.

"Then I imagine she hopes you'll now take over that role?" Leofwine prompted.

"My father has little time for his children. Even after the Battle of Dean, he still thinks me a child."

"All fathers believe their children are still children, even when they long to be treated as men. He has set you up with your own household now. I would have thought a marriage would be next on the list for you." If Leofwine thought he'd cheer Athelstan with such words, he was mistaken. Swift fury settled over Athelstan's face.

"I can't agree with you, lord Leofwine, although I wish I could. I hope you have the right of it, but only time will tell." Once more lapsing into taciturnity, the ætheling stood and bowed smartly, and returned to the front of the church, taking his knees before the coffin.

Only now did Leofwine bow his head low, his thoughts more reverential now he'd recovered somewhat from his journey. All the same, he couldn't help but worry about Athelstan's evident dissatisfaction with his father. It didn't bode well for the future.

THE FUNERAL TOOK PLACE NOT LONG AFTER DAYBREAK THE FOLLOWING DAY.

The royal family arrived with the watery sun, and Leofwine watched from a respectful distance as all of the children progressed into the church, even the youngest, skipping with joy, clearly unaware that their grandmother was dead, and would never be seen again.

Leofwine felt a twinge of sorrow for the younger children who had little possibility of remembering their grandmother when they were older. They would hear only of her exploits, and perhaps have little to remember her by but the memory of a hug or a kiss. Maybe that would be enough, but Leofwine remained unconvinced.

The king looked regal in his thick clothes, his cloak festooned with furs and his royal regalia. His face was drawn, sorrow etched into his pale skin, his blond hair beginning to thin. He didn't wear his crown, and that revealed a great deal about the king's state of mind.

Æthelred came here to sorrow for his mother, not to show respect as a king to a dead queen. It was both touching and a little strange. But then, Leofwine was only too aware of the problematic nature of Lady Elfrida's relationship with her son.

Bishop Ælfheah of Winchester officiated over the ceremony, several other bishops and abbesses in attendance, most notably from Lady Elfrida's other religious establishment, and also the sisters and the abbess from Wilton.

It was a sorrowful affair, and when the coffin was lowered into the ground beneath the altar, the thud of the massive slab of stone settling back into position sent shockwaves out into the church that Leofwine couldn't help but think would percolate to the very edges of England's coastlines, if not beyond.

Lady Elfrida, it couldn't be denied, had been a woman of exceptional skills and talent. Leofwine couldn't imagine that he'd ever see her like again in his lifetime.

15
AD1002

The Raiders of last year, it transpired, hadn't really left England, choosing to settle on the Isle of Wight during the winter months instead. Provided they didn't launch any attacks, Leofwine decided he was prepared to leave them there for the time being. He realised that only with the better weather would they venture out from their hiding places to steal and murder once more.

Messengers had raced between Leofwine and the king for much of the winter. After the funeral of Lady Elfrida, when the king had barely spoken to Leofwine, he'd made the decision to return to Mercia and bide his time.

The king's easy acceptance of the pitiful excuses offered by Ealdorman Pallig continued to infuriate Leofwine, and he doubted that the king would ever take action against Pallig, not now his mother was dead. If anyone could have convinced Æthelred of Pallig's duplicitous nature, it would have been Lady Elfrida. That hope was now gone.

There had been no news or further threats from Swein of Denmark, or Thorkell the Tall or Jarl Erik, but Leofwine knew that the man hadn't forgotten his threat or his intent toward England.

Swein was merely waiting for a better opportunity. The not knowing was almost worse than if Leofwine had known all of Swein's intended actions.

The king eventually called his ealdormen to him at Winchester on a cold and frosty February morning. There was a great deal of complaining from the ealdormen about the terrible timing of the meeting, and Leofwine noted that lord Ordulf was noticeably absent, as were the king's children, even Athelstan, who by rights should have been there to support his father, as Lady Elfrida had once done.

With a smirk, the king began to speak to the assembly, and Leofwine felt a swell of apprehension form in his stomach.

"I intend to marry again." Leofwine wasn't overly surprised by the revelation. The death of his wife had been sudden and unexpected. The king was still a young man.

"And my bride will also cement the defensive alliance with the Duke of Normandy, for I will marry his sister, Lady Ælfgifu. She's somewhat younger than I, but the duke assures me that she'll be a suitable wife and that she has all the characteristics needed to make her a queen of England."

Ealdorman Pallig looked uncomfortable at the news much to Leofwine's delight. Perhaps, after all, the king wasn't as blind to Pallig as he'd thought.

The dukes of Normandy had provided support for the Raiders for the last few years, giving them both a safe haven if the king's fleet pursued them, and also allowing them to launch attacks on England from Normandy.

The king's attack on Normandy had sped up the process of reaching an accord, and it seemed the deaths of the king's wife and his mother, made the potential match even more appealing. The Duke of Normandy's sister would soon be the queen of England.

Leofwine was unable to stop the smile of joy from spreading across his face. It was a bold move by the king and one he hoped shocked all the men in the room, not just Pallig.

"My congratulations to you," Leofwine spoke genuinely to his king at the first opportunity, clasping his forearm.

"With thanks, lord Leofwine. I must say I've long envied you and your choice of wife. I hope that Emma, as she'll be known at the court, will prove to be to my taste. I'm not yet an old man and shouldn't be alone in my bed each night."

Leofwine grinned. "Indeed not, My Lord. But your first wife did produce fine sons and daughters for you."

"She did, she did, and I'm proud of all my children. I did, to be honest, consider allowing Athelstan to have the girl, but I'm not minded to give him such an advantageous bride just yet."

Leofwine laughed along with his king. He'd been a good and faithful husband to his wife. Ælfgifu had never had the ear of the king other than in the bedchamber and had always played second place to his domineering mother. Or that was how many had interpreted the situation.

Wulfstan had once told Leofwine that he shouldn't believe something just because he'd been told it. The words had forced Leofwine to reconsider the relationship of the king's wife with the king's mother. Perhaps, after all, Lady Ælfgifu had never wished to be a queen. Perhaps, apart from her untimely death, Lady Ælfgifu had been content with her marriage to the king. After all, she'd survived the treason of her father.

"The wedding will take place as soon as the season turns. All the ealdormen, holy men and women will attend the occasion. It will be a grand occasion, to remind everyone of England's great wealth and success in defeating the Raiders."

The announcement made, the king had dispersed his witan, only for a new scandal to rock the king's intimate coterie of allies and ealdormen that occasioned a fresh witan.

Ealdorman Leofsige had not escaped the ravages of the year before unscathed. His lands might not have been attacked, but his support for paying the Raiders off had earned him the scorn of those who wished to battle the Raiders, as had his allying with Ealdorman

Pallig, restored to the king's confidence, but smothered in conspiracy.

At the hastily convened witan to sentence Leofsige for his crime of murder, the unease amongst the small number of remaining men was palpable. Outside the joys of early summer were rolling across the land with the promise of warm weather and new crops, but inside the king's hall, the atmosphere was icy, and not even the king's impending wedding thawed the tension.

Leofsige was defiant as he stood before them all, attempting to explain his actions in killing one of the king's reeves.

"My lord king, the man was belligerent. He incited the attack. I confess, I lashed out at the man, but when I would have willingly taken his apology for his peremptory tone in demanding the increased tax, he became violent toward me." Outrage coloured Ealdorman Leofsige's words, his face almost purple with rage, but Leofwine knew that the ealdorman was adding his own slant to a story he'd heard many times already, and with a different outcome.

Leofsige had viciously attacked the reeve, leaving him battered and dead on the floor of his hall, the rest of the inhabitants and the reeve's guard too shocked to intervene before it was too late.

LEOFSIGE'S FACE WAS DRIPPING WITH SWEAT AND HIS CLOTHING DAMP BELOW his armpits, as he tried to excuse what had happened. It was, Leofwine surmised, impossible for Leofsige to talk his way out of this debacle. Bad enough that he'd killed one of the king's reeves, he's also done so because he'd not agreed with the king's command that increased taxes be paid to compensate for paying off the Raiders from the Isle of Wight, an outcome that Leofsige had begged the king to implement.

Leofwine eyed Leofsige with distaste as he lied and floundered through his testimony.

"My lord king, my apologies that my actions have brought such disrepute to your name and my own reputation. I intended no such things, and I'd not malign the name of the dead man, but he did draw his weapon in my home."

There were cries of "liar" from the family of the reeve, and the men of the reeve's household were called upon one by one to testify that the ealdorman had lied. Leofwine was unsurprised to find that Leofsige had no oath-givers to support his case and that he called on no one from his family to help him escape the inevitable outcome.

Ealdorman Ælfric had committed treason and blamed his son to evade punishment. The king's father by marriage had been banished for his own treachery, as had Ealdorman Ælfric Cild, before his own involvement in English affairs had become more deadly, and he'd been executed for his crimes. For the murder of one of the king's officials, Leofwine knew exactly what punishment Leofsige would face, even if the man himself were in denial.

It was clear that while Leofsige protested his innocence, he was resolved that his king wouldn't find him innocent. Usually, the judgement handed down would have been one of death, but he was the king's ealdorman or at least had been.

In the end, the king decreed Leofsige be exiled, with or without his family as they saw fit, and all the land the family had owned would be transferred back to the king. He also had to pay the man's death fine both to the king and the family of the dead man.

Leofwine kept his thoughts to himself but felt it a pity that the king could be so lenient. The execution of a traitor to the king's peace would have reinforced the king's desire to ensure England was as safe and secure as in his father's lifetime.

Leofwine watched almost incredulously as Leofsige thanked the king for his clemency and left the witan without another word, escorted on his way by the king's household troops, tasked with ensuring the man left the country as he should.

Leofwine worried about the eventual repercussions of the actions, especially after what had happened with Ealdorman Ælfric Cild, allying with the Raiders. Leofsige knew much of the inner workings of the land. Penniless and landless he'd easily find succour amongst the Raiders, and perhaps Swein of Denmark would welcome him with open arms.

Before he left for good, Leofsige and Pallig had a brief conversation, unheard by any others, but witnessed by Leofwine who wondered what they discussed. Was it just a parting of one-time allies or was it something more, perhaps even the words that Leofsige needed to hear to know how best to approach Swein of Denmark.

Leofwine wished his king had ordered Leofsige's execution. Far better a dead enemy than one who could foment more trouble.

16

AD1002

As the quickly convened witan drew to a close, Æthelred was left visibly deflated by the experience with Leofsige. With a tired countenance, he called Leofwine to him.

"Leofwine, this business ... it weighs heavily on my soul and yet I know I couldn't have acted any differently."

"No, we can't countenance the murder of men acting in your name. I'm afraid that I always found Leofsige to be too keen to act without due consideration." Leofwine spoke as he found, pleased to finally be able to tell the king how he truly felt.

A fatigued smile graced Æthelred's face. "Too true, but it did make him an interesting man to have around if a bit of a liability. My mother did warn me against him, in the end."

"Anyway, to the crux of the matter." Æthelred's tone had changed, hope colouring his voice. "His unexpected banishment from the court leaves me with an issue that I hope you'll be able to solve. It was Leofsige that I'd arranged to collect my new bride from her brother. I'd hoped that you would do the honours in his place. Before you interrupt me, I appreciate your concerns; your last overseas trip was not that pleasant."

Leofwine held back his flare of anger at the king's casual mention of his disfigurement and almost death.

"But, you're the one man I can trust to send. Ealdorman Pallig has shown himself unworthy, and I don't wish to tempt fate by sending him over the seas where he may, or may not, meet up with Swein of Denmark. Ealdorman Ælfric is no longer a young man and has always been keener to see to his own needs. Ealdorman Ælfhelm is needed in the north. And, of course, it would allow you to use your ship again."

The king ended his speech on a wheedling tone, and Leofwine smiled a little to be reminded of his beautiful ship. The king was correct. He didn't get to use it much and hadn't travelled anywhere out of sight of his homeland since his return from the Outer Isles.

Still, he didn't look forward to a voyage away from home, across a sea known to be a hunting ground for Swein and his men. Neither did he relish the idea of having to tell Æthelflæd and Wulfstan, but it was good to know that the king wanted to make such a public affirmation of his trust in him.

With a heavy heart, he spoke, "My lord king, it would be my honour to collect your bride for you, and as you say, it would be good to use my ship. When should I depart?"

"As soon as possible; I'd arranged with the duke to collect her when the winter storms had finished, which I think they should be by now."

"I'll seek out my shipmen and ask them for their advice and depart accordingly. I'll send word when we leave so that you can know when to expect us to arrive."

Æthelred grasped Leofwine's arm, "You have my thanks. Your steadying presence is always to be welcomed."

Leofwine was, as always, taken aback by the king's praise, but before he could comment further, the king had turned away, dismissing Leofwine from his thoughts.

. . .

The day he set foot in his ship again was a stunningly still, bright day. He was relieved to see the vast ocean so calm, but his shipmen commented darkly about it being a bad sign. He ignored the men, as he felt the almost forgotten but memorable roll of the waves beneath his feet.

Æthelflæd had taken the news surprisingly well. Wulfstan hadn't. He'd insisted on coming with Leofwine until he'd been convinced that Horic was the man for the job. With the Mercian lands needing to be managed in his absence, Oscetel couldn't be spared. He was tasked with overseeing Mercia, while Wulfstan was to watch over the Hwiccan lands with the aid of Horic's sons.

Horic's oldest son was a fine man, and Leofwine was keen to advance him where he could. He was also astute enough to take orders from Wulfstan even when he didn't agree with them, and then make any changes necessary.

Having ensured his affairs were in good order should the worse happen, Leofwine felt reasonably confident as the ship was oared into deep water. Æthelflæd and his children hadn't come to see him off, instead staying in the house in Lichfield where he knew they were well guarded and far from the attacks on the southern coast.

The king hadn't come either. Æthelred had stated that if it was too dangerous for him to cross the sea to meet his bride, it was also too risky for him to venture near to the coast. Leofwine had agreed – almost.

However, Athelstan and Ecgberht had journeyed with him to the southern shore. Leofwine wondered what dark thoughts they harboured at the idea that they might soon have new siblings with a claim just as good as their own to the throne. But whatever their thoughts were, the young men kept them to themselves, and only on rare occasions said anything that could be deemed a criticism of the king.

Athelstan had grown in stature and reputation since the battle of Dean last year. Leofwine was sure that all the men who served in his household troop would lay down their lives for Athelstan, and he did worry that none would gainsay him either. Leofwine knew only too well how important it was to have men serving you who could, on occasion, disagree with you and offer sage words of advice.

Ecgberht, he didn't know as well. He'd seen him and spoken to him at the witan, and of course in the wake of the battle of Dean. He was the spitting image of his brother in all ways, and Leofwine didn't doubt that within a year or two, he would have the solid muscled build of his brother to match.

Both young men were keen warriors, and Leofwine was pleased that he was on the same side as them as he watched them spar with each other in the evenings when they camped for the night as they journeyed to the coast.

Horic was joyful to be on board the ship again. He insisted on rowing along with the men and had them all joining him in rowdy songs that Leofwine wished he didn't understand. Ælfric, the ship's captain, chortled with glee at Horic's antics and allowed the men most of the morning to acclimatise themselves to the seriousness of the endeavour they'd been given.

They did not sail alone, either. On either side, two ships from the king's army flanked Leofwine. Leofwine had worried that any absence from the fleet would be detrimental to its ability to protect the coastal regions. Now as he watched the ships fly through the water to either side of him, he felt comforted by the knowledge that he travelled not only with sixty men who swore allegiance directly to him as their lord but a further two hundred who did to the king, and by association, Leofwine, while they were away from England.

Leofwine thought the ships, gleaming in the early summer sun and with new brightly coloured sails to power them if needed, looked magnificent as they plunged through the gentle waves. Only Horic's raunchy songs made them appear anything less than a lethal force of Æthelred's. Hopefully, there were none close enough to hear of what Horic sang.

The journey was a short one, almost over before it had begun. With no sign of any enemies, Leofwine jumped from his ship onto the harbour at Cherbourg to be greeted by men the Duke had sent to welcome him.

They were not a large party of men, but there were enough in beautiful, luxurious clothing to make Leofwine think that the Duke was keen to establish far better relations with the English king than they'd enjoyed for some years.

They were welcomed in their own language before being escorted to a large wooden church built a short way inland.

Leofwine, alert as ever, became suspicious of the Duke of Normandy's intentions as soon he noticed the significant number of horses tied up outside the church. There was no need for such a large force when they were supposedly allies. Entering the large wooden structure, Leofwine soon realised the peril his small collection of men were in.

As his own king would do, the Duke was seated at the front of the church on an ornately carved wooden chair, gleaming in the light from the candles. Men of his church surrounded him, as did those Leofwine assumed formed his most intimate council.

The Duke was a good-looking young man, with bright eyes and a casualness that belied the power and wealth at his fingertips. At his side, on a less ornate chair, sat a pale young woman, her hands held protectively over her slightly bloated stomach Leofwine supposed carried the Duke's first child.

The Duke and his Duchess hadn't been married long, but it already looked as though their marriage had been fruitful.

However, in active attendance on the Duke was a face Leofwine had hoped never to see again – the disgraced ealdorman, Leofsige. Leofsige wore a huge grin on his round face, and he also held his hands protectively over a fat belly as though he was trying to hold all the excess in.

With Leofsige was another face that Leofwine had never actually seen before, other than in his nightmares and thanks to the image concocted by listening to Finn and Horic's stories.

Without any introductions being made, he was sure that Swein of Denmark stood before him. He too was a huge man, well built, eager and evidently well skilled enough to strike fear into the hearts of any who went against him. While he carried no weapons within the church, his physical presence was sufficient threat. Leofwine stared at him openly with interest.

Swein's face, covered with a long beard and dropping blond moustache, was elongated with a sharp mouth and well-formed nose. Leofwine noted bitterly that his face bore no scars from his many battles, but then, Leofwine doubted Swein had ever suffered the ignominy of being burned alive in his own home.

Swein was laughing and talking to Duke Richard, as was Leofsige as if they'd been friends for many years. A silence quickly descended, as Leofwine's presence was made known around the room with a hush of whispers. With no hurry, Leofsige and Swein bowed their way out of the Duke's company.

Leofwine, with Hunter at his heel, strode confidently to where the Duke sat. He couldn't let his fear, or his horror at seeing the man he thought might be Swein of Denmark, distract him from the duties the king had given him. Leofwine stopped before he reached the slight platform upon which the Duke sat and bowed his head respectfully.

"My lord Richard, I am Leofwine, ealdorman of King Æthelred, and I've come to claim his bride for him."

The Duke rose from his chair to step forward and clasp Leofwine firmly on the forearm.

"Well met, my lord Leofwine. It's good that you've managed to make the journey so early in the season. I'm sure my sister ..." and he stopped to point out a slight girl, looking intently at Leofwine and his dog, "... will be pleased to know that her husband-to-be is so keen to marry."

A small malicious smile played around his lips, and Leofwine immediately realised that the Duke and his sister did not, perhaps, see eye to eye on everything. This marriage might not be to the young woman's liking.

"Come Ælfgifu, introduce yourself to lord Leofwine."

The young girl, for she could be no older than fifteen years, stood quickly from her seat close to a brazier warming her and a small army of other women, and strode confidently towards Leofwine.

She was slight with long wavy blonde hair, unbound and free-flowing down her back. She was richly dressed, and jewels sparkled at her neck and from her dress brooches. She shared her brother's face and quick eyes and curtseyed when she came close to Leofwine.

"It's good to meet you, my lord." Her voice was low and soft as she spoke in his language and stumbled in places over the unfamiliar words. Leofwine attempted to answer her with the words that Horic had assured him would mean 'welcome' in her own language.

Her hand was feather-like on his forearm, as she too gave him a traditional greeting. She smiled at his words and when she walked away, back to her seat. Leofwine wondered if his king would appreciate her fully. If he wanted more sons and more daughters, he should perhaps have chosen a more solid-looking bride, but it was too late for regrets now.

"I hope she meets with yours and your king's approval," Richard said, his eyes watching her critically for any misstep.

"She's a beautiful woman, and I'm sure that Æthelred will be more than pleased with her, and hopefully she will be with him."

Richard laughed at the words, the noise echoing in the quiet atmosphere, "Well, he better be pleased. This marriage is a hard-fought piece of diplomacy, and I don't want it to fail. However, we do have some small problems we must discuss first."

"Indeed, my lord, I'd expected no less." In all honestly, Leofwine had hoped the treaty could be formulated without any problems, but the presence of Swein and Leofsige made that impossible.

"But come, we'll drink and feast in my hall, and then, we'll turn to business."

Abruptly Duke Richard stood, and waiting for his wife to do the same, he strode from the church, indicating that Leofwine should follow. Feeling a little uncertain, Leofwine hesitated a moment and then felt a soft hand in the crook of his arm.

"I'll show you," Ǽlfgifu said, as she walked beside him, her words carefully formed.

"Your dog, what is her name?"

Hunter glanced at Leofwine, where she walked in front of him, and Leofwine smiled. The dog always seemed to know when she was being spoken about.

"Her name's Hunter, and she helps me to see."

"Hunter ... it's not a girl's name?"

"No, not at all. Why?"

"My brother says that I must adopt another name in your country – Emma. Is that a girl's name?"

Leofwine studied the girl for a moment. She looked pensive as she both fought for the words she wanted and attempted to keep her composure. Perhaps the king changing her name to suit himself, because it had also been his first wife's name, was a step too far for her.

"Yes, a girl's name and a beautiful one at that. I take it someone explained why the king might wish to call you by another name?"

She looked at him quizzically,

"Is it not that he just doesn't like the name?"

"No, that's not the case. It's that you, unfortunately, share a name with his first wife."

The girl flushed brightly at the mention of the king's previous wife, looking uncomfortable and faltering in her steady steps.

"I'm sure that in the privacy of your own rooms, your servants may still call you by that name."

The young girl brightened at the words and strode a little more confidently through the open doorway to the outside world.

Now that Leofwine wasn't fixated on where he was going, he was able to take in the view around him. Far out to sea he could see tiny boats fishing, and down the hill they'd just walked up there was a tidy collection of houses and small fields with animals or plants growing.

Behind the church and obscured by it until they'd walked all around the wooden structure, was a large hall into which the Duke was leading his entourage. The ground they travelled across was hard-packed earth, dry for now, but he wondered if, when the rains came, it would descend into mud and puddles.

Behind him, he knew Horic walked close to him, as did Lyfing and Ælfhun, but he felt vastly outnumbered as he saw the stream of men coming from the church behind him.

Amongst the number strode Leofsige and Swein. The thought was not comforting, and with a quiet word, he sent Lyfing and Ælfhun running back to the ship to collect another ten of the best fighting men.

Leofwine felt confident for the moment that nothing untoward would happen, but he didn't wish to risk it. He'd understood this mission was one of peace and reconciliation; he didn't yet know what Leofsige and Swein's presence meant but knew it couldn't be good.

The Duke presented Leofwine with a huge feast to mark the occasion of his arrival and had Leofwine sit beside him at the front of his great wooden hall so that all could see the wounded English ealdorman.

Candles lit the dark interior, and a massive smoking fire was contained within a huge fire pit in the centre of the palace. Its smoke drifted lazily in the still air and occasionally erupted through the small smoke vents in the ceiling.

The men of the Duke's court were seated in rows facing their Duke and Leofwine, and throughout the feast, Leofwine felt their scrutiny and scrupulously avoided looking in the direction that Horic had told him Swein of Denmark occupied. Still, he could feel the man's eyes on him, and he couldn't help but notice that the Duke often glanced his way, a distracted look on his mobile face.

At his side sat Ælfgifu, neatly picking her way through the food placed before them, and beside her, Horic was robust in his consumption of the feast and verbose in his conversations with men who spoke his own tongue. Throughout the long evening, his full-bodied laughter could be heard ringing out, and each time it did, Ælfgifu tensed a little at his side.

Leofwine and the Duke made conversation of little consequence until after they'd eaten and the food had been cleared away. Then, with a cup of mead in his hand, Richard turned towards Leofwine, his face intent.

"My lord, you'll see that you've caught me at an inconvenient time. My lords Swein and Leofsige have come to me and asked me for assistance in getting Leofsige back into the favour of the king. If I'm not able, they've threatened to attack my lands as well as your king's."

Leofwine had expected no less from the disgraced Leofsige. He'd wondered why he'd so casually taken his leave from the country of his birth.

"That is, as you say, most unfortunate, but I think it has no bearing on my being here."

Richard openly glared at Leofwine's attempt to sidestep the issue.

"Ah, but I think it does. And I believe you agree as well, for all your nonchalance. The agreement with the king was for this wedding to put a stop to attacks on each other's lands. It was never my intention that it should bring me into conflict with the king of Denmark and one of his followers."

Leofwine raised his eyebrows in surprise,

"The thought that it might bring you into conflict didn't cross your mind then?"

Richard spluttered a little at the direct question, "Well no, that's not true, but I'd hoped to have had her wedded and bedded before anything happened. At the moment, it's still a theoretical wedding, and I could refuse to let it go ahead."

"But then you'll earn yourself the hatred of the king of England, who sits on your doorstep, as opposed to the king of Denmark who, unless he's a man far stronger than I think, can only send his ship army against you. My king could, by right, have his household troops sent to your lands, and they could ravage and burn as they go."

Richard turned away to stare pensively at Swein of Denmark and nodded in understanding,

"You do make a good point there. But Swein has huge numbers of ships to call upon. Your king, I think, does not."

"To attack your lands, king Æthelred doesn't need huge numbers of ships. It's taken us less than a day to get here and would take less than a day to journey back. Think, in six days, we could transport almost the entire population of England here. I don't think that Swein has that ability."

The Duke swallowed nervously at Leofwine's words and turned to scowl at him,

"You again make a convincing case for my continued support of Æthelred. But I think you don't fully understand the terror of one of Swein of Denmark's attacks."

A bitter laugh at those hastily muttered words earned Leofwine a penetrating glare.

"Apologies, my lord, I'd forgotten the nature of your wounds. If it eases the situation, your scar is so much a part of you that I didn't see it when we first met."

Leofwine shrugged, "It doesn't ease it, but it's good to know that my scar has faded from something to stare at to something to ignore, and as you say I'm only too aware of Swein of Denmark and the strength of his warriors. When did he arrive in Normandy?"

"Only yesterday and since then he's done little but bend my ear about how worthless your king is, and you in particular."

"And Leofsige, I don't think he really wants his land back. He's too busy enjoying the comforts that Swein can offer him. It's a pretext and nothing more, but still, the man is here, and he's brought ten of his ships with him and his warriors have made a point of parading themselves through the town and scaring my people. I don't like it."

"I'd not like it either, but ten ships? Is that all he thinks it'll take to scare you from your alliance? I think he sells you too cheaply."

The remark hit home, as Richard flinched, "And your king doesn't; he sends only three ships."

"But we came in peace, my lord. We didn't come to threaten you and yours."

The Duke again turned his gaze back to Swein of Denmark. The man was blatantly staring straight back, aware he was the subject of their discussion.

Leofwine turned to watch him with interest, finally looking at the man without fear. Putting the person to the name was liberating in a way he'd not expected. In his mind, Swein had somehow become an omniscient God capable of anything and everything in his quest to take England and exact his revenge on Leofwine.

It was refreshing to realise that he was just a man, as fallible to injury and death as any other. Whatever Swein hoped to accomplish, he only had the resources of any other man at his fingertips.

"I'll think about this more, but I imagine I'll eventually agree with you. But be warned, Swein of Denmark doesn't wish you and your king long life. If I let you leave here with my sister, I expect some reassurance that she'll not be captured by them and borne off to be one of their bed slaves. She's a delicate creature and must be treated with respect."

"Of course, my lord, I'll guard her as if she were to be my own wife. Already, some of my best men are within your hall and standing guard outside. The king of England trains his men well and ensures that they're well equipped. And of course, many of these men rescued me from the Outer Isles and saw me safely home," Leofwine added as an aside. He didn't want the Duke to forget that he already had a claim of revenge against Swein of Denmark.

. . .

THAT NIGHT LEOFWINE WAS OFFERED A ROOM WITHIN THE DUKE'S HALL that would have been impolite to refuse. Still, Leofwine slept little and woke the next morning hoping that the Duke would've decided that they could leave and take Ælfgifu with them.

She'd been a charming companion throughout the long night of feasting and Leofwine had detected a certain feistiness in her that he thought his king would enjoy discovering. If he'd not been quite so happy with Æthelflæd, he might have felt a little jealous at his king's good fortune in his new wife. After all, he'd never met her.

As Leofwine broke his fast in the same spot he'd occupied at the feast last night, Ælfgifu and Richard walked towards him, a small tight smile on her face while he looked resolute and determined, his step long and confident.

"Good morning, my lord."

"Good morning to you, my lord and my lady." His choice of words clearly irritated Duke Richard as his face blanched a little of colour. Leofwine hid his amusement. The Duke must have only just realised that his sister would soon be a queen whereas he would remain a Duke.

With a composure that Leofwine admired, Duke Richard spoke again. "After much consideration, I've decided that the wedding will go ahead, and the treaty will be ratified. You may leave today. Ælfgifu is packed and ready to leave, as are her servants who'll accompany her. She also carries a letter with her that I trust your king will act upon with all haste. It's a small favour to ensure the safety of my sister."

Confusion knit Leofwine's brow as he debated what provision the Duke might have stipulated. He was in the unfortunate position of not being able to ask the Duke what he wanted of his king while having to agree to it, all at the same time. Long moments had passed before he spoke.

"I'm sure that no favour you ask of my king will be problematic. He's keen for the wedding to take place with all speed, and as such, I'll pledge my word in the place of that of my king's."

"As I knew you would, my lord. And now, to the less welcome news."

Duke Richard had already dismissed Ælfgifu from his thoughts, and she stumbled towards her seat, uncertainty on her young face. Her brother had told her she would leave today but had offered no further words as to how she should proceed and so she chose to eat as she would on any typical day.

"Less welcome news?"

"Yes, I have reports that Swein of Denmark and lord Leofsige left during the night with all their men."

"My lord?"

"They'd not moored at the harbour as you had, but a little distance away. My men tell me that all the ships are gone, but I'm unsure which way they travelled. Hopefully, it was not towards England." The news was far from welcome.

"Hopefully not. Perhaps it would be best if we departed in all haste from this place. I'd sooner reach England today."

"Of course, lord Leofwine, I entirely agree. But first, I must insist on a small mass of celebration for my sister's impending wedding and then we'll allow you to leave."

"As you will, my lord." Leofwine bowed his head and strode from the hall. He had messages for his men, and he wanted to ensure that those still on the ships were aware of the possible threat.

He wished he'd managed to speak to Swein of Denmark and Leofsige, but the Duke had kept him occupied throughout the evening, and when he'd finally had a chance to seek out the pair, they'd long departed from the feast.

He'd thought to speak to them today, offer Leofsige what support he could in the hope that he'd not ally with Swein. It appeared that he'd been denied the opportunity and he wondered whether it was at Swein's prompting or Leofsige's own.

. . .

The mass was, thankfully, a short affair as the Duke had dictated and by midday Leofwine was aboard his ship with the soon-to-be queen and on his way home again.

Ælfgifu had become tearful at leaving, but once out on the slightly rolling sea, she'd calmed and become intrigued by Horic and his songs. She blushed quite prettily in places, and Leofwine decided it was best not to ask his men to stop their loud singing; it was working well as a distraction.

She and her four servants, hunting hound and a small amount of luggage were safely stowed in the middle compartment of the ship, where they were sheltered from the occasional wave that washed over it, the sea gentle.

She clutched the letter to her chest that her brother had given into her safekeeping, and as much as Leofwine wanted to grill her on its contents, he did not. He fervently hoped that his king wouldn't be angry with him for whatever it was he'd unknowingly agreed to.

Just out of sight of his homeland, Ælfric shouted a warning to Leofwine. Horic stood abruptly and stared hard at where Ælfric pointed and then swore, long and hard.

Leofwine wasn't able to see anything where the men looked, but he feared he knew what it was, and when Horic stopped his tirade, he had his fears confirmed.

"Swein of Denmark and his bastard ship army are following us."

"Just following us?"

"Just following us, he says, like it's of no importance," Horic railed, his worry colouring his words and making him speak without due deference to Leofwine. Leofwine decided to ignore it, a thread of fear making him as unguarded as Horic.

"For now, yes, they just follow us, but if the wind changes and the mood so takes him, I'm sure he could catch us."

"I hardly see how. He has the same number of men as us, and the wind is hardly favourable although he does have his sail raised."

"I'd love to agree with you, Leofwine, but if there's one thing I've learnt, we northmen can row bloody fast when there's easy prey to be had."

"With thanks for calling us all prey, Horic," Leofwine spoke with asperity.

"Apologies, my lord, but that's what we'll be seen as. I was worried they were lying in wait for us, and now it appears as though I was right."

"Ælfric, can we go faster?" Leofwine turned to his helmsman and saw him peering forward, rather than backward.

"Aye, my lord, we can. I don't much like Horic's words that the northmen are faster. I'm sure we can outrun them."

"Then that's what we'll do. Come, signal the other ships and, Horic, I suggest you show us just how fast you can row."

"My lord," Horic said, striding back to his space along the side of the ship,

"Come on, men, the faster we row, the faster we can find ourselves with our wives, and we can enjoy ourselves."

Horic's words occasioned some laughter, and then the ship took off to the increased pace of the oarsmen. Leofwine stayed standing, even as the boat bounced and crashed through the waves.

Ælfric stood at his side, and the pair kept a silent vigil watching the spectre of the other ships float in and out of clear view. Ælfgifu, having understood most of the conversation between the men, stayed silent, but her gaze never left Leofwine's face, watching it intently for any sign that her future might become doubtful. She too refused to look behind her.

As the sun began its descent into the western view, Swein's ships became even harder to see as the clouds and sea merged into one expanse, but the welcome sight of their coastline quickly came into sight.

Still, Leofwine didn't let up on his shipmen. Only when they reached dry land would they be safe, or so he hoped. He did allow the image of Swein and his men surging onto English land to enter his mind, but he quickly banished it, more out of hope than any assurance that Swein wouldn't attack.

Within clear sight of the port they'd left from only yesterday morning, Leofwine allowed the sweating, heaving men, to slacken their efforts. They were exhausted after a full half-day of heavy rowing, and Leofwine could clearly see more of his king's ship army stationed around the port and hustling to ready themselves and escort the ships in. They'd seen the enemy too.

Swein of Denmark took the opportunity to skirt perilously close to Leofwine's ship, not wholly within boarding range but not far off either. From his place at the front of his vast ship he called mockingly, "My blind lord, you escort your precious cargo well. But I could've caught you if I'd wanted to."

In the half-light, Leofwine struggled to focus on the man and his ship. It was a large vessel, containing far more than the sixty men that Leofwine's own held, and for a moment, doubt entered his mind. Could he have caught them? Or had this all been a ruse to scare the king, his new bride and his ealdorman?

"If only that were true, king Swein; your men couldn't have caught us even if we'd dropped our oars into the sea and paddled with our hands."

Behind him, Leofwine heard Horic's quiet chortle of appreciation at the barb.

"And now if you'd be so good, I suggest you leave these shores. You're not welcome, and neither, I'm afraid, is the one-time ealdorman who you harbour."

Swein glowered angrily at Leofwine, his ugly countenance easy to determine even at a distance and in such bad light.

"Mark my words, Leofwine, we'll meet again, and you'll be my enemy, and I'll be your nemesis."

"As you will, Swein. Now, before the king's fleet surrounds you, I suggest you and your men leave, and I'd also request that you do not return."

Swein glowered ineffectually at Leofwine for a long moment, but

Leofwine felt his fear for the man dissipate. He was just a man – a man with a lot of ships and men, but a man just the same. And he was not going to have England's future queen.

Turning his back confidently on Swein he signalled for the men to resume rowing and as they did he felt more than saw the mass of the king's ship army swirl around his own ship and out towards where he assumed Swein was turning away, his threats hanging limply in the damp evening air.

17
AD1002

Athelstan had mounted a guard at the port waiting for Leofwine to reappear. His brother had returned to the king to report that the escort had left and that the king should muster to meet his new bride.

When Leofwine stepped ashore, the king's son was busily introducing himself to Ælfgifu, or Emma as she must now be publicly called, and Leofwine noted with wry amusement that he quickly fell under the spell of the lovely young woman.

The king would perhaps have been wise to let his son marry her after all. In only a few stilted sentences, Athelstan had her chuckling, and her alert eyes were bright as they took both him and her surroundings in, her first sight of England coming with the dusk.

"Thank you, lord Athelstan, for awaiting my return."

"My pleasure, my lord; I wanted to personally ensure that both you and ... lady Emma made it to the king in one piece. Do you know who's been chasing you?"

Athelstan nodded towards the sea, where the specks of the fast disappearing ships could still be seen.

"Regrettably, yes: Swein of Denmark and his men."

"Swein," Athelstan repeated, suddenly looking far more intently out to sea, "Do you think he planned it or was it just an unhappy occurrence?"

"Oh, planned it, definitely. Swein was at Duke Richard's court with the disgraced Leofsige."

Athelstan didn't speak, taking his time to consider his next words.

"Then, I think you've done admirably well, my lord. The king will be pleased."

Athelstan's face was grave, his concern palpable as he considered what could have happened. Leofwine nodded in agreement.

"Let's hope the king agrees, for the Duke has made a final stipulation in a letter that Ælfgifu ... sorry, Emma ... carries about her person, and I'm not aware of what it is. I can't imagine it to be anything too catastrophic, but I have my fears."

Athelstan's young face twisted in worry at yet more disturbing news.

"There's little point in worrying now. We'll just have to wait until we see the king."

In a flurry of activity, Athelstan escorted Emma and her small band of servants towards the welcoming lights of the nearby hall, and Leofwine turned back to his crew.

"Aren't you coming, lord Leofwine? I've arranged for a welcome meal."

"I'll be in shortly, my lord. I just need to speak to my men and relay some messages."

"With thanks, my lord Leofwine, for your care of me," a small voice spoke up, and Leofwine bowed towards the young woman he'd escorted across the sea.

"It was my pleasure," and he meant every word of it. Even meeting Swein had been a delight for he felt he'd learned a valuable lesson in preserving his future.

. . .

The following day they were to meet the king at his palace in Canterbury, a straightforward and short enough journey to make.

In the mid-morning sun, they set out happily enough, escorted by Leofwine's men and those of Athelstan's. Athelstan rode with his soon-to-be stepmother while Leofwine and his men rode on ahead, ensuring the way was clear.

There'd been no clear indication that Swein of Denmark and lord Leofsige had left their coasts the previous evening and Leofwine was nervous. They could easily have come ashore further along the coast and ridden to try and intercept the bride before she could be wed to her new husband. Leofwine would be surprised at nothing either of the two men tried.

The still morning air didn't herald any attackers, but Leofwine didn't relax. Ealdorman Leofsige knew this part of England well, and Leofwine felt sure that something else would be attempted.

Almost within sight of Canterbury, a mounted force suddenly came upon them. Leofwine reined in quickly, his command echoing between the remainder of his men, although all had seen the threat.

Belatedly Leofwine remembered the river they'd recently crossed.

Swein of Denmark had no doubt ordered the attack, although he wasn't part of the force as far as Leofwine could see. Leofwine thought the river had been too small for the large vessels to navigate along, but clearly, he'd been wrong.

Athelstan, alert to the threat almost as quickly as Leofwine, had his men surround the young queen-to-be and her entourage. She disappeared from Leofwine's sight behind a human screen of men who'd dismounted from their horses and were in a fighting stance, shields raised and weapons of choice in their hands.

The horses were led away by the younger men who were not yet full fighting members of Athelstan's household troop.

"Lord Leofwine, I believe you may have misunderstood my intent," a large northern man called from his position in front of them, his thick accent slurring the words. He stood blocking the road they were following, his warriors to either side of them. In the bright day, their weapons flashed dully, and Leofwine could tell just from looking at them that the men were warriors by trade.

"When you've put down your weapons I'll apologise for my misunderstanding. If you'd be so good as to tell me your name, I'll name you as you name me," Leofwine retorted, his sword firm in his hand and his helm in easy reach if he needed it, even though he still sat on his horse, able to see the land clearly for some distance to either side.

"I fear this will not go well for you, my half-blind ealdorman," the warrior quipped. Leofwine was pleased he'd not noticed that he also faced one of the English king's sons. He was sure that it would have made the man even more determined to beat them. Leofwine was convinced that Swein would still welcome one of the king's sons as his hostage.

"You slur me with words which have no impact on me and are those, I assume, of your king, Swein."

"I'm doing what needs to be done if that's what you mean," the man said, still not mentioning his name but pulling his helm firmly over his face, twirling his war axe in his hand as though it were no more than a toy. Leofwine could feel Horic behind him, just itching to be set loose against the northern Raider.

Leofwine glanced behind him to ensure the rest of his men were ready. Only then did he too pull his helm over his head, marvelling at the man's utter stupidity for attacking in broad daylight. The enemy was either confident because he knew something that Leofwine didn't, or utterly stupid. Leofwine slid from his horse and ordered Hunter to lead the animal away.

"As you will, stranger; I hope your death is quick and brief," Leofwine hollered.

The man growled a response that was lost amidst the war cry that arose from the men behind Leofwine as they slowly advanced toward the crew of forty men.

Horic's roar of anger almost deafened Leofwine as the man took up his preferred position at Leofwine's side.

"You're a coward, you horse's ass, and now I'll enjoy watching you bleed. Don't think I don't know who you are, Ulf." Horic's words cemented Leofwine's belief that he faced one of Swein's trusted warriors.

Released by Leofwine's order to attack, Horic went straight for Ulf, the force of his first hammer blow unbalancing the man, while Horic screamed in triumph. Leofwine raised his shield to ward off the blow from the man immediately before him.

"Swein of Denmark has called for your death," the man roared, and Leofwine found himself laughing at the fury on the man's barely visible face.

"I care not for your king Swein!" Leofwine screeched. "He's just a man, and he'll fall before my blade, as will you."

Leofwine raised his shield to ward off a blow from the man's axe and took the opportunity to poke his blade between the man's exposed legs, sliding upwards as he went. The man howled in rage as he was severed high up his thighs and blood burst in a red-hot stream along Leofwine's ungloved hand.

Leofwine continued to laugh, a battle fury he'd never before experienced taking hold of him so that for every shriek of laughter he gave, Horic countered with a booming cry of rage.

The clash of metal on wood resounded, interspersed with the cries of wounded and dying men.

At one point an ear-piercing scream erupted from a female mouth, and Leofwine looked around in shock, recalled abruptly to his real duties here. It was not a cause for concern, though, just Athelstan forcing Ælfgifu to retreat with his men, leaving Leofwine and his own to face down the enemy.

It was a good move and one that caused the fury of Ulf's troops to double, and their fighting skills to become less and less accomplished.

Leofwine cut down two more fighters before he found himself

standing before Ulf, fighting for his life against the mighty Horic who rained blows from his hammer about the northman's shield.

Blood covered Ulf's face, and Leofwine noted with no small satisfaction that Horic had ensured a nasty cut now sliced the man's face. Pity he'd not live to be ridiculed for his injury, but Leofwine had had enough of the man's arrogance.

Wading to the side of Horic, Leofwine shouted his intent, and then stepped forward and landed a mighty stab of his sword through the exposed back of Ulf. Ulf stilled as the wound registered, howling with rage as Horic spat in his face.

"Swein is welcome to you," Ulf screeched, turning to face the man who'd killed him, recognition flashing instantly on his face.

"I'm welcome to Swein, I think you mean," Leofwine retorted, with no remorse for his actions. Ulf crumpled to the floor face first, and Leofwine roughly pulled his sword free from the man's back, using his foot as leverage when it became stuck.

"Apologies, Horic – the kill should have been yours."

Horic shrugged in easy acceptance, "It's better that you be remembered as his killer. It'll ensure Swein of Denmark realises you're not to be toyed with."

"Then you have my thanks, Horic."

"If you don't mind, I might help myself to the insufferable fool's armbands."

"Help yourself. I've no use for more treasure. Reward yourself."

With little prompting, Horic bent to his grisly task of removing anything of value from the body of Ulf, Leofwine noting with pride that none of the forty enemy men still lived. His men were even then digging a shallow grave for the dead men, and copying Horic in dividing the spoils.

Leofwine wiped the blood from his face. It should have been a beautiful day for a wedding but that it had also proved to be a good day for a fight was not lost on Leofwine. He just hoped his king would be as pleased with the killing of Ulf as he was sure to be with his new wife.

. . .

THE KING'S GREETING FOR HIS YOUNG WIFE WAS A CLEAR INDICATION THAT HE was pleased with his choice and Leofwine experienced a moment of satisfaction when they arrived in Canterbury. He'd served his king well.

If the king was concerned at finding Leofwine's men covered in blood, he masked it well, his gaze on his intended bride.

Yet, as the evening progressed, Æthelred, incandescent with anger, called Leofwine to a personal meeting. Leofwine had been expecting a brief thank you and some form of a gift. What he received was very different.

The king paced angrily within his room alone. Leofwine entered the room at his instruction and stood attentively, waiting. When he saw the parchment crushed in his king's hand and the angry mask that seemed to have clamped over the king's face, Leofwine knew with a sinking heart that whatever Duke Richard had demanded, it was not a good thing.

"I take it you agreed to ... to this?" The king's voice was a harsh whisper as he shook the crumpled letter in his hand.

"I agreed to the addition to the treaty, my lord, yes. I wasn't made aware of what it contained."

"And do you know now?"

"No, my lord, Ælfgifu ... apologies my lord, Emma ... was faithful to her brother's word and kept the letter with her. She wasn't aware of its content either."

"Good, then if none know but duke Richard and me, then hopefully, I'll not have to act upon it."

"My lord, what has he written?"

"Don't concern yourself with it, Leofwine. The Duke has attempted to play you and me for fools. I understand from Athelstan that the bastard Leofsige was there with bloody Swein of Denmark."

"Yes, the two men seemed very close."

"I don't doubt it, and I know whose idea this ... this outrage was.

Now go with my heartfelt thanks. You're not to blame for this ..." Æthelred shook the letter angrily, "and you have my permission to remind me that I said so if I ever do try and blame you."

"With thanks, my lord," Leofwine stuttered, wondering what Duke Richard had enclosed in the letter while at the same time relieved that he didn't know. The look on the king's face was one he'd never seen before – a mixture of anger, hurt and defeatism all rolled into one. Hastily, he bowed his way out of the king's presence and returned to the great hall. The king didn't appear for the rest of the evening, leaving his new bride-to-be sitting attentively before a mass of men she didn't know, on show for all to see.

The wedding was to be celebrated at Canterbury a week later. That allowed Leofwine just enough time to rush to his Mercian lands and assure himself of his wife's safety, and that of the king's lands.

The king waved him away impatiently when he asked to be allowed to return home, his countenance not quite what it had been on seeing his bride, but it was clear that he was trying hard to brush aside whatever had disturbed him the day before.

Æthelflæd had never attended a royal wedding before, and Leofwine returned to a household in an uproar and a woman who was almost too busy to do more than offer him her cheek to kiss. He'd been expecting a little more and felt disgruntled throughout his day at home, and even more so as he and Æthelflæd rode back south.

Northman was to accompany them, but the other children were left behind in the capable hands of their house servants. Leofric grumbled and grouched the entire time Leofwine was home and he almost dissolved and allowed his second oldest to accompany them. Only Æthelflæd's outraged cry that he had nothing to wear prevented him from speaking out.

Leofric had apparently realised his intent though and as he turned to leave the boy finally gave him a hug of welcome and smiled in his direction.

Æthelflæd was flustered throughout the journey south. When Canterbury came into sight, three days later, did Æthelflæd relax the tight stance of her shoulders, and smile genuinely for the first time. He wasn't sure why a royal wedding should cause quite so much worry, but he knew better than to ask.

As Leofwine was thrust into an elaborately decorated tunic on the morning of the wedding, he wished he'd had nothing to wear and been excused from the wedding. The tunic was of the finest quality cloth, but as every part of it had been covered with some form of decoration, it was hard to tell. He refrained from saying that actually the costume could have been made from the roughest hemp and instead endured a day of fidgeting and trying not to scratch.

Northman's tunic was just as finely crafted but without so many embellishments and he spent much of the day strutting around.

Æthelflæd looked stunningly beautiful in her soft gown of pale blue ringed with neat stitching. But it did make Leofwine stop and stare at his wife with a frown for surely her stomach was a little rounder than usual and her breasts a little fuller. She was clearly pregnant again but hadn't yet informed him. He imagined it was because he might, just possibly, have prevented her from coming to the spectacle of the wedding and so he held his tongue. He'd speak to her after the wedding.

Emma, as she was officially known, looked delicate and beautiful in a flowing dress of finest purple linen with a white wimple around her head. Her dress was deeply embroidered around the neck and had tight sleeves with golden threads. Æthelred was dressed in an elegant tunic to match his new wife, and he glowed with happiness.

The wedding passed with no incident, and the huge feast that followed was raucous with the cries of the king's young sons and all their friends. Leofwine watched with amusement as cup after cup of mead was consumed amongst a deteriorating quality of toasts to their father.

Abruptly Leofwine was overwhelmed with a dread that he was getting old, as was the king, and that before him sat the new generation who would be facing the Raiders. His young son, face aglow with excitement, would be a part of that next generation, as would all his children. The thought was not the most comforting.

With only four ealdormen, the king's men were stretched ever thinner over more extensive areas, and he was the youngest of them all, and they all faced threats from the Raiders. What would the king do if he were suddenly to lose all his ealdorman, which was not such an impossible thought? Yes, his sons were getting older and growing in stature, but the king had so far not gifted any of them with great commands.

Leofwine wondered if it was time to call his king to account for his plans but then, on the following day, signing second on a royal charter awarding him land, his thoughts were banished in a swell of self-congratulations. Perhaps there was the possibility after all that his king would see him as the premier ealdorman and seek out his counsel more and more often.

With his king wed and the geld paid to the Raiders who'd been harassing the south since the year before, Leofwine rode for home, hopeful that the Raiders were gone for good and that whatever Duke Richard had demanded of his king would come to nothing. He couldn't have been more wrong.

According to reports received from the king, the Raiders left gloating over their massive hoard of treasure and as a parting shot they set fire to every religious house and manor they came upon as they retreated to their ships in the far south. The king's anger was immediate and as Leofwine later discovered, with the threats from Duke Richard hanging over him and some minor attacks from Swein of Denmark and lord Leofsige, the king's patience with all things Danish ceased.

In a moment of blind panic, Æthelred ordered his reeves to rid the country of all people of Danish blood outside the Danelaw by killing them where they stood. Leofwine's instructions arrived too late for him to carry out his king's orders on November 13th and by then the king had recanted of his anger. But it was too late. Many

Danes were murdered at the king's hands, including ealdorman Pallig and his wife, Swein's sister.

When Leofwine learned of the terrible atrocity, he demanded that masses be said for the souls of the dead, and also for those of the English people. He didn't think that king Swein would be pleased when the news finally reached him during the winter season.

Where usually, Leofwine would have let his men rest throughout the dark time of the year, he insisted on drills and the riding of the borders. He spent his days assuring those in the Danelaw that the king's words had been taken out of context by over-zealous young men, keen to do their duty for their king, and he prayed, and he prayed that the birth of his fourth child would not occasion another conflict-inspired name.

18
AD1003

The year began with a scream, the clang of swords on shields and a death. When Leofwine looked back as the year turned from bad to worse, he couldn't quite decide which event affected him the deepest.

Clearly, the birth of another lusty baby son was fantastic news, and he thanked God for his bounty by arranging for more land to be set aside for the monastery at Deerhurst, but it was all marred by the death of his faithful Hunter.

She'd looked ill for much of the winter and often he'd been forced to leave her behind, taking with him one of her children that he'd half-heartedly been training to replace their mother.

But planning for the future and accepting that she was gone were two entirely different things. He'd not invested enough time into training his new companion dog, and it showed.

His young children had aptly named the dog Hammer, after a lengthy and long-running debate after his birth two years before. Northman and Leofric had insisted on a 'proper' name for the dog but had then proceeded to spoil him and make him more pet than Hunter had ever been. Even before Hunter had been called upon to be his eye, she'd been a dog of activity, not prone to spending any amount of time seeking attention.

Hammer loved his children, as he saw them, and tolerated Leofwine and his commands when he must. He was the opposite of any dog Leofwine had encountered, keen to growl at the master and a playful puppy in the hands of the master's children.

To curb his frustration with the dog, Leofwine finally announced that Northman was old enough to escort him as he went about his duties. Northman was ecstatic, but Leofric and Ealdgyth didn't share in the joy, and Æthelflæd grew tired with their constant moaning and bewailing that their dog had been stolen away by their father.

Leofwine's own frustration high, having tripped over yet another obstacle the damn dog had failed to alert him to, he told the children he would get them their own puppies provided they trained one of them to help him. Æthelflæd laughed at him then – the first time he'd heard her relax since the birth of their son – and she queried whether the new child would have his own dog too.

When the entire litter had arrived from the old farmer that Leofwine had initially sought advice from when first training Hunter, his household descended into happy chaos that, surprisingly, Hammer calmed and could order.

Ealdgyth sat for hours grooming her small puppy, whereas Northman had his and his father's dog-to-be, outside undergoing a harsh training regime that he'd devised himself. Leofric squirrelled away with his own puppy and the one for his new brother, and belatedly Leofwine realised that the two brothers were in competition to see who could raise the best-trained puppy.

Much to everyone's surprise, Hammer took his responsibility as a surrogate father to the five puppies very seriously and by the time the Raiders' attacks were well under way, Leofwine felt as though he commanded an army of dogs and children as well as men. He was proud of his sons. They'd make good commanders of men one day if their puppy training were anything to go by.

The clang of swords on shields had come from his men, who'd

not taken a single day off from their training during the short winter days. There was a palpable air of unease amongst his people ever since the massacre of the Danes on St Brice's Day. Something was coming, and they knew, as Leofwine did, that it would be Swein-shaped and not pleasant.

Swein of Denmark didn't hesitate in his efforts to avenge his sister and brother-in-law. Whether the men had seen eye to eye in recent years was something that Leofwine could never determine, but one thing was clear: it was all the excuse the king of Denmark needed.

Swein's attacks on Wilton and Salisbury the following day were carried out ruthlessly and without warning. He and his men bypassed Southampton and stole horses and marched or rode as fast as possible across the open expanse of land until they reached their targets. The fyrd, under Ealdorman Ælfric, had not even assembled when the towns lay in burned ruins. And still, Swein sent no word to the king of his intentions or demands.

King Æthelred, secluded with his heavily pregnant queen in Woodstock, was far from the atrocities committed during the two days of rampaging. When Ealdorman Ælfric belatedly arrived with his household troop and the men of the fyrd, he was more than happy to negotiate than face the wrath of the twenty shiploads of men that Swein of Denmark had with him.

Leofwine, too far away as usual to do more than hear the news after the events had occurred, cursed the king and Ælfric in equal measure. Ealdorman Ælfric was spineless; he always put himself first, and his king and country second.

While Leofwine was prepared to accept that Ælfric had faced the enemy more times than any other and could draw on that experience, he held it as no excuse for Ælfric's actions. He might well have seen friends and relatives die but really, did he want to save himself only for others to experience the same pain?

Leofwine was disheartened to hear that lord Leofsige was still with Swein. The former ealdorman was making good use of his knowledge of England to enable the Danish king to attack to maximum effect. Salisbury and Wilton, a mere day's ride from the king's usual haunts of Cookham and Wantage, were a personal threat that Leofwine didn't miss.

Swein's next move was also heavily infused with meaning, for he fled back to his ships and sailed straight for Exeter, part of the new queen's dower lands. As she heaved the king's son from her belly, her reeve treated with the king of Denmark and let him take her town.

The queen, unpopular simply because of her marriage to the king, became the subject of scorn. Rumours spread the length and breadth of the country that the Duke of Normandy, unhappy with Æthelred's attempts to rid the country of the Danish, had instructed his sister to allow Swein of Denmark to take her lands as a blatant attempt to throw the country into further upheaval.

Leofwine didn't listen to the rumours that summer. He had no time. He and his men vowed to protect the land of the Mercians and the Hwiccans, and they spared no energy in ensuring the safety of the people as they grew and then harvested their crops for the coming winter.

Leofwine kept in constant contact with his king, but not once did he journey to the king's witan, content to allow messengers to run between him and the court. While Swein no longer scared him, news of the carnage Swein caused as he passed almost unimpeded through the western lands as if he were punishing the area and the people for the deaths of his sister and her husband, was unhappily received.

Leofwine wanted to send a message to Æthelmaer, entrenched as he was in the lands his father had held, but he knew it would be foolish to risk the lives of his men on an errand that would accomplish little. The king hadn't called out the fyrd of the western provinces, and now it was too late to do so.

Leofwine prayed each night for those he feared slaughtered at the hands of the Raiders, especially the churchmen, and every night, nightmares filled his dreams and drove him to the comfort of his wife's arms.

He loved her more thoroughly that year than he ever had, each sexual encounter tinged with a little sadness as if they both realised it could well be the last time that they kissed and held each other as tenderly as Swein came ever closer to their homeland.

His young son grew well and robust, cocooned as he was in the heart of the Mercian lands, and Leofwine wished more than once that he could offer the same protection for all the people of the English territories.

19
AD1004

The winter months stopped the Raiders from carrying out any further attacks, but they kept their camp on the Isle of Wight, a constant threat to the king and his people. Leofwine wondered how Swein of Denmark could govern his lands when he was never there. And then Leofwine questioned who Swein could trust enough to protect those areas for him. Perhaps Swein was luckier in his choice of ealdormen than his own king.

Ealdorman Ælfric grew more and more adamant that Swein must be bought off, and Æthelred was more and more adamant that he shouldn't be. The king decried the enormous wealth they'd already expended on the Raiders and insisted on a new coinage being issued that showed him in a warrior stance. Æthelred demanded that the royal officials spread the word of his military prowess and remind anyone who would listen that they'd had a great victory only four years before.

Leofwine hoped that no one reminded the king of the defeats that the last four years had also bought about.

The king seemed unhappy with all of his ealdormen, when the witan convened, calling them to task for minor infractions that had never been censored before, and Leofwine grew uneasy. The king was planning something, and Leofwine wondered what it was. Would the king finally decide to replace all the ealdormen with his sons from his first wife, or would he pick new ealdormen from amongst the royal officials at court?

Only then the king received the excellent news that seemed to restore his faith in his ealdormen. Swein moved his arena of attack from the far south to the lands of the East Angles, raiding Norwich and burning as he went.

With Ealdorman Leofsige banished, Æthelred had not named a replacement for the area, but had made the decision to have Ulfcytel, an accomplished but young warrior stationed in the area with his household troops and the king's backing to raise the fyrd if and when needed; and to treat with the enemy, if necessary. And that was precisely what Ulfcytel did and with quite dazzling results.

Initially caught unprepared, Ulfcytel sought peace with the Danes. Swein, by all accounts, had laughingly agreed, with Leofsige at his side clearly enjoying the discomfort of his countrymen. When Swein subsequently broke the agreement, Ulfcytel reacted with stunning clarity of vision, raising the fyrd and meeting him in battle at Thetford.

Ulfcytel, a member of the Danelaw political elite, had been a skilled warrior since he could hold a sword; his endeavours had often been the subject of praise in the past, and this time he excelled himself. Rumour had it that Swein of Denmark only escaped with his life because those of the men tasked with destroying Swein's ships while they raided inland failed to carry out the order promptly, allowing Swein and his men to escape in the remaining half of the ships they'd arrived in.

It was a pity that Swein survived to continue his concentrated attack on the English lands, but it gave the English people heart to carry on with their efforts. As Leofwine had discovered two years before when he'd met the man, the English people realised that Swein was a man, not a God, fallible if the right conditions prevailed.

The king called together his fractured witan once more, and Leofwine entered the great church at Wantage with some trepidation. The king could surely not allow the current situation to continue.

He wasn't surprised to discover the church almost bursting with men and women, come to pay homage to the king and hear his words about the raiders.

Ælfric, the old and wizened Archbishop of Canterbury, was rumoured to have made the journey, even at his great age, to show his support for his king. When Leofwine entered the preternatural calm of the church, he was not surprised, therefore, to find the man there and surrounded by as many of the leading churchmen as Leofwine had ever seen before.

Wulfstan of York had also travelled to support his king, and Godwine, the new bishop of Lichfield, had journeyed with Leofwine from the Mercian lands, taking advantage of their joint trip to discourse at length on the king and the state of the country as a whole.

The churchman had not alluded to the great massing of churchmen that was going to take place at the witan, and Leofwine felt unhappy that the man had thought the information not worthy of sharing. He'd worked hard to develop a good working relationship with his predecessor, but clearly, he'd need to build a new connection if he was to share his secrets with his ealdorman.

All in all, a significant swathe of bowed head greeted Leofwine on entering the church. The men took up two full rows of chairs at the front of the church. Leofwine wondered if the king had summoned them or if they'd come voluntarily, but then Hammer cut him up short, and he stopped abruptly, unsure what had upset his hound.

The dog had improved no end when tasked with keeping order amongst the herd of dogs Leofwine now commanded, but still, on occasion, something untoward would make him forget all his training. Leofwine bent down and offered the dog a few words of encouragement and Wulfstan gently nudged the disobedient dog with his thigh. Hammer walked a little more confidently into the room full of men he'd never met before.

The king hadn't yet arrived, but his vast collection of sons formed a band of support almost as extensive and broad as that of the churchmen. By comparison, the group of three ealdormen would make a dismally poor showing, and Leofwine's unease grew as he took a seat near the front of the church. The conversation swelled around him, but he paid little attention, instead seeking out Ealdorman Ælfric and Ealdorman Ælfhelm, but neither man had arrived yet.

Leofwine instead turned to the king's sons and caught the eye of Athelstan. He was sat quietly with his brothers, barely speaking, but impeccably dressed in a finely embroidered cloak clasped together by a dull red gem that reflected the candles from the altar. He nodded and smiled at Leofwine before turning away to glance at the rows of young and old men alike who served the king as his royal officials.

One of the men caused Athelstan to stare openly, and Leofwine turned to glance at the man. Vaguely he recalled the well-built young man, his youthful face unmarked by any battle scars and his auburn hair neatly trimmed. His clothing was not the best quality and yet he sat with confidence that spoke of some inner calm. Leofwine speculated as to why Athelstan marked him out so openly.

When Athelstan turned back to meet Leofwine's eye, his eyes were hooded. Clearly, there was some unspoken message there.

He turned aside to Wulfstan sat calmly beside him, talking to Horic.

"You see that young man over there, in the row with the royal officials. He has a young face, auburn hair and his clothes are a little rough."

Wulfstan turned slowly to look where Leofwine indicated, making it appear as though he only turned to scan the crowd behind him.

"Yes, I see him."

"Do you know who he is?"

Wulfstan nodded as he turned back to face the front of the church,

"Yes, he's a bit of a rising star in the king's confidence. I'm sure I've mentioned him before. He's Eadric. He heralds from some long-dead and obscure royal line in the Mercian lands."

Beside them, Horic too scanned the crowd,

"Ah, yes, I agree with you. That's Eadric. He's ... a keen individual."

Leofwine turned an amused expression on Horic, "And what do you mean by 'keen'?"

"Oh, you know. The king could tell him to swallow his own tongue, and he probably would. I've heard that he's made it plain to all who'll listen to him that he plans on gaining the ear of the king and reclaiming whatever misbegotten part of Mercia he claims as his own."

"I've heard the same, Leofwine. He's certainly worth watching out for. Why do you ask?"

Leofwine explained that Athelstan appeared to have pointed him out to him.

"I'm not surprised," Horic muttered, "that's one of the other rumours flying about. He and Athelstan don't exactly see eye to eye and being so close in age it's grating on Athelstan that the king sees Eadric as someone worth cultivating, whereas the king stole the bride intended for him."

"Is he really so high in the king's favour."

"Yes, he is. He seems to be magnificent at insinuating himself into situations that are none of his concern."

Again Leofwine caught Athelstan's eye and nodded to him to show his message was understood.

"I think we might need to have a little chat with the young man."

Beside him, Horic offered a short bark of laughter, and then all the men scrambled to their feet as the king and his wife walked into the church.

The king finely dressed and looking younger than ever before if that was possible, walked with his petite queen, a radiant smile on his face, as his young son Edward was carried in beside them.

The king had dressed to complement his wife, but Leofwine couldn't help but note that it drew attention to the age gap between the pair of them. As young as the king now looked, it was clear to see that he was double the age of his bride. She would have been far better suited to his eldest son.

Emma caught Leofwine's eye as she was escorted to her seat and favoured him with a bright smile that he returned fully. The king caught her glance and looked to see whom she rewarded so freely with her favour. Seeing Leofwine, the king waved in greeting and then gestured to his archbishop to begin the service.

Archbishop Ælfric spoke the words of the mass firmly and precisely as if defying all who commented only on his age. Leofwine smirked at his clipped tones and business-like demeanour while appreciating it. He loved his God dearly, but sometimes he did think the churchmen he knew expounded a little too much at all the wrong times. For today's sermon, Archbishop Ælfric preached on renewal and new life while offering a caveat that what was older and more known was still to be trusted.

Leofwine looked to the old man with interest. It was clear that he was not the only one aware that rumours were circulating that the king planned some form of shake-up amongst his court. Not for the first time, Leofwine wondered if his time away from the court, when he was busy in the Mercian and the Hwiccan lands, was harming his hard-won acceptance from the king.

Leofwine shrugged the thought aside; he didn't serve the king for his gain, but for the good of his people and his king. He took his position seriously but didn't allow the lines to blur between what was his and what was the king's.

The king could, if he wanted, remove Leofwine from his position as easily as he'd given it. While Leofwine didn't relish his role so far from the fighting and the exposed coastlines, he wouldn't want to serve his king in any less capacity. He enjoyed his position. Otherwise, he would not have fought so hard to keep it.

The sermon done, the king welcomed his followers and asked for a brief recounting of activities from Ulfcytel. Leofwine was surprised by the king's decision to have him speak so openly before the assembled witan. Never before had the ealdormen or the reeves had to justify their activities. It worried him for as long as it took him to realise that the king's face was creased with a broad smile. Obviously, this was not a public humiliation but a public affirmation of the king's man.

Ulfcytel spoke well in concise sentences, his description of the battle and his confrontation with Swein of Denmark bare-boned and devoid of superfluous information. Leofwine listened with interest, waiting to see if Swein had reiterated his threats towards England. When Ulfcytel finished speaking and turned questioning eyes on his king, it appeared not.

"There have been reports directly from Swein's fleet that he was only able to escape because not all of his ships had been destroyed. He's gifted you with an additional name – Snillingr. It means 'bold', he believes you acted as quickly and curtly as he would have done had the situation been reversed."

Ulfcytel looked questioningly at his king and opened his mouth to reply, but the king spoke first.

"I'm not asking for excuses or apportioning blame, so please, let me speak. Gentlemen ..." and the king turned towards his rapt audience. "I wish to commend the actions of Ulfcytel and the men of the fyrd. I've had masses said for the many that perished in the fighting, driving Swein of Denmark back from our shores and to his poorly guarded ships." A faint smile played around his mouth as he said the words.

"The man grows too arrogant as he tries to strip the wealth from my land, and this action by Ulfcytel is what is necessary. I need men who can think as well as fight. I need men who will do what is necessary to keep our land safe. If with one breath we make peace, and it's breached, we must with our next back up our threats with actions that make Swein of Denmark believe that England is not open for the taking."

"We must make him openly admit after each altercation that he failed in his endeavour because we out-thought him or outwitted him, or – and I know this to be true – we are better than him."

There were cheers from those listening to the king, and even Leofwine felt pride and hope swell within him. The king continued, clearly enjoying his moment, "And as you would expect, men who act as they see fit and in my name need rewarding. Ulfcytel, please come forward to me."

Ulfcytel did as bid, standing confidently before his king, his height exceeding Æthelred's. "And Wulfhilda, my dear, would you also stand before me."

Leofwine felt his head swivel in shock before he could stop himself. He'd not even noticed that the king's daughters were in attendance. Now he saw that behind Athelstan a row of almost identical girls sat paying attention to their father. The oldest stood and walked forwards. She blushed as she went, uncomfortable with being the object of everyone's attention but her small steps were steady over the floorboards, and she'd been expecting what was to happen now.

Leofwine watched understanding dawn on Ulfcytel face as the young woman approached him. He looked a little dazed and clearly appreciated the girl's beauty. She had the look of her father and shared his bright eyes and blond hair, artfully arranged in layers of plaits down her back.

Wulfhilda, her headscarf gleaming with stitching and jewels, curtseyed for her father and placed a kiss of welcome on each of his cheeks before turning back to face everyone in the church as her father clasped her hand in his.

"I know you're barely acquainted, but hopefully time will cure that small impediment to this marriage between you and my daughter."

Audible gasps could be heard from the farthest reaches of the church, and Leofwine shook his head in amazement that the majority of people hadn't realised the king's intent already.

"My lord king, you honour me, and I hope I'll honour your daughter," Ulfcytel spluttered in shock.

"I'm sure you will. Shall we celebrate the wedding today or would you prefer tomorrow?"

The poor man gasped again and opened and closed his mouth in shock, "I'd prefer today please, Father. I don't wish to delay my marriage any longer." Wulfhilda's voice was young and bright and yet assured all at the same time.

As the light caught her face, Leofwine had a flashback to her grandmother, Elfrida. The thought flashed through his mind that Ulfcytel might well have just received a gift from the king that he might not always appreciate, just as the king had said to Leofwine when handing him the Mercian lands.

The king laughed at his daughter's self-assurance. "As you wish then. Perhaps one of my holy men would do the honour when we are finished here."

Archbishop Ælfric jumped to his feet, an act that astounded Leofwine. Did the man not appreciate his own age?

"It would be my pleasure, my lord king, and I'm sure that bishop Wulfstan will assist me."

Bishop Wulfstan stood as well and bowed to show he concurred.

"Excellent! Excellent! But my dear ..." and he turned to his daughter, "... first, we must discuss some important matters. Perhaps you and your sisters would prefer to return to the palace and wait for the wedding."

Wulfhilda curtseyed to her father again, and with a last lingering look at her new husband-to-be, she walked demurely from the church accompanied by her two younger sisters, all speaking in whispers as they went. At the end of the aisle, Wulfhilda abruptly stopped. "Father, apologies, but would it be acceptable if Emma accompanied me?"

The king's calculating look passed from his daughter to his queen, but Emma was already on her feet, beckoning the woman who carried her small son to follow her. "It would be my pleasure," she trilled, her voice rich with amusement.

"I must prepare her for the wedding; as her mother, she is correct." Considering Emma was only just older than her step-daughter, Emma was pushing the boundaries a little with her choice of words, but it was clear that she was keen to help her step-daughter. Leofwine doubted the king was quite as pleased with their closeness as he ushered his wife down the aisle.

Ulfcytel stumbled back to where his followers sat, overwhelmed by what had just happened, and Æthelred returned to his place on the dais. The enjoyment of moments ago had drained from his face, and it was clear that he still had more to say and that it was not going to be agreeable.

"My lords and ladies, now that the pleasant part of the day is over we must turn our minds to the task of defending our land and our people. Swein of Denmark toys with us at every opportunity, and we must stop him."

The king abruptly stopped speaking. His eyes focused on someone further back in the church. Leofwine turned and was not unsurprised to see that the man Athelstan had pointed out to him was on his feet.

"Yes, Eadric, you wish to speak?"

"With your leave, my lord king, I would."

"As you will," the king replied, his voice offering no sign of whether he was pleased to be interrupted or not.

Eadric nodded to his king in thanks, and then, to the shock of Leofwine, stepped from his seat and strode confidently to the front of the church. He stood beside his king facing all before him.

The king hadn't been expecting his actions, and from where he'd retaken his seat, he glowered a little at the activities of the youth.

"Thank you, my lord, for allowing me to address the witan. As some of you may not know who I am, I'll introduce myself. I'm Eadric, and my family was once a member of the Mercian royal line." His gaze flickered to Leofwine as he spoke and Leofwine admired the audacity of the man, to stand so prominently and make his intentions so clear.

"We have for many years, shared a border with those of the Welsh. Like Swein of Denmark and his men, the Welsh are fond of lightning strikes and causing as much devastation as possible in as short a space of time as possible. I think we should learn valuable lessons from those altercations of the past, and I believe that if we attack in as random a fashion as they do, that we'll have some success."

Leofwine stifled a cry at Eadric's words, for surely he was merely suggesting what Leofwine had told his king so many years before.

The king turned his suddenly hooded eyes onto Eadric, "And just where would you have us attack?"

"I suggest we take the fight to them, as we were forced to do with Normandy. I propose that we attack their homeland, Denmark."

There was a huge roar of sound at the carelessly tossed words and even the king rose from his chair, his broad fur cloak sliding to the floor to pool at his feet. At Leofwine's side, Horic muttered a foul oath before apologising to the Christian God for speaking so in his house.

Wulfstan looked at Leofwine with amusement, "Now that's how to get a reaction from everyone. Suggest something so daring that it might just work."

Leofwine looked from Eadric to Wulfstan, intrigued.

"You think the king should attack that blatantly?"

"I'm not saying he should, no, but it's a tactic worthy of Swein of Denmark himself."

"It is. Swein would think more highly of Æthelred if he did attack," Horic interjected.

"We northmen see honour in our adventures, but few have ever dared to attack us in our own homeland. We believe our reputations protect us from attack from any but other northmen. It's a worthy and audacious thought. One, I think, the king will not appreciate."

The king was outraged by the suggestion but was doing his best not to let it show as he watched heated words fly between his advisors and councillors. The king's son, Athelstan, was glaring at Eadric with hatred and beside him, Ecgberht was shouting into Athelstan's ear, his words unintelligible from such a distance. Leofwine could only imagine what the king's two oldest sons were thinking.

With an effort, the king called his witan back to order. His face flushed with the effort. Eadric had not moved, enjoying the chaos his words had caused, a smirk on his face.

Finally, an unhappy silence was restored, and the king gestured for Eadric to reclaim his seat. Eadric bowed to his king and did as he was bid, suddenly meek in his demeanour.

"With thanks to Eadric for his interesting ideas on how to defeat Swein of Denmark. I see that it has some merit, but I'd ask that we don't rush to make any decisions. Eadric," and he looked squarely at the man, "I assume you've investigated this idea thoroughly before presenting it to the witan. Do you have ideas of costs and the number of men involved and if we have the resources to mount such an audacious attack?"

Eadric reddened at the king's words, "In truth my lord king, I've not done so. It was just an idea that I thought should be considered."

The king's eyes narrowed, "I believe it is, but first, you must give the matter greater thought. My ealdormen and senior royal officials already know this, and I'd request that you do the same. If after due thought has been applied to the idea, it's deemed worthy of consideration by the entire witan then we'll do just that, but for now, the idea can't be pursued."

Eadric's face drooped with disappointment, but he nodded to show he understood the king's words as he retook his seat.

With a more pensive expression, Æthelred took in the mass of faces looking at him and quirked an eyebrow at Leofwine. He took his cue from the king and stood. Clearly, it was his duty to make some good from Eadric's upset.

He stood and bowed to his king.

"My lord king, I think young Eadric has the right of it in another area. His mention of our neighbours in the west makes me realise that we should make more efforts to reach an accord with them, one more lasting than any before."

"While there have been some small incursions in the past, I'd imagine that at some point they'll realise that they can take advantage of our preoccupation with Swein of Denmark and his men."

Æthelred nodded in appreciation of Leofwine's attempts at changing the direction of the witan's thoughts.

"I agree. Perhaps you and Eadric should spend some time together and agree on a way forward."

"It would be my pleasure."

Out of the corner of his eye, he saw Eadric sit a little straighter at the mention of his name, and Leofwine broke eye contact with the king to offer him a look of acknowledgement. He would have the perfect opportunity to root out whatever this young man had on his mind, and that was fine with him.

Ealdorman Ælfric then claimed the king's attention with a lengthy discourse on the state of his fyrd and his land following Swein's despoiling. The king listened attentively, although Leofwine doubted that anything he heard was new to him. Ælfric was often with the king, not that he didn't need to be: his actions were so ineffectual that he needed to excuse himself continually.

Finally, the king declared the witan concluded for the day, his frustration with excuses threatening to chase away his good mood at the impending marriage of his daughter.

20

AD1004

Leofwine was true to his word, and he had Horic seek out Eadric during the feast for Wulfhilda and Ulfcytel's wedding. The king's pleasant disposition had made a welcome reappearance, and the young couple had been pleased with each other as they'd exchanged the words that married them before the archbishop and bishop, and the rest of the witan.

Eadric appeared a little the worse for too much mead, staggering and holding on to the casually offered arm of Horic. Horic looked unimpressed and unceremoniously dumped him onto the wooden bench Leofwine occupied at the wedding feast.

"I think this might not be the best time to have any sort of discussion with him. He's clearly had too much to drink." Horic's words made perfect sense to Leofwine as he glanced at the younger man.

Eadric's eyes were glazed as he swept yet more mead into his mouth, and Leofwine felt a twinge of concern. He'd not expected the slightly rash young man to lose his self-control so entirely in the king's hall. He'd thought to offer him advice on how best to advance into the king's confidence, now he wasn't so sure that Eadric was worth the effort.

"My lord Leofwine," he slurred, "I've come at your request."

"Eadric, you have my thanks. I'd hoped to speak with you about your Welsh neighbours, but perhaps, now is not the best time."

"Why is that, my lord?"

"You're enjoying the feast?"

"What of it?"

"I think you might have enjoyed it a little too well," Leofwine said the words somberly.

Eadric laughed so hard at the words that spittle spilt from his curved mouth.

"I think you might enjoy it too little, my lord," Eadric mocked, careless of the shifting of Horic behind his shoulder. "You, my lord Leofwine, are always the most proper and most attentive of the king's ealdormen, and yet it does you no good. The king still sees you only as his puppet to manipulate as he sees fit. You mark my words, my lord," he spat again, "the king doesn't value you, and I'm going to use that to my advantage."

Now it was Leofwine's turn to laugh, in amused outrage.

"Your words are brave, and my role in life is to serve my king. If he sees me as his puppet to command as he sees fit, then I'm content. You would do well to learn the lesson. The king is his own man."

"The king is no more his own man than I am," the youth chortled into his mead.

"He's constrained by rules and regulations and constraints that prevent him from acting as he wants." He coughed a hard laugh, banging his cup of mead against the table. "And when he does act as he wants, as he did with the Danes, all the gates of Hell break forth, and Swein of Denmark comes pouring through; and if it's not Swein, it's another of the northmen."

Leofwine was growing outraged by the words boiling from the lad's mouth, and that he spoke so openly of his contempt for his king.

"Eadric, I must protest at your words."

"You can protest all you want, you half-blind bugger. Your words mean nothing to me. Neither should they to you, or the king. Your opinions count for nothing. The king has shown that to you so many times and yet you, the faithful puppy, come running back to do his bidding whenever he decides he might benefit from you."

"Even today, after I spoke out, he turned to you to repair the problem. He didn't ask his other ealdormen, the men he respects, even though they're self-centred fools. No, you're his man through and through. I imagine that before you even piss at the witan, you seek his approval."

Before Leofwine could reply, Horic had grabbed Eadric about the shoulders, and in a parody of the support, he'd earlier offered him, dragged the drunken boy away. Eadric didn't even fight the northman, but continued to laugh and shout insults to Leofwine as he was hauled away.

At a nod from him, Wulfstan followed Horic to ensure he did no real harm. Horic had been tempered by his years of living amongst Leofwine's men, but when the mood took him, he could still adequately act the Viking marauder. For all Eadric's current lack of position within the court, it was evident that some saw him as a man of importance. It would be impolitic if he should come to harm at Leofwine's hands.

Leofwine watched the shuffle of Horic and Eadric, and the more sedate walking pace of Wulfstan, with disgust on his face. Who was this upstart? Why did he think his opinions counted for so much at the king's witan? In frustration, Leofwine grabbed for his cup of mead, missed it with his outstretched hand, and dashed it all over himself. Hammer growled in disgust at being covered in the sticky substance and shook himself roughly clean, covering Leofwine as well.

In revulsion, Leofwine stood abruptly. With a bow to where the king sat surrounded by his older daughter and first son-in-law, laughing and enjoying his brief moment of triumph, Leofwine stalked from the hall, his anger fuelled by the knowledge that the young fool was more than half correct in his interpretation of his relationship with the king.

21

AD1004

THE ATMOSPHERE OF THE WITAN, LIKE LEOFWINE'S MOOD, TURNED SOUR THE next day.

The king may well have temporarily distracted his officials with the marriage of his daughter and the raising of Ulfcytel to a new position of prominence, but it wasn't enough to distract from the attacks of Swein of Denmark. The rumours that abounded about Ulfcytel's new position – not quite an ealdordom, to be sure, but something else entirely – were swirling with high speed.

The king had never before been able to offer his daughters as some sort of reward to his men, always too young. But the king had three daughters, not just the one, and while the youngest was far too young to be married anytime soon, Edith was only a few years younger than her sister, Wulfhilda. Others would have realised as well.

Leofwine knew he'd not be alone in wondering if it was to be a new policy for the king. No more ealdormen, but instead men beholden to him through marriage and more personally accountable to him because of that.

Others within the witan had thought long and hard about the

implications of yesterday's activities with the young men of the royal court calling for a concentrated attack on Swein of Denmark. They jostled amongst themselves, and the king laughed to see the lot of them, the next more keen than the previous, to ride forth in the name of the king and defeat the enemy and claim their royal bride as a prize.

Whether the king intended chaos to rule after his actions of yesterday, Leofwine didn't know. If he hadn't, he'd stumbled upon the means to call his men to arms in a way that Leofwine had never seen before. Even Ealdorman Ælfric seemed a little keener to face the Raiders. Perhaps he was dreaming of royal grandchildren, even at his age.

Only Ealdorman Ælfhelm of Northumbria seemed bemused by the complete change within the witan. He'd arrived late yesterday, offering words of apology that rang too hollow for Leofwine's liking, and he'd snarled and bluffed his way through the council meeting and wedding ceremony. Now he sat surrounded by his followers, openly glaring at his king.

King Æthelred was not enjoying the scrutiny and often stared back at his ealdorman. Their relationship, always precarious in the past, appeared to have reached a new impasse and Leofwine wondered what he was ignorant of that had made Ælfhelm so angry with his king.

Luckily, Leofwine didn't have long to wait. When the young men of the witan had gained the agreement of the king that they could command a small raiding force of their own and scour the countryside for Swein and his men, Ealdorman Ælfhelm rose slowly to his feet.

"My lord king," he bowed low and Æthelred hailed him with a faint narrowing of his eyes. Leofwine was confident that he knew precisely what Ælfhelm was about to say, but he had no option but to let him speak; it was after all the witan, the place where the king was answerable for his actions.

"I've come here, as you bid, but I'm unhappy to be leaving my lands when we're so vulnerable. More than that, I'm unhappy that my people are being forced to pay to finance expeditions against the Raiders which occur far from their land and have no impact on them."

Leofwine hadn't heard Ælfhelm complain quite so publicly before, although he knew there had been mutterings to that effect from among the general people. He'd encountered some small disagreements from those in the Danelaw. They didn't need to defend themselves from their distant relatives or pay for them to leave. The northmen left them well alone, accepting that they may well live in the land of the English, but they were not to be taxed by the activities of their old countrymen.

The king shifted in his chair as Ælfhelm spoke, but it was Wulfstan of York who answered him, having garnered the king's attention by standing even while Ælfhelm still spoke.

"My lord, you do, of course, talk with the views of your countrymen paramount, and I perhaps more than anyone else in this room, can understand their frustration. They're hounded from the north by the kingdoms from beyond the Wall, and the lands are not free from Strathclyde's menace, which has resurged in the last few years, but still, we're a united country, and we must work for the good of all."

Ælfhelm's face twitched as he listened to the holy man. It was evident that he respected Wulfstan for all that he was now advocating the policy of the king in contrast to his own complaints.

"Archbishop, you're correct that you more than anyone would know, but surely, you've heard the rumours and discord amongst the people. They can't fight battles and pay for actions elsewhere. They need to maintain their borders and their own way of life. But," and here he held his hand up to forestall any other from interjecting, "we don't ask that we go free from the burden of protecting this land. We only call for some acceptance that we have our own fyrd to maintain and our own household troops. We would simply like to negotiate for a smaller sum to be paid from the Northumbrian ealdordom."

The king's face had lost its pleasant cast, and he scowled at Ælfhelm.

"My lord, these words are not mine alone; I've been approached by the farmers and the nobility and as their representative at the witan. I must relay their unhappiness."

"Indeed, my lord Ælfhelm," Æthelred spoke through tight lips. 'But you must remember that you're my representative and that you have to talk with my voice as well."

"I do, my lord king, but even you must recognise that the lands of the north are far away from the fighting here in the south. You've never stepped foot within the Northumbrian lands. The people see you as a faceless name."

"I'm no anonymous name. My name is on our coinage for God's sake. And the people of the north are most welcome to journey to the witan or my palaces and see me in person. And I have visited York." There was solemnness in that statement, and Leofwine recalled that the king's first wife had been buried in York.

"I appreciate that my lord king, I simply ask for your consideration."

"I know what you ask, and I ask you back: what would my people of the northern lands do if the fyrd of the south were not able to protect these lands? What if the northmen ran amuck and attacked them from the Mercian lands because all the men of England had fallen for lack of resources and funds."

Ælfhelm's gaze swept the room, looking for who knew what, but he must have found it for he turned back to the king.

"My lord king, we're all aware that this land is rich – richer than even you can adequately determine. That wealth and its portability drive Swein of Denmark and his men to attack us. Our currency is the envy of all our neighbours and news of our wealth travels far and wide, but – and here is the problem – some of that wealth must stay in the hands of those who work for it. That is the argument of the Northumbrian men and women. They work hard and see too little for their efforts."

Realising that the two men were content to argue the matter away for the rest of the morning, Leofwine abruptly stood, unsure what he was going to say but keen to avert a war of words that would carry far from this room. Their enemies didn't need to know of yet another rift between the king and his ealdormen that could be exploited.

"Might I suggest, my lord king and my lord Ælfhelm, that as with young Eadric yesterday, some thought be put into both what the men of the north would count an acceptable sum to pay and what the Treasury knows is the amount that needs to be paid. I'm not saying that it's a viable option, but perhaps we could appease the Northumbrian lands if we consider it, at the least."

Smouldering eyes turned his way, and Leofwine felt his resolve waver under the king's gaze. Ælfhelm glared his way, too, and Leofwine felt, as was often the case, that he was stuck in the middle, trying to appease when it was unlooked for by the two protagonists.

Wulfstan of York was still standing and he, at least, didn't glare. "I think the ealdorman has the right of it. I'd be happy to assist in this matter. My priests would be more than willing to garner opinions, and I could report them back, say at the winter witan."

There was a silence as the king considered the words moodily, his face clouded as he weighed up the limited options he was faced with.

"Very well, you may do so, but ealdorman Ælfhelm, I'm unhappy that you've allowed the views of those in the north to influence you so. Remember, you're merely my representative, and you must govern and act in my name. I'm surprised that a man whose primary wealth stems from those Mercian lands you talk about so freely should allow the Northumbrian men to worry you so much."

Ælfhelm bobbed his head to show his understanding of the situation, but his eyes flashed dangerously as he swept both Leofwine and Wulfstan a fuming look. It was apparent that the king had angered him, and Leofwine thought king Æthelred a fool to do so.

Ælfhelm was the king's barrier in the north; his view of the northern lands being subsumed under a wave of Raiders could so easily be reversed if the borders of the north were breached and the men of the lands of the Scots rushed through. They could reach Leofwine's Mercian lands within days, and with the focus of the small army almost exclusively on the borders and the exposed rivers, it could be disastrous.

Unease inundated Leofwine. His hard-won security in the Mercian lands suddenly felt compromised in a way he'd never considered before. He'd always thought his family safe, his appointment almost more of a punishment than a reward, just as his king had laughingly told him on the day he'd given him the post. It deprived him of the opportunity of facing the Raiders when they attacked, and he'd chafed at the constraints. Now he thought himself a fool for not realising before just how exposed his protected lands really were.

22
AD1004

THE WITAN THAT BISHOP WULFSTAN OF YORK HAD HINTED AT AS OCCURRING in the early winter months was ultimately delayed by months, forcing Leofwine to journey to Headington in the dark days of December. His temper, already frayed, snapped at the thought of being compelled to travel through the frozen landscape.

Winter was his time at home, to spend with his wife and his children. He should not be playing court to his fractious king, even if he served only as the king saw fit and acknowledged that openly.

Æthelflæd laughed at his foul temper and drove him from his house with promises of things to come when he returned while Wulfstan point blank refused to attend.

His injury from the battle four years earlier had healed well, but in the chill of winter, it twinged and made him as grumpy as Leofwine on his worst day. Æthelflæd didn't appreciate his caustic humour, but she agreed with him with a roll of her eyes and a conspiratorial look above the whitening hair of their friend when he told Leofwine he was staying where he was.

Stomping from his hall as his second son would do when thwarted by his older brother he called his Hammer to him and grouchily set out, his thick winter cloak pulled tightly around his neck. He would go. He would serve his king, but he didn't have to be bloody happy about it.

Neither did his temper improve at the king's court when he discovered that Ealdorman Ælfhelm hadn't even bothered to attend; he'd sent a messenger to say that concerns with the border kept him away from the witan. The king received the news with a rage that Leofwine shared. Ælfhelm had already publicly quarrelled with the king and his no-show, as inconvenient as it was to travel from the far north with snow lying on the ground, could only be interpreted in one way: direct defiance of their very public agreement.

Wulfstan of York had made the journey, but then, as he made public knowledge, he'd arrived some time ago to attend to his other diocese in Worcester. He'd gone on at some length about the depth of snow even in November when he'd travelled south, and the king appeared to be mollified, although Leofwine remained unconvinced.

Once again, Leofwine was fearful that the king was considering, as he'd done once before, having a clear-out of men he thought no longer useful to him. This was a perfect excuse to get rid of another one.

Ealdorman Ælfric, stumbling around the palace, was not doing the reputation of the ealdormen much good either, and neither was the knowledge that once again Swein of Denmark was overwintering on the Isle of Wight. He was a potent menace, waiting to show his head when the weather improved.

Leofwine was overly aware of the young faces presented to the king. Eadric with all his pomposity was in attendance if anything grown a little higher in the king's estimations. The king now spoke to him and asked for his opinions during discussions, much to the annoyance of the king's oldest son who sat mostly silent throughout the proceedings, his brothers also conspicuous by their absence.

Leofwine wondered if they'd been warned off or had simply decided that if their father did not heed their advice, they wouldn't offer it.

Little was decided throughout the short, always tense, gathering. Leofwine was little pacified to find he was asked to attest a charter for only the second time in second place; it was no significant advancement when there were only two ealdormen in attendance. If he looked at it in the right light, he was still the least favoured of them all, as he always had been.

On his journey home across the frozen landscape, he pushed his horse hard, desperate to be back and shake the dread that was welling within him. For all the king's preparations and his show of faith in Ulfcytel, Leofwine feared that the following year would test them all and he didn't relish the thought.

23
AD1005

THE WINTRY WEATHER PERSISTED LONG INTO THE EARLY SUMMER MONTHS, stunting the winter crops and forcing the farmers to question when they would plant the summer crops.

The Easter influx of new animals shivered and perished in the constant chilly conditions. Those who survived to be led out into the early summer warmth suffered when an unexpected and late snowstorm covered the land, forcing the farmers and the shepherds to return those animals who lived to the comfort of their winter homes.

And then, when the snow finally cleared and the excess water was blown away by fierce storms, a great drought swept the land, damaging those seeds that had been sown and causing entire crops to fail.

The people groaned under the harshness of the weather, and when Swein of Denmark and his men began to attack again, many fled before him deciding that the little they had was not worth saving. The only highlight of the horrendous year was when Swein himself withdrew from the English shores.

Sadly, as Swein left England's shores, he thought of Leofwine, and a messenger arrived on the pretext of sending Horic news of some kinsmen who'd either perished or thrived, Leofwine did not recall the cover message the man carried. He was more concerned with his gifting of a small, bloodied knife, intentionally never cleaned and with the message that it was a reminder from Swein of Denmark for him.

Horic had delivered the message and knife personally to Leofwine, his reluctance clear to see. With each passing year, Leofwine quietly voiced the hope to Horic that Swein might have forgotten about him, once and for all. It was evident that was never going to happen.

With so little food for the men because of the drought, and realising that all the gold and silver in the land couldn't buy that which didn't exist, king Swein returned to his homeland threatening to return when England's fortunes improved.

The king stewed throughout the prolonged summer heat, quick to anger and even quicker to blame anyone who dared put a foot wrong. He called on his churchmen to explain why God punished his people as they did. While they tried their hardest to offer words of support, Æthelred began to internalise what was happening to his land and began to see it as some sort of punishment for actions taken by those around him.

Leofwine sought advice from Wulfstan as to how he should deal with the difficult man his king had become, but Wulfstan could only offer words of caution. He remembered the changes that had brought Leofwine his own position. On that occasion, the king had removed all those he blamed for bedevilling his youthful exploits following the defeat at the Battle of Maldon, the battle that had left Leofwine's own father dead. Wulfstan offered no comfort to his weary ealdorman.

Little was accomplished through the king's governance. He didn't call his witan together; he didn't promulgate any new laws. All he managed to do was produce another squalling child, a daughter, to add to the list of those who needed a good marriage.

Rumours and counter-rumours spread about the king's intentions. Ealdorman Ælfhelm seemed to be embattled in the north, and his sons were much maligned. Their entire party became ostracised and Æthelmaer from the Western lands, their long-time confidant, was forced to create distance from them.

Æthelmær wrote to Leofwine to express his disquiet with events, and all Leofwine could do was agree with him and assure him that he acted in his own best interests. He'd not yet fully gained the king's trust as it was. If Æthelmaer wished to replace his father in name as well as deed, he needed to ensure the king continued to think highly of him. After all, the Western Provinces was still lacking an ealdorman ever since Pallig's death.

Ealdorman Ælfhelm appeared to have sealed his fate with his king and sadly his sons were implicated along with him in the alleged treason. Leofwine had always thought highly of Wulfheah and Ufegat; they'd formed a close group at the witan that Leofwine had on occasion been a little jealous off, even though he knew they'd only been favoured because of Lady Elfrida's influence.

Leofwine would have appreciated knowing that other men within the witan had his back as the sons did for their father and their uncle, Wulfric Spot. Now, if the gossips were to be believed, it appeared that even their careful networks of supporters would not keep them from their king's wrath.

And with the news that the aged Archbishop of Canterbury, Ælfric, had died, Leofwine felt the year ended on as dismal note as it had started. He didn't long for the coming year, knowing that it was going to be full of renewed attacks from Swein of Demark, and with his king on the warpath as well, even amongst his closest supporters, it promised to be anything but peaceful.

24
AD1006

THE WINTER WAS LONG, COLD AND HARD AND THE SUMMER LATE IN ARRIVING once more. Even in the affluent home he kept they were reduced to eating what little could be found, slaughtering the skinny animals they could no longer feed and eating the stringy creatures.

Leofwine laboured under no illusion in his home near Deerhurst about what the new year would bring. There were stories and counter-reports circling and somehow, even though he tried not to listen, they all came to his ears. His primary cause of concern was for Ælfhelm, the northern ealdorman.

Ælfhelm had made no effort the year before to reconcile with the king, and his sons were more often than not the subject of virulent speculations. Keen warriors, the both of them, they'd turned reckless with the king's lack of intent.

Leofwine sought solace in the arms of his wife, discovering in her warm kisses and pliant body, the chance of finding oblivion from his worries. But it was never quite enough. He still woke from his hard-won slumbers to the weight of dread.

With the coming Easter, he knew he'd need to force himself to action and make himself available to his king but dragged his feet, dreading the arrival of the king's messenger more than he ever had before. Then the decision to act was taken from him, and he cursed his slovenliness.

On a blustery March morning, the sound of horses at his gate alerted him to visitors. The men's calls were reasonably civil to each other, and he assumed it was a friend. The man who walked through his doorway, bringing with him a blast of chilly air, was neither his friend nor yet his enemy.

Eadric carried weight and muscles on his previously slimmer frame, and his every step implied threat. His broad smile of welcome saved the expansive entrance he made from being a violent act as he flung open the wooden door and strode into Leofwine's home.

"Well met, Eadric," Leofwine spoke, standing from his chair near the fire pit where he'd been playing a game of boards with Northman.

"Well met, my lord Leofwine. You've an excellent home here."

Leofwine accepted the compliment, although unease thrummed through his body.

Eadric was busy surveying the interior of the property and the number of men who lay sitting or sprawled, in an unruly formation around the fire pit.

"The famine hasn't been too severe here?"

Leofwine heard his benign words but understood behind them a criticism.

"Yes Eadric, it's been severe, but with Æthelflæd's careful management of food and animals we hope to make it through to the better weather."

Eadric was more intent on inspecting his home than listening to his answer, and Leofwine's voice trailed off uneasily. Why had he come here? He'd entered the house alone, but from outside the noises of many men on horseback could be heard. Had the king sent him or had he come alone to enforce his will on the man who stood in the way of his ambitions?

Beside him, Æthelflæd appeared and handed an elaborate carved wooden welcome drinking horn to Eadric. He grasped it within his large hands as Leofwine introduced his wife. Eadric made no pretence of his appraisal of Æthelflæd, and she faltered slightly in her routine of welcoming guests.

"And your children, they're here somewhere?"

Leofwine took a moment to steady himself: he shouldn't let the man disconcert him. After all, he was the older, more experienced man, more able in his role than this young upstart who was still to make his way at the witan. That Eadric was working on gaining the king's ear, and heart, should not distract from his hard-won self-belief.

"Northman, please come and introduce yourself to Eadric, and you Leofric, you can come too."

Northman had initially slunk away from the game board when his father had stood, but he now strode forward confidently, a broad smile on his young face. At ten years old he was a tall boy for his age, with unruly long auburn hair and intelligent eyes.

Leofric at eight was younger and if possible, more confident than his brother. He had an easy demeanour with everyone and would sit and chat to any who would engage with him, from the oldest crone to the tiniest baby. Godwine was too young to be introduced to anyone. A robust toddler, he was playing with his nurse oblivious to the atmosphere in his home.

Leofwine was proud of both older boys and watched with a wry smile of amusement as Northman offered this imposing stranger an arm clasp of friendship. His voice was high and youthful, but he carried himself well. Eadric smiled at the lads, and much to Leofric's disgust ruffled his hair.

"And daughters? Do you have daughters?"

"I do, just the one so far, but as you can probably see, there may be another on the way."

Æthelflæd flushed at his words, and Leofwine grinned at her, enjoying her obvious embarrassment.

"I hope to have a large family myself – soon."

"Family is something to treasure. Do you have a bride in mind already? I was probably about your age when I first wed."

"I do, my lord, and I just need to convince the king of my desires," he said, watching Leofwine's face intently.

Leofwine kept the smile of pleasure on his face that talking about his family always inspired, but he felt his resolve slip a little at the news. At last Eadric was coming to the point, and it was clear that he thought it would upset Leofwine.

"Well, the king chose my bride for me."

"So I've heard. Only I think, perhaps, I may be a little more fortuitous in my choice of a bride."

Leofwine didn't need to look to Æthelflæd or his oldest son to know that they both bristled at the disdain in the words. He chose to bide his time, though; he was intrigued by where Eadric was going with his line of conversation.

"One of the king's daughters will, I hope, become my bride." The smug grin on Eadric's face was almost unbearable to look upon, and yet Leofwine managed to speak clearly.

"They're beautiful girls. I've seen them on more than one occasion at the witan."

"The one I propose to take is a beauty, but she could look like the back end of an ox for all I care. All that matters to me is that she's the king's daughter and that he'll allow me to marry her."

Eadric drawled his words as he casually sat in Leofwine's wooden chair adjacent to the fire pit. He'd not removed his cloak, and Leofwine admired that he could stand the sudden heat while being perplexed by the intent behind the words.

"The king had no daughters at the time of my marriage to be marrying them off, and certainly I'd not have wanted to wait until they were old enough to get married. As you know, Æthelflæd is the sole survivor of the old Hwiccan dynasty."

"A dynasty as dead as this land," Eadric droned.

"Eadric, I'm unsure of the meaning behind your words. My land isn't dead, and clearly, my lady is alive and well, and her children are the heirs of her body and this land."

"But they're not related to our king."

"And neither are you," Leofwine remarked, the words rushing forth before he could stop them.

"I intend to be soon, and my sons will have a claim to the throne. Yours never will."

"I've never expressed a desire to be a king, or to have my children be kings."

"Then you don't seek enough for yourself and your children. Like this land, you are stagnant and will soon die back."

Leofwine's anger was starting to coalesce at the sheer audacity of the man sat before him. What right did Eadric have to walk into his home and start belittling his accomplishments and those of his family?

"Was there a reason for your visit today, Eadric?"

Eadric laughed loudly at the strained words, "Yes and no, my lord. Firstly, I came to see what of yours I should be coveting; and second, the king asked me to visit you and impress you with his need to see you at the witan when it's convened in April. I'd expected more of a welcome from you, but I see I may have been misinformed about your great hospitality."

Leofwine weighed the words again. Eadric was clearly saying something without speaking it aloud, and as Leofwine sifted the words, he finally realised what was being implied.

"We suffer with our people, as the king does. We don't take what's not ours or demand that we're fed by the farmers at their expense. We all work for our food and our health. I'd suggest it's a lesson you might benefit from. You're welcome to join us for a meal, but the portions will be slight. The weather is yet too cold to know when we'll have our early harvest."

Eadric stood abruptly. "There's no need, but my thanks for your offer. I've not travelled far today, and I'd not want to 'take from your people' as you say. Good day to you, my lord, and I look forward to seeing you and your sons and wife at the wedding – whenever it may be."

With a curt nod to Æthelflæd, Eadric swept from the room, leaving in his wake confusion and anger in equal measure. Leofwine strolled to the doorway Eadric purposely left open behind him, allowing the chilly wind to penetrate deep within the room, and watched Eadric mount his huge black horse and turn back towards the open road.

Eadric travelled with only four other warriors and a handful of squires, his arrogance in his superiority showing even in his small war band. Leofwine considered what would happen if they were ever attacked for there were too few to mount a meaningful counter-attack, and the thought did not disappoint him.

At the gate, Eadric stopped his horse and wheeled it around to face Leofwine. He raised his hand in a gesture of farewell and kicked his horse to a canter. The beast lurched forwards, and the echo of Eadric's loud laughter could be heard ringing through the icy air.

Leofwine called his men to shut the gate and stomped back inside to the warmth of the fire, left partially smoking in the breeze from the open doorway. He closed the door with care and instantly, Æthelflæd was at his side.

"What was all that about?"

"I think that was a message from the king that I need to be a little more compliant with his wishes. That man Eadric, he's dangerous."

"Why did he ask about the boys, and about Ealdgyth?"

"He was just making a very pointed comment that he thinks he's to marry into royalty, nothing more. Don't worry."

"I'll not worry when you don't worry. Until then, I suggest you remember that we're a partnership. You might be the ealdorman, don't interrupt me."

He'd opened his mouth to speak but shut it again.

"But I'm your wife and your representative in Mercia when you're serving the king. If I could be the ealdorwoman, then I would be." She grabbed his arm as she spoke, gripping it tightly. "I may not wield a sword, but I have my powers and skills. Do you wish you'd married into the king's family?"

Her voice shook slightly as she spoke and while he meant to respond angrily, he instead, closed the gap between them and lowered his head so that he could kiss her angry red lips. The kiss was brief but passionate.

"No, I don't wish I'd married into the king's family. I married you, and I'm happy and content."

"Only happy and content," she said, a slight smile on her concerned face.

"You could maybe make me more than happy and content," he whispered against her lips, and she laughed a sweet girlish chuckle.

"I could, yes, I suppose. But I will not. I carry your child within me already, and I think that might be all the proof you're going to get today of my love for you. We've more important things to do."

He groaned at the reminder that he had responsibilities and a household to run, but he stole another kiss before Northman could announce loudly that really it was disgusting when old people kissed. Leofwine cuffed the boy around the head good-naturedly and sent him outside to train with the men on the hard packed surface that now surrounded his home. The mud ruts were frozen into place and precarious if you didn't look where you were going.

Northman ran happily to the task, and Leofwine pensively watched him go. Eadric's interest in the boys, unwelcome as it was, opened up a possibility regarding one of their futures that he'd not considered before.

It was just a pity that he was starting to detest the man and could not imagine sending one of his sons into his domain, even if he was to rise in the king's confidences, as Eadric intimated he would.

25
AD1006

Leofwine attended the king at his witan, as demanded. He found him short-tempered and quick to anger from the moment he entered the royal house at Enham.

The king airily gave the churchmen permission to hold their own meeting and to discuss who would replace the dead archbishop Ælfric of Canterbury. As soon as the men of God had retired to their counsel, the king began a long monologue on the condition of his kingdom and the state of his ealdormen.

The only kind words he had to speak regarded Archbishop Ælfric who'd bequeathed the king his best ship and sailing equipment, complete with sixty helmets and sixty coats of mail. Leofwine was astounded at the generosity of the archbishop before he remembered that on his own death, he'd also have a ship and its quota to pass on to someone. If he didn't have children, the king would be the most obvious choice.

"My lords and ladies," the king began, his tone caustic, his sarcasm evident. "It's come to my attention that there are those amongst you who work against me; those who don't like my policies, and instead of coming to me with their disillusionment, work to undermine my reputation. I've decided that it's time to act. As I was punished last year by God with the death of my beloved son Ecgberht, I've decided that in this case, it's the sons who will be punished for their fathers' sins."

Leofwine winced at the anger in the king's voice. It was barely contained, and although Leofwine could appreciate the king's grief at the death of the young man and how it might have made him lash out at those who displeased him, he greatly feared what he was going to say next.

"Ealdorman Ælfhelm of Northumbria is to be deprived of all his lands that belong to me, and his sons will, on my wishes, be blinded."

There were audible gasps of shock from those at the witan, and Leofwine found himself on his feet before he could stop himself. He needed to protest. He knew what it was like to live without sight. He couldn't let others suffer the same fate.

"Please sit, Ealdorman Leofwine. I don't wish to hear your sniffling attempt at diffusing the situation, and any appeals to my better nature will fail. So please sit!" The king's voice was low and even, deadly in its delivery.

Leofwine sank into his chair, looking around in disgust at those who cheered the king's words. He also hastily sought out Ealdorman Ælfhelm on the row of fellow ealdorman and wasn't surprised to discover he was not in attendance.

"As you will all no doubt realise, none of the men I speak of is here to have judgment passed on them. Instead, I'll reward whosoever can carry out my wishes. All I ask is that you act in my name, and carry out only my wishes, nothing further. Ealdorman Ælfhelm should be brought to me, to stand trial for his treason, and his sons should be brought here as well. I wish to see the effects of their punishment on them."

A few of the young men who were royal officials were talking excitedly amongst themselves, but it was Eadric who stood abruptly at the king's words and strode from the hall in a jaunty style. The king smiled tightly as he watched his departing figure.

"Ah, I see there are some who realise that my actions are not to be debated. I only wish there were more of you who would act as Eadric does."

There was a muffled throb of conversation as the impact of his words was felt, and Leofwine noted a few other men rush from the witan. As his eyes swept across the now intermittently empty seats, his eyes came to rest on Athelstan, sitting tall and erect, his face a perfect mask hiding all his emotions.

Belatedly Leofwine noticed the space next to him, where in the past Ecgberht would have sat. He wondered why Edmund, the next oldest brother, did not sit there, and then he turned away in shock. Of course, the king must have decreed that his place not be taken.

All the king's sons sat quietly, eyes tightly forwards and focused on their father. They must have been instructed on how they should act.

"And Wulfric Spot," the king's voice was low, "do not think for a moment that your association with Ælfhelm has gone unnoticed. You're to be deprived of all your lands, and you'll never step foot inside this witan again, now be gone."

Wulfric Spot, from his seat behind Leofwine, looked up in shock at his king and Leofwine felt instant pity for him. He'd been the only one brave enough to face his king, and while he might be escaping with his life for his troubles, he would have no means to support himself.

"My lord ..." he began, stuttering in shock as he slowly stood to face his king, his face grave with fear and worry.

"Don't gainsay me, Wulfric. Be gone before I change my mind and blind you too, or worse – and don't think of joining Swein of Denmark and his men either. If I hear that you've betrayed me not once but twice, I'll have you killed wherever you are – and don't think I won't."

Æthelred held the gaze of Wulfric for a long, slow heartbeat and then Wulfric bowed and clattered noisily from the palace hall, his feet sounding loudly in the sudden silence of the room.

It was not often that the king made such a public display of his displeasure and his anger. It was a shocking reminder that he was their king, and although he ruled with the support of his witan, he could displace and remove his men as he saw fit.

Beside him, Wulfstan gripped tightly on Leofwine's thigh, willing him to let the king have his moment without interfering. Leofwine couldn't meet his eyes, shame flooding him that he would sit idly by while the king ruined the lives of his faithful men, all on a whim that he had somehow been betrayed.

Internally Leofwine cursed the man. Why hadn't he made more effort to keep Ælfhelm by his side? Why had he not pursued the idea of allowing the men in the northern lands some leeway in the taxes they must pay?

With the commotion over and some peace restored to the witan, the king spent long moments looking over those who now served him. Leofwine and Ælfric were his solitary ealdormen, although Ulfcytel also sat with them, the commander of the army in the eastern lands, bound through marriage to his king and yet not quite an ealdorman.

Behind them sat the king's remaining older sons, the four of them sitting forward, attentive to their father, the space between Athelstan and Edmund speaking of the king's loss.

And yet further on sat those of the royal officials who'd not been touched by this turmoil, and there were few of them and few that Leofwine could name – Æthelmaer, Æthelwold, Ælfgar and Godwine, not much more than names to Leofwine. He knew of them from their time together as royal officials but the last ten years seemed to stretch empty between them, almost as if he'd become an ealdorman and had left them behind.

Leofwine now looked at them with intrigue, wondering what the years had done to them as men. Were they still who they once had been or had time wrought changes on them that couldn't be seen on the surface?

Æthelmaer was a good-looking man and sat as smartly as the æthelings before him. He was beautifully dressed in a tunic with elegant embroidery around the cuffs and neck and yet there was something about him that disturbed Leofwine. Did he look a little too pleased with himself?

Æthelwold was a much older man, a remnant of the time when Leofwine had sat amongst the royal officials before his king had raised him to his ealdordom and seen fit to send him across the seas to be blinded.

Ælfgar was another relic, but he was closer to Leofwine in age. He looked fit and healthy and was alleged to be keen with his sword and his war axe. He enjoyed a good battle although he'd not often faced the Raiders in any huge numbers.

And Godwine was another of Leofwine's generation. He was a good man, not often speaking up against the king, but as reliable as they came. If the king had ordered him to kill a convent full of nuns, he would have done it without compunction. His unquestioning nature left Leofwine disturbed on occasion and clearly the king as well, for he'd never risen from his position to anything more significant.

There was a vast host of faces that Leofwine little knew, and he cursed himself for not spending more time cultivating alliances. If the king called him to answer for any deeds seen as untimely, he was aware that none would stand up for him.

Not even Athelstan who he'd once hoped saw him as more than his father's servant. Leofwine vowed that if at the end of the year he still had the king's goodwill, he would spend his winter months making friends with any who would have him.

As the king's voice penetrated his thoughts, he turned back to stare at the man who'd suddenly become an unknown quantity to him.

"And now my lords and ladies, we must turn our minds to more pleasant tasks. As you all know, Swein of Denmark and his men left our shores last year when the famine was at its worst. This year, they'll be back. Already I've heard from Swein of his intention to return unless we pay him forty thousand pounds to stay away."

There was, understandably, an outcry at those words, and Æthelred held his hand up to restore quiet.

"I entirely agree. The thieving bastards have taken enough of what's ours and have done little to earn it. I'm therefore calling out the fyrds of the Mercian lands and the heartlands of the royal family, Wessex."

"As before, we'll arrange for small troops to be spread across the land and they'll watch and wait for the northmen. As soon as they're upon us, the household troops will inform the rest of the fyrd, and they'll march to defeat them. We'll make a stand. We'll drive them from our shores as God did last year, with his less than bountiful harvest."

Grins and looks of apprehension touched the faces of the king's councillors, and then a slow clap of support started and worked its way around the less than crowded room.

King Æthelred smiled as he watched to see who supported him and who did not. Belatedly Leofwine began to clap and nodded to show Oscetel, Wulfstan and Horic that they must do the same.

Æthelred looked on with his eyebrow raised quizzically and a contemptuous smile upon his lips. Leofwine nodded towards his king, but he'd turned away, his interest on those men who he could yet raise to positions of greater prominence. His eyes seemed to fasten on one particular person, and Leofwine followed his line of sight. A boy no older than seventeen years stood on his feet, a look of delight on his face as his king looked at him.

He was clearly a warrior, his clothing a little shoddy, but his sword was at his waist, gleaming brightly, and a jewel nestled within its scabbard, caught and reflected the flames of the candles, hinting at his prowess in battle.

Beside him, Horic whispered, "Uhtred, from the far north. He is –

and even I must say it – a fine warrior and happy to spend his life killing those from across the border. I think the king may have designs on him for Northumbria."

"What? He intends to replace Ealdorman Ælfhelm so soon?"

"Rumour has it, my lord; and he'll make a fine replacement. He's regrettably a little stupid. He does as he's told without thought and never seems to regret anything. If the king told him to jump off a cliff, I think he probably would."

Leofwine turned to glare at Horic, who was chuckling quietly to himself,

"The king seems to have devised a new ploy. If all the men he surrounds himself with can't think for themselves, then they can only ever follow the king's orders. Perhaps, my lord, I could suggest a lesson in how to never think again."

Leofwine's glower relaxed into a half smile.

"I think you may have the best of me, Horic. Thinking has always been the cause of my trouble. Clearly, something you don't suffer with!"

Horic roared with laughter at the words, not caring that the king fixed him with a penetrating stare.

"You're to do my thinking for me, as once Olaf of Norway did, and to be honest these days, it's mostly my wife."

Wiping tears from his eyes, Horic turned to Oscetel who looked as stern-faced as the king, "What do you think?"

Oscetel watched the king as he spoke.

"I think you might have the right of it, about your wife at least," Oscetel spoke slowly and gravely, his words contrary to how he uttered them and even Leofwine felt a grin spread across his tight face.

"But, with a herd of your look-alikes running around your farm, I'm not surprised. For all your brawn and bravery, without a little bit of thought and common sense you, my good man, would starve even as your fields grow dense and ripen and your animals grow full and fat."

Horic's laughter dried up abruptly.

"Well, when you put it like that you might be right," Horic muttered darkly, fixing Oscetel with a less than congenial stare before turning back to Leofwine.

"My lord, I agree, someone must do the thinking, but I can assure you it's not always our king." His voice had fallen to a whisper. "Don't let the king rule us too much. Perhaps a little more contrition in your actions and all will be well."

Beside them, Wulfstan hadn't spoken, his eyes a little glazed. Leofwine nudged him, and a semi-snore erupted from his mouth that had Horic chuckling again,

"Wulfstan, I'm sorry if all this discussion bores you," Leofwine spoke quietly, as his friend turned to look at him blankly.

"Why have I missed something?"

"Only most of it," Leofwine muttered quietly, trying to keep the worry from his voice and failing entirely.

Wulfstan looked stricken and then his face darkened,

"I'm afraid I grow a little too weary of court politics in my old age. The king is no fool, and yet his decisions are often poor. He gives too little power to his sons and too much to men who are foolish but who amuse him. I've been watching the same mistakes since he was a small boy."

Wulfstan spoke so quietly that Leofwine strained to hear him. "I'm part of a group of councillors who are now all long-dead, and sometimes I wish I were too. He's a wise and just king. Yet his words today fill me with sadness, and they should you as well. Horic has the right of it: follow a little blindly, but keep your wits about you. And now, if you don't mind, I'll return to my ruminations."

Leofwine looked at Wulfstan with sadness. Just as with Hunter, the spectre of death was creeping slowly over his oldest friend, and he was too stubborn to see it. He should have let him stay at home, but he'd wanted his closest supporters with him. With Horic, Wulfstan and Oscetel behind him, he always felt empowered. Perhaps from now on, he would let Wulfstan do a little less and give a bit more to his oldest son. He didn't want to make the same mistakes that his king was making.

His king, happy with the decisions he'd made, rose to leave the witan but turned back at the last moment and stood for a moment. "We are all of us warriors in our own ways. Let's show these northmen what it means to be proud of our land and ready to die for it."

A cheer greeted Æthelred's words as he walked out, and a small smile played on his lips. For all that, Leofwine thought he looked unhappy, weighed down by fears and worries that never seemed to leave him. Perhaps being the king of a country always under the threat of attack was more a trial than Leofwine had thought.

26
AD1006

Swein of Denmark arrived back in England to the news of attacks in the north from the Scots and a king who now had fewer ealdormen than at any point in his reign. While Swein would, through his spies, know that the king had called out the fyrd of Mercia and Wessex, he would also know that the kingdom was riven by strife and division as the repercussions of the king's decisions at the witan were still being felt up and down the country.

Leofwine had returned to Deerhurst after the witan, collected his wife and children, and leaving Horic once again to see to the safety of his ancestral home had departed for the Mercian lands. Regardless of his king's thoughts on the matter, he knew that he would defend the kingdom well.

Almost as soon as he arrived in Lichfield, leaving an ill and grumpy Wulfstan to Horic's tender ministrations, news from the north came in the form of a messenger. He jumped from his horse where Leofwine stood surveying a training session in which Northman was playing a part; he was a good strong young boy, smart with his choice of attack and defence, and Leofwine enjoyed watching him outfox the older boys in the war band who served as squires for his men.

"My lord Leofwine," the messenger spoke, ducking his head. He was travel-stained, and his horse looked weary. Signalling to Leofric, who stood rapt with attention watching the fighting with his father, that he should take the horse away for some food and water, he turned his full attention to the man.

"I'm Aldric, my lord, Uhtred, sent me to inform the king and his people of an attack on the land near Durham."

Leofwine hid his shock well, "And who attacks?"

"The Scots, my lord. About six thousand of them, or so Uhtred reckons."

Leofwine relaxed a little. The Scots – that was at least a familiar menace.

"And how does Uhtred fare?"

The messenger cracked a smile across his mud-splattered face. "Well, my lord, he has an eye for how to exploit every weakness and, of course, he knows most of those who've risen against the king, and that helps too."

Belatedly, Leofwine ushered Aldric inside his house for refreshment and noted that the man limped.

"And you, did you assist in the attacks?"

"Regrettably not, I wounded my leg some time ago, in a border skirmish. Since then, I've served Uhtred as one of his messengers. It's easier to ride than to walk."

"I don't doubt that at all. Well, come, take sustenance and tell me what your instructions are from here. Are you to seek the king, or would you prefer one of my men to do that?"

"If you could, my lord, then I can return to Uhtred. I'd not want to miss out on all the action."

Leofwine grinned at the bloodthirsty lust of the man.

"When I left, Uhtred was offering the women of Durham a fine fat cow in exchange for one of the Scots' heads, cleaned and mounted on a stake for all to see. I'd not want to return when the heads are all rotted away."

A grimace of disgust swept briefly across Leofwine's face, and Aldric laughed.

"I didn't think you'd have a soft heart, my lord, for the bloody Scots."

"I don't, but still, when a man is dead, he should be buried and not displayed as if he were a toy. It's the way of our religion."

"They'll be buried eventually, my lord, don't fret so. When the heads have all rotted, and the birds have finished pecking out the eyes, they'll be buried in a pit. Mind, I don't think they'll be reunited with their bodies," Aldric added as the thought struck him.

Aldric spoke with a slight accent, easy enough for Leofwine to understand, and as he drank from a large cup of mead and grabbed at a meal Æthelflæd had produced from somewhere, spittle and food flew from his mouth as he laughed at the tender heart of the ealdorman of Mercia.

Leofwine tried to enjoy the grim joy of killing the enemy, but couldn't stop himself from thinking how he would feel if it was his sons or his father whose head was spitted and laid out for all to see.

Calling to Leofric again, he asked his young son to inform the men that a messenger was needed.

"Do you have word of where the king may be keeping his court?" he asked Aldric.

Aldric glanced at him for long enough to shake his head as he chewed and swallowed as fast as physically possible.

"Did Uhtred not provision you before you left?"

Aldric looked contrite for a moment, "He did, my lord, but I confess, on my travels, I came across a family in need and rather than take succour from them, I gave them my own."

Leofwine laughed at the man's rueful tone, "Who are you, to be quibbling about my soft heart?"

Aldric laughed long and hard at his words, "My lord, I think you've the right of me after all. I don't suppose you have any to spare for me to take back the way I came, do you?"

Æthelflæd, eavesdropping from her spot by the open fire, had already signalled for one of her maids to put together some rations for the messenger, and so Leofwine merely nodded in compliance.

"Do you have any other news, other than the victory?"

"Well, yes, my lord. I can tell you everything that has happened in Northumbria in the last few months if you care to listen."

"Yes, go ahead. I've heard little since the last witan. How does the disgraced Ealdorman Ælfhelm fare?"

"My lord, you're behind with your news. I'm afraid that Ælfhelm is dead and, rumour has it, murdered at the request of the king."

Outrage consumed Leofwine,

"And from who have you heard this?"

"It's common knowledge throughout the lands above the Humber. That's why Uhtred has taken command of the fyrd. Ælfhelm is dead at the hands, or so rumour has it, of a certain Eadric who is said to be high in the king's estimations, and his sons are twice blinded – useless to all if you'll beg my pardon for saying so."

Leofwine closed his one good eye in sympathy. To be blinded entirely was a torment he couldn't imagine. He suffered enough with his one eye and his dog. To have no comfort of even the smallest amount of sight was terrifying.

"Aye, My Lord," Aldric spoke quietly into the silence that had fallen at his announcement. "I'd not wish it on anyone. There's outrage in the northern lands. Æthelred is lucky that Uhtred is so committed to his land and his people and prepared to step into the breach to save them. His thoughts are not, I'm afraid to admit, of helping the king when he faces the Scots."

Leofwine acknowledged the words with a slow nod of his head. The king had allowed things to progress too far, and if Eadric had been the man responsible for the actual murder of Ealdorman Ælfhelm and the blinding of his sons, he feared Æthelred had found too willing an accomplice to his desperate actions.

Aldric took his leave a short time later, frantic to get back to Durham. He was laden with food for his journey and for any in need he found as he travelled. Leofwine knew the story he told was a familiar one. The land had yet to fully recover from last year's famine, and he knew the people would only mend when the land did. It was going to take the time that many didn't have.

Æthelflæd was marshalling their supplies as best she could, aware that they must help where they could. The church was acting similarly. Any who had excess were asked to donate to someone with less than them. Those who had nothing gratefully received anything from a chicken to a cow to a smattering of barley.

Leofwine had been pleased by the support each and everyone had given to others, but still, he knew there were areas of deprivation where no one had anything. He'd tried to discover all such villages but was unsure if he'd been successful. His land was a maze of tiny farms and hidden villages over every hill and under every hill and, frustratingly, the records kept by the church were not complete. Not everyone could be accounted for in a population that swelled and retracted with the weather and the harvest.

Oscetel meandered through the hall, looking for his lord. On seeing him, he sat and watched him intently. Leofwine, lost in thought didn't notice him until he spoke a greeting.

"What news, my lord?"

Leofwine focused on him and grimaced.

"The Scots raid the Northumbrian lands; the king allegedly killed Ealdorman Ælfhelm, and his sons are blinded. I wonder where his daughter is?" His voice trailed off as he spoke.

Oscetel waited for a beat and then opened his mouth to speak, but Leofwine continued.

"Apologies. Yes, Uhtred won the battle for the king or rather, as the messenger says, for himself and his people. Even now the good wives of Durham are beheading the Scots, combing their hair and washing their faces and leaving the heads on spikes for all to see. He rewards the women with a fat cow."

Oscetel laughed at the news. "He's a true Northumbrian man, never afraid to do to the Scots what they would do to us."

Leofwine cocked an eyebrow at Oscetel.

"Come, my lord, even you must see the truth in that. Uhtred and his family have held their land for centuries, longer than almost any other family. They're brought up on a diet of beheading the Scots before they've broken their fast. There'll never be peace with them, and the stupid fools will never stop raiding even though they win so rarely. I admire their continual optimism, as misplaced as it is."

Shaking his unpleasant thoughts aside, Leofwine thought about Oscetel's words. He was a true Mercian and had ties to this land that stretched further back than Leofwine's own. The Northumbrians had long been their neighbours, and so, he must assume, knew their temperament better than most.

"We would do well to learn from the Northumbrians. If the Raiders are here for the long haul, and I fear they are, we must raise our children on a diet of blood and war. We must make them fear nothing and fight for what they believe in. As your sons do, the boys must train with the men, for if all the men fail, it will be the boys and the women who hold Swein of Denmark and his men at bay. I almost pity them should they meet Horic's wife."

Oscetel laughed as he spoke, pushed up from his place on the bench and walked outside, taking the smell of sweat and iron with him. Leofwine appreciated his attempt to lighten the mood, but it hadn't worked.

Beside him, Æthelflæd snaked her arm around his neck and then waddled to the chair that Oscetel had just vacated. She was hugely pregnant, and he knew she was struggling to stay as mobile as she liked. He stood and kissed her lightly on the head before reseating himself.

"My lord, you are again, beset with worries."

He smiled wryly, "I am, my lady. Are we to be formal throughout the conversation?"

She smiled at him warmly, and slapped at his hand, reaching out to take hold of her own.

"I thought a bit of normality, and due respect might make you feel as though the world wasn't crumbling beneath your feet."

"I appreciate the sentiment, but facts must be faced."

"Yes, but not every moment of every day."

"No, I suppose not. Did you want something?"

"Only to see you smile and your shoulders drop from their hunched position. Otherwise, I'll spend my night relaxing you, and with this huge child of yours in my belly, I think it's time that you relaxed me."

Her words did the trick, and he laughed out loud.

"Have you thought of a name yet?"

"No, we have not." She stressed the 'we'.

"You mean I get a say? That's a first."

With mock anger, she slapped at his chest.

"If you're here when the child is born, I'll let you name it. It's not my fault if you're never where you're needed."

He sobered at that. She was right – almost.

"I was there for Leofric, and still you named him."

"Yes, well, you weren't supposed to remember that. Or you were to have been too much a gentleman to remind me. Either works for me." She glanced at him as she spoke, her beauty highlighted by the fire before them, casting her features into relief, her hair splayed behind her like an angel's halo.

"Come, turn around, and I'll rub your back for you. You look almost crippled over with pain. I suggest you grow them a little less well in future."

"Really, Leofwine," she huffed, rising to her feet and reseating herself so that her back was to him, "for a seemingly intelligent man, you do say the most stupid of things. It's you who makes them so big. It's nothing to do with me. You feed me up each time I'm with child, and then complain when little giants erupt from me."

He supposed she had a point. All four of their children were hale and hearty, and by God's will, none had succumbed to childhood illnesses. He was proud of his growing boys, Northman, Leofric and Godwine, and knew his wife was besotted with Ealdgyth – she was going to be as tyrannical as her mother when she grew to womanhood. She was already well used to getting her brothers to do as she commanded. He pitied whoever became her husband.

He let the gentle movement of rubbing his wife's back distract him and felt calmness settle on him. Leofwine felt as though for the last ten years he and his wife had faced a growing list of difficulties and still, in their own little world, they were happy and content. Whatever came his way, he knew that with her stalwart support, he would make it through.

27
AD1006

Leofwine reined his horse in so abruptly that mud clots flew through the air and landed with loud thuds on the ground before him.

In front of him, a vast host of men had assembled: the fyrd of Mercia.

So many men and not even the whole host of them, he thought. He'd asked his men to arrange several mustering points, and so he rode into Coventry expecting a multitude of men. Still, it was a shock to see so many swords, shields and axes in one place. And the men meant business. A quiet rage emanated from them, and he thought that in mere moments, they could be roused to great anger. They were a potent force.

He'd already been to Derby and seen the fyrd there, given his orders and sent his men on their various errands to protect the land, some to the borders with Strathclyde, some to stand inconspicuously on the borders with the Danelaw, and yet more to guard the burhs and the people. He wouldn't be caught unawares.

After Coventry, he would return to Lichfield and then travel towards the lands of the Welsh, where the men of Shropshire and beyond were gathering. Or so he hoped.

News had reached him that Eadric was planning on leading the men from his land, but Leofwine had heard no official word from King Æthelred, and until he did, he'd continue as intended. He didn't much relish the thought of Eadric storming in and taking the honour for provisioning the men so well, but he was trying to be pragmatic; as long as the land was safe, it little mattered who led. Or so he told himself.

Before him, the host of men fell silent, and he felt himself the focus of many eyes. For the first time in years, he felt conscious of his wounded face and held his hand firm on the reins of his horse to stop from touching it. These men were his to order, and yet he knew too few of them. He was as curious about them as they were about him, but he didn't stare, unlike the men who bowed their heads briefly to acknowledge him before returning to their open staring.

Oscetel had travelled before him and had arrived with enough time to spare that he'd managed to gather all the commanders together to enable Leofwine to speak directly to them.

While others of his men mingled with the crowd, inspecting the equipment that the fyrd members had provided or been given, Leofwine dismounted from his horse and strode towards Oscetel. He was surrounded by a large group of men, from the young to the old, all looking smart, if not lethal, in their war gear.

Leofwine held back a smirk at seeing the pompous stance of one of the older men, clearly enjoying the attention of the younger men, new to their posts, who had surrounded him and were asking for advice on matters that concerned them about any coming battle.

Oscetel rolled his eyes as Leofwine drew closer, alluding to the rotund man at the centre of attention, and Leofwine smiled in welcome to cover his laughter. The older man reminded him of Northman at his most engaging, puffed up with his own self-belief. However, he doubted that this man would be quite as quickly deflated as Northman could, once reminded of who he was and his actual accomplishments.

Oscetel strolled forward and began to introduce the men.

"My lord Leofwine, let me introduce you to Eadnoth, the king's reeve for the area."

The large man shuffled forward, a broad smile across his round face. He offered his arm in a handclasp, and Leofwine reciprocated, looking over the man's elegant tunic, wholly unsuited to any military action that may soon be coming.

"Well met, Eadnoth. You've gathered the men together well."

Eadnoth was further visibly inflated at the words of praise, but before he could speak further, Leofwine turned aside; he was more interested in the young men, and Oscetel would know it.

"And this is young Godwine and Brithwold, both commanding for the first time this year. They offer firm assurances that this will not be their first battle."

"Indeed, where else have you encountered the raiders?"

Godwine coloured a little, and Brithwold spoke first, "Well, my lord, perhaps battle is too fine a word for the skirmish we had with some Raiders who were travelling across our lands."

"Any contact with the Raiders will stand you in good stead, even if all you did was catch sight of them and drive them from Mercian land."

The men both straightened at the words.

"There was an entire ship full of the brutes, but they returned to their ship soon enough when they saw us."

"And did you see them as men or as the enemy?" Leofwine asked.

"As both, my lord; they are men, but they are our enemy and as such just as fallible as we are."

Leofwine nodded vigorously in agreement,

"And that's perhaps the best lesson you'll ever learn. The stories and rumours we hear of these men can be terrifying – and believe me, they're terrifying to encounter in full battle. But like us, injuries will fell them or kill them, and at the back of their minds must always be the knowledge that if they want to return to their families and their homes, they must decide whether fight or flight is best."

Leofwine felt the men who encircled him still at his words, and he wondered if he'd spoken incorrectly. The revelation to him that Swein of Denmark was just a man had been a liberating experience, but perhaps it was not so for everyone.

Godwine was the first to speak. "That's an important lesson, my lord, and one I'll ensure that all I meet are made aware of. We mustn't turn these men into the devil if it's not necessary."

His words were finely spoken, but his voice wavered a little and Leofwine felt a sense of foreboding. These men were young, barely tried, and yet they had the security of the country to ensure. He wondered if the men were actually capable of it. Perhaps this was the problem with calling out the fyrd. The force might well be massive but the men, not used to military action, too timid to be truly useful.

Before he became mired in thought, Oscetel called him to attention and the rest of the afternoon was spent in a noisy training exercise, not unlike that which had occurred before the Battle of Chester six years ago. He pitted his forces, one against the other and saw how the commanders handled the different situations. What he saw did not fill him with fear, but neither was he convinced that this stretch of Mercia would be protected, as it should be.

Calling to Oscetel, he spoke a few brief words, and an agreement was reached that he'd work with the commanders for a few days more before setting the men on their respective paths to protect Mercia.

His return to Lichfield and his family was a muted affair. Æthelflæd was labouring to bring his new child into the world.

As he sat and waited through the long night, wincing at her cries and grateful that he'd not had to endure every one of the previous births, news arrived that Swein of Denmark had returned.

Swein was focusing his attacks on Æthelred's Wessex homeland.

No matter his hatred for Leofwine, it appeared he was happy to torment the king with his sneaking attacks into the Wessex heartlands. Leofwine imagined that Thorkell the Tall and Jarl Erik were using the knowledge gained at Dean to infiltrate the Wessex kingdom.

Leofwine hoped the fyrd would drive the raiding King Swein back but set out with all haste as soon as he could to visit the borderlands with the men of Powys. He was curious to see whether Eadric held his place there or whether he'd rushed to the king and was even now, busy defending the Wessex lands.

Although it pained him to leave his new son and jubilant wife, the new birth spurred him to more significant efforts. His family would be protected, at all costs.

28

AD1006

MESSENGERS FROM THE KING FOUND HIM AS HE APPROACHED HIS MEETING with the king of Powys near the old dyke. The news they brought was not good, but neither was it terrible.

Swein of Denmark was busily attempting to infiltrate the old lands of the kingdom of Wessex, but for now, the fyrd were competently keeping them at bay. The king, however, was less than pleased with Leofwine.

Leofwine smiled his way through an interrogation by the messenger, who it soon transpired was a member of Eadric's rapidly growing household.

"Well met, my lord," the immaculately dressed messenger started, but then his eyes narrowed, and his next question was no question at all.

"The king demands details of your movements and a full report of any incursions by the Raiders. And I must say it's taken me many extra days to reach you, here, in Eadric's territory. I suggest you answer me quickly so that I can return to the king. He was anxious about your intentions before I left the court. I'd not be surprised that he now fears you dead and has replaced you."

"And your name is?" Leofwine countered, forcing himself to calmness at the sharp tone of the man.

"I'm Wulfric, commended man of Eadric of Mercia, not that it's any concern of yours."

"And you've travelled all this way alone?" Leofwine could barely keep the surprise from his voice. The man, now free from his horse, laughed loudly at his words.

"I don't fear the Raiders, my lord, not in the safe Mercian lands of my lord Eadric; they should fear me. Have you not heard of my prowess? I was assured details of my encounters had spread far and wide."

"Not to the ealdorman of Mercia's ears, no," Leofwine countered, an amused half smile on his face. It seemed as though Eadric was drawn to men similar in mannerism to his own. Leofwine hoped that made for dull conversations.

The man faltered at the firm denial of who he was, and behind him, Leofwine heard Oscetel chuckling quietly as he saw to his horse's needs. Wulfric glanced sharply to Oscetel's back with a look of annoyance.

"And where were you sent to look for me?" Leofwine asked, attempting to distract the man.

"Why, to your home in Lichfield of course," he stated as if it should be obvious.

"And who suggested you go there? Surely not the king, for he knows his instructions to me were to travel far and wide throughout Mercia."

"Well, no, I think my instructions came from the king through Eadric. He was perhaps ... mistaken about your current actions."

"I should think he was," Leofwine retorted, "and neither is it his place to demand to know what I'm doing. You're clearly not the king's messenger, and in light of the menace ravaging our lands, I find myself disinclined to inform you of what I'm about and what my plans are. The king knows what he ordered, and he knows that I'll follow his instructions."

Leofwine's tone was benign enough, but he felt a steely resolve.

How dare Eadric take it upon himself to have him chased around his lands like an errant child?

"And your master, he's helping in the effort against the Raiders?"

Wulfric, already uncomfortable that his half-truths had been so easily discovered, paused a moment before responding, and that was all Leofwine needed to know.

"Eadric, of course, assists the king. Even now he's in attendance upon him and helping him with the war effort." Wulfric puffed with pride as he spoke.

"So he's not in the saddle then, chasing down Swein's men? No, I think not," Leofwine continued, not allowing Wulfric time to reply.

"Eadric is dancing for the king and keeping his feet clean. If you wish to be your master's messenger, I suggest you inform him that I've been surveying the lands of Shropshire, which he claims as his own, and I find the dyke in a terrible state of disrepair and relations with the kingdoms of the Welsh to be less than cordial. Inform him, from me, that I'll see to his lack, but that I'll be advising the king when I next see him."

By the time he finished speaking, Leofwine's anger was challenging to hold in place. With a curt nod towards Wulfric, Leofwine turned away to hide the livid tinge of his face.

Oscetel had ceased his actions and was watching his lord closely, ready to respond to any command he gave. Leofwine tried hard to smile at the man. Their long years together meant that Oscetel would have instantly realised the genuine anger bubbling away inside him, but if it surprised him, he didn't show it. Instead, he signalled for his squire to lead Wulfric away.

"You're well, my lord?" Oscetel asked quietly. Leofwine could only nod his response as he worked on composing himself for the next unenviable task his king had set for him.

In the distance, he could already make out a small group of riders coming towards him, some on horseback and some running alongside. This was the king he'd come to meet, or so he hoped.

Llewelyn, king of the Welsh kingdom of Powys, was a man of a similar age to Leofwine, and he rode with a calm confidence that Leofwine instantly appreciated. Here he was, come to meet a representative of a hostile king, to discuss a mutual enemy, but he looked calm and self-assured. Instantly, Leofwine knew that he and Llewelyn would at least be able to have a meaningful meeting.

Llewelyn dismounted from his horse and walked the last short distance to where Leofwine stood to wait for him, on what was officially the king of Powys' land.

Llewelyn was a tall man, dressed as Leofwine was, in his byrnie and with his sword strapped to his back. He had a small and tidy beard and moustache, and his hair flowed to his neckline and was neatly cut, only recently, as the stark straight lines were still in evidence.

He held his hand out in welcome and Leofwine grabbed it, grateful that Llewelyn was happy just to meet with him without the need for any ceremony or pomp. They'd not met before but had communicated via messengers in the years that Leofwine had guarded the Mercian border. Both wrestling with external forces had taken it upon themselves to meddle with the often uneasy accord at the borderlands.

Some here called themselves Powysian's and some English, and the king of Powys and the ealdorman of Mercia had allowed the situation to remain as it was. There was little point in making an English man look to the Powys king if he didn't want to, and vice versa the same situation applied. There was no point stirring up trouble with the unruly border dwellers. They really were a law unto themselves.

"Ealdorman Leofwine," king Llewelyn spoke first, "it's good to finally put a face to the name."

"Indeed, it is. But before we proceed, how should I address you?"

The Welsh king spoke his language without hesitation, and Leofwine was again relieved. He knew that the Welsh had their own tongue, but Llewelyn was expert in English.

"Just Llewelyn, Leofwine – that will suffice while we're away from the court. I suppose that if we ever meet under more formal circumstances, we must revert to king and lord, but for now, my name is adequate, as I hope yours is?"

"Of course, you honour me, and you have my thanks."

"But now to business; it's not the nicest summer day, and I fear rain will be falling on us soon, and so let us discuss what we need to consider and then I, at least, can return home." He spoke quickly and concisely, and Leofwine warmed to the man even further.

"As no doubt you're aware, my king finds himself under attack from the king of Denmark. I know that you too suffer from some attacks from the lands of the Irish, and I wished to speak to you about your intentions regarding the attacks."

The king of Powys raised an eyebrow at him, clearly admiring his forthrightness. "If you ask if we intend to attack them, then I can tell you that I don't intend to. They're an annoyance, but they're like smoke and air: one moment before me, and the next, vanished."

"The lands around here are riddled with caves and valleys where it's easy to hide. Even my own people don't know the full extent of the places they inhabit, but it makes it impractical for me to attack. As such, I intend to drive them from my land when they harass and, regrettably, that does mean they're herded onto your own lands if they make it this far."

"And you wouldn't be willing to redirect them?" Leofwine asked.

"No, not if it puts the lives of my own warriors and people at risk. I just wish them gone. I don't care where."

"And would you be happy if we extended the same courtesy to you?"

Llewelyn laughed joyfully,

"I'd not be the happiest, I admit, but again we both have no loyalties to the other, and so, yes, I'd accept it. But we'd do our best to get them back on your side of the border."

Leofwine smirked at the man's honesty.

"Would it, perhaps, be best to have my men stationed here?"

"Probably, but then you've many more warriors than me," Llewelyn indicated by pointing to the team of troops and squires who were busily setting up a camp on the Mercian side of the massive earthen rampart that ran as far as the eye could see. Leofwine had spent some time examining it in detail.

It seemed such a simple device, built so long ago under the orders of the then Mercian king, Offa. The organisational skills it must have taken to accomplish, the men and women who must have laboured to dig so deeply into the muddy earth spoke volumes as to how sophisticated the long-dead king's administration must have been. And it was successful too. It did what it was supposed to do. Even now, Llewelyn and his men eyed it with distrust and didn't attempt to bring their horses too close to it.

"And if they cross into your land, what would you have my men do?" Leofwine probed further, watching expressions flit across Llewelyn's face as he either chose his words with care or decided on an actual answer.

The men behind him stirred on their horses as his silence dragged on, and Leofwine noticed that a small wind had picked up and was scattering the piles of detritus being dredged up from the bottom of the dyke. Still, he waited patiently, as he would for his own king. Llewelyn might not be his king, but he deserved respect nonetheless.

Finally, Llewelyn sighed deeply, "Well, I think you've the right of it after all. I will station some of my own men near to here as lookouts for any Raiders who may come our way. It would be counterproductive if your men banished them from your lands, and the buggers simply made merry on my own. And now that's settled, I must ask you for news of this Swein of Denmark and why he desires your lands, and you specifically, as much as he does."

Leofwine felt a faint flush envelop his face. He'd not expected to be questioned by the man but felt that he should offer an explanation. He could feel Oscetel's eyes on him, and he wondered what he thought. Did he remember the state that Leofwine had returned home in from the Outer Isles? He'd surely heard the stories about the event.

Horic, while he didn't enjoy recounting his tale of how he'd saved Leofwine and Olaf that night could be called upon to offer his own version of events if he was drunk enough. For once, Leofwine was pleased that Horic and Wulfstan were absent; it would allow him to speak of his injury in the way that he wanted to, without interruptions and recriminations.

Turning back to Llewelyn he spoke, "I'm afraid the personal enmity between Swein and I stems from my being in the wrong place at the wrong time, and of course, my personal involvement with my king, Æthelred. When I escaped from the burning hall where Swein was attempting to slay Lord Olaf of Norway, I set in motion a chain of events that I've not yet been able to counter.

"Swein of Denmark holds me responsible for Olaf's wealth, which he negotiated without consulting Swein, although he'd also been a part of the raiding party in England. Swein wished to stop Olaf from ever reaching Norway, but he was unable to, and Olaf became the king of lands that he thought of as his own, and which he still either desires or lays claim to. I'm unsure whether he now counts himself as king or not of Norway. Events move too fast for me to keep track of, and of course, we hear little from the traders, as most are really Raiders in disguise."

"As to his hatred of the king, that has a similar basis as it was the king who negotiated with lord Olaf of Norway. As to why he wishes to claim our lands, I think wealth holds the key to that."

"I know little of the way the Northern kings tax and govern their people, but my man Horic, from the lands of the north, has alluded enough to the state of affairs there that I've reached my own conclusions. England is rich in land, portable wealth, people and good farming land; it's surrounded on almost all sides by exposed coastal areas, and we are, believe it or not ..." and here Leofwine felt a self-deprecating smile tug at his tight face, "... quite peaceful in our intentions."

Llewelyn had listened attentively as he spoke, nodding his head with understanding and smiling along with Leofwine's final comment.

"However peaceful you are, My Lord Leofwine," the use of his title alerting him that the words Llewelyn would now speak were severe in their intent. "I can assure you that those warriors you have are well skilled and well armed. We don't enjoy engaging with you English but sometimes we must. You're not better at combat than us, but you are different. I always think the Raiders attack in a similar way to my own people. Perhaps that's why we are so much more successful at driving them off."

Leofwine let the sting of his remarks ease before he spoke.

"We all have our own ways, I suppose. It's just a matter of learning how to defeat them. You and your countrymen have a habit of melting away into the mists and caves of your homeland, whereas mine has a habit of standing and fighting. While the Raiders, well, they love nothing more than to retreat to their ships and sail for home. I wonder who of us all will ultimately be successful."

Now Llewelyn shot Leofwine a stern look at his neat summing up of affairs and let the comments float away in the summer breeze.

"All I can say is that I don't envy you and your king the constant bombardment. But that is all for now. I'll return home, and I hope that we have little contact over the coming months. However, I assume I can always be assured that any messengers I send will be safe in your lands and that they'll find you either in Lichfield or at one of the king's palaces."

"Of course, Llewelyn, and you have my thanks for agreeing to meet with me in person."

"In person is always best. Messengers can sometimes cause more problems. Good day to you, and Leofwine ... good luck. And one more thing: keep that oaf of a man Eadric away from my borders; he's none of your charm and a mouth that can only utter depravities. I'll not treat with him as I do with you."

As Leofwine was bowing to acknowledge the words the king

spoke, he felt the thud of the horse's hooves. Leofwine raised his head and watched him leave with interest. Perhaps they had more in common than he had at first realised. He wondered if there was a way he could exploit the king of Powys' hatred of Eadric to his advantage.

"Well, my lord," Oscetel called loudly, breaking Leofwine's train of thoughts, "what do you think of him, and do you think your trip was worth all the trouble?"

Oscetel's face held genuine interest, and Leofwine shrugged an answer. "He seems to be a man of honour, but that's much to say after only a brief conversation. I just hope he holds true to his words regarding the Raiders."

"Now, we must discuss whom we'll trust to stand a guard here and not irritate the man. His agreement was, I think, more hard-won than that brief exchange indicates. He's clearly thought long and hard about the Raiders and Eadric. I'm curious as to who he currently counts as his greater enemy."

"I'd think Eadric, my lord. There have been comments from the men that you might not be aware of. The closer we come to his alleged ancestral lands, the greater the hatred of him seems to become. He's not a good ally for the king, as you've implied before. But, he is beguiling to those he wishes to gain from."

"You tell me little I hadn't already suspected, but you have my thanks all the same. Everywhere I turn, there seems to be an enemy. It tires me Oscetel. And then it angers me."

"And then your wife takes you to bed and calms you down," Oscetel interjected.

"Yes, she's certainly a calming force. But what do you think?"

"I think you're correct in your summing up of England and yourself in particular. The king is not a bad king, but his judgement can be poor. He surrounds himself with men who don't have this country's best interests at heart. He whines and moans when planned actions don't go as he'd hoped."

"He has active and influential churchmen at his side; Wulfstan of London and York is a man who gains respect wherever he goes, and his words are always listened to carefully. He has sons and daughters aplenty, and yet he doesn't use the boys as the tools they could be, and then he stirs up more trouble by marrying again and having more sons. It'll not end well, my lord, and it is all in his remit to prevent, and yet he doesn't. Æthelred is his own worst enemy and you, my lord, it pains me to say, are his tool – and a misused one at that."

Leofwine looked anywhere but at Oscetel as he absorbed the words. There was little new in his summation of past events, and he was certainly not the first person to tell him the king saw him as only someone to manipulate. At least he'd been a little more sensitive in the vocalisation of his thoughts than Eadric, but still, it stung.

Of all the king's ealdormen, he was the only one who worked for his king and with the people paramount in his thoughts, and it did him little good. The king may well no longer see him as an invalid and may have made him ealdorman of Mercia, after rescuing his children and mother from Dean, but it was an uncomfortable position to be in.

Mercia was safe from attack, mostly, with little chance for great battles that would reach his king's ears, and Leofwine felt that it robbed him of the opportunity to excel for his king while at the same time keeping him too busy to attend the king as often as he'd like.

Annoyance warring with satisfaction over his agreement with Llewelyn, Leofwine turned his mind to more pressing matters. Did he want his lands overrun just so the king would respect him a little more? It was a sobering thought.

29
AD1006

Leofwine jumped from the back of his horse, anger infusing his every footstep over the dry summer grass that surrounded his home in Lichfield. He'd recognised the horses that milled around his house the moment he'd been able to see them, and his joy at being home had quickly turned to fury. What was Eadric doing in Lichfield?

As he strode purposefully through the open front door, he heard a murmur of voices, some raised more angrily than others, and he was greeted with the sight of his wife, clearly roused from an afternoon slumber with her new child, arguing forcibly with an insolent-looking Eadric. Eadric lay sprawled across the wooden benches close to the fire.

Æthelflæd's face was flushed with annoyance while Eadric drawled responses to her sharp questions. Behind him, he heard the welcome footsteps of Oscetel and noticed belatedly that Wulfstan was in attendance on his wife.

"Eadric," Leofwine called loudly. Both Eadric and Æthelflæd had been oblivious to his entrance for all that it had not been quiet. "What brings you to disturb my wife?"

Eadric fastened Leofwine with an annoyed glance, apparently

unhappy that he'd returned to interrupt whatever it was he was doing.

"My lord Leofwine, it's nothing for you or your wife to worry about. Just a little matter for the king," he drawled, looking anywhere but at Leofwine.

"And if it's such a little matter, why have you roused my wife from her birthing bed?"

"It's not I who has forced her to meet with me. You must ask that old fool Wulfstan if you want answers."

Wulfstan was working hard to contain his rage where he stood behind Æthelflæd, and Leofwine felt a moment of pity for his old friend. It was one thing to know you were getting old, but quite another to have it so publicly shouted aloud.

"Well, I'm here now so perhaps, Eadric, you would do well to inform me of your intentions!" Leofwine spat, his annoyance growing with every breath he was forced to take in Eadric's presence.

"It was merely something the king suggested, and I thought I should come and see if it met with your approval."

Reining in his anger at the news that this was another sign of the king meddling in his affairs, Leofwine indicated that Eadric should continue.

"The king and I were discussing your ever-expanding family, and the king happened to mention that perhaps one of your sons should become my squire. When I mentioned to Wulfstan that I'd come to collect the boy, he was most unhappy about the arrangements."

Leofwine bit back the bile that had formed in his mouth, "And you would expect him to just hand over my son at your words?"

"Well, they are not my words, they come from the king."

"Why? Has the king ordered that my son becomes your squire?"

"Well, not exactly, I suppose it might not have been an order. But certainly, I didn't think that the plan wouldn't meet with your approval. Now quick, get the boy packed. I've other matters to attend to."

Taking a calming breath and grateful that Wulfstan saw to

Æthelflæd's care by sitting her in a comfortable chair as far from Eadric as it was possible to be, he considered his response.

"Eadric, if you had the intention of taking my son as your squire, then really you should have communicated the news to me. There's much to discuss before I could let him leave with you."

Eadric's hooded eyes turned to glare at Leofwine before settling on the suddenly small shape of Northman, who sat huddled next to his mother, his face a mask of misery.

"It's an honour for the boy. You shouldn't stand in the way of his advancement. Even if you don't seek honours for yourself, I'd have thought you'd be pleased that a man such as I, such a close confidant of the king, would wish to take in one of your runts."

"I've not said it's not an honour, nor have I said it is. What concerns me is your presumptuous manner of laying claim to him without consulting me."

"My lord, I sent a messenger to you when you were on the Borders. He informs me that you didn't let him give you the entire message."

"He didn't carry a message about my son, and you well know it." Leofwine could feel his words coming faster and faster as his anger grew at the audacity of the man. "And even if he had, I've been away, in service to the king. How would I have had time to return home and discuss the situation with both my son and my wife?"

"Leofwine, you're the master here; your family should do as you say. What is all this about discussions?"

"I'm master here, thank you Eadric, you are correct. However, my children and my wife are allowed their opinions. I'd hope that garnering the view of others was something that you pursued in your house."

Eadric laughed a little at the words. "Then you are very mistaken. I'm the master of my house, and my wife, when she is my wife, will do as she's bid. As will my children. Now is the boy to come with me or not?"

"No, he's not. He's too young and your arrival too soon. I'm happy to converse further about him becoming a squire in your household, but nothing more. And now, as you're clearly busy with other business, I suggest you leave. I'll discuss this at the next witan. Good day, Eadric."

Leofwine moved backwards to stand beside the open door, indicating that Eadric should step through it. Eadric took his time rising from his chair and with a last insultingly languorous appraisal of Æthelflæd, he walked beyond Leofwine.

"You'll regret this, my lord, I assure you of that," he muttered darkly as Leofwine slammed the door shut on his departing back and then fought for composure.

Silence reverberated around the large hall, the solitary noises coming from where Eadric could be heard shouting commands at his men to "bloody hurry up" and "no, the boy wasn't joining us".

Only when the sounds of the horses' hooves over the hard-packed earth had faded to nothingness did Leofwine move, and then it was to both crush his wife and his son in his embrace. Æthelflæd shook in his arms and Northman had dirty tears streaking his face.

Wulfstan opened his mouth to speak, but Leofwine forestalled him, "You did the right thing Wulfstan, don't think any differently. Eadric's a menace."

Wulfstan nodded to show he understood and moved to step away. Before he did, he placed his arm on Leofwine's shoulder.

"Welcome home, son," he whispered as he shuffled towards the closed door.

Grief pierced Leofwine's rapidly beating heart as with those words his oldest friend acknowledged his advancing years.

30
AD1006

FURY SURGED THROUGH HIS BEING AS HE STOOD, FEET FIRMLY PLANTED ON the as yet unharvested field of golden corn, facing his enemy similarly arrayed further along the field. The Raiders had made an impressive show of themselves, and as they hollered and shouted insults at the equally impressive collection of Englishmen, Leofwine let his anger have its way – a rarity for him.

Months of sneaking attacks and lightning-fast strikes across the homeland of the Wessex homeland had brought them to this moment, and for once Leofwine's fear at what may happen in the coming battle had flown from his head. He knew the strength of his men, and he knew the tight fighting formations that would make them a formidable force to attack. He harboured half a hope that he knew these men before him as well, perhaps better, than they knew themselves.

Away from their homelands and with nothing but their lives to sacrifice, they would fight as best they could, but as they fought only for treasure and gold, he didn't think they'd be too keen to die.

And that was what he'd planned. Along with Oscetel and Horic, collected from Deerhurst as they'd shot south to meet the Raiders from the heart of the Mercian lands, they'd devised a plan whereby they hoped to inflict upon the enemy as many deaths as possible. With a heap of dead and dying men, a force that showed no signs of tiring and that could continuously be replenished from the other fighting units of the fyrd, they all believed that Swein of Denmark's men would head back for their ships – once and for all.

The king's messages had reached him not long after his return to Lichfield from Powys, demanding that he bring as many of the fyrd as he thought could be spared to the lands surrounding London and further south. The king had mentioned they might need to travel towards Canterbury, where Swein's men were inflicting irreparable damage upon the nation and its people.

Putting aside his annoyance that once again the king could not rely on any effective military action being taken under the command of the ageing ealdorman Ælfric, Leofwine had ordered a full half of the Mercian fyrd to gather near London. Stationing half the men there, he and his own household troop had advanced deep into the lands of Wessex before coming across the Raiders almost within spitting distance of Winchester.

Hasty messengers to the king had ensured he travelled further north with his wife and young children, while messengers to his own fyrd in London had the men flying into the Wessex homelands.

And now, all assembled, they stood ready and waiting to drive the Raiders decisively from their shores. Leofwine had spoken to all his commanders, imparted words of advice and assigned roles to those he knew would be able to follow through with his orders or countermand them as events unfolded. Those incapable of such quick thinking had been forced to form up beside Leofwine in such a way that he could issue commands as and when needed and ensure they only took actions he felt would win the battle.

Neither was he alone. Athelstan, winning the king's blessing to join the fight, had brought his own household troops and commanded a sizeable force of the king's men. Surrounded by his own commanders, young Morcar and Sigeforth, Athelstan had confided in Leofwine of his worries surrounding his father's ever-growing closeness to Eadric, who was notable by his absence.

The ætheling's actions now mirrored Leofwine's own. Whether or not the king chose wisely in the men he surrounded himself with, Athelstan didn't wish Swein of Denmark to gain any more at the expense of the English. He was here to fight, and not just for his father's honour.

Leofwine admired Athelstan's courage and decisiveness. It could not be easy to serve a father who held him back and refused to impart any real authority on him.

Leofwine was struck with the thought of how different their current predicament would be if only Athelstan were king and not his father. Not the most pleasant of thoughts, but the respect he'd once had for his king was being eroded by his consistently less than astute decision-making. The developing relationship with the man who was vocal in claiming Leofwine's jurisdiction was not helping the situation.

Leofwine's anger reawakened within him, and he relished its heat. He was going to prove his worth to his king by being the man to finally oversee the banishment of Swein's men. He only wished that Swein was leading the men, but from the information his scouts had so far discovered it seemed as though Swein had felt no need to leave his haven near his ships.

Leofwine thought him almost as much of a fool as his own king: better to be involved and show his value as a leader than hiding until the action was all done with and then claim the glory. It would make him look an idiot.

With a cry of authority, Leofwine ordered his men to advance, shields before the men in the first row and also above their heads, held there by the men in the second rank.

The jeering and calls of derision from the motley collection of Raiders didn't stop but grew louder at their tactic, and Leofwine smiled. They were all bloody half-wits. His men, led by Oscetel and

Horic, stopped a hundred paces or more from the assembled enemy and hunkered down behind their shields ... waiting.

Long moments passed as the cries of Swein's men slowly died in confusion. This tactic they'd not seen before. In the distance, Leofwine could see the opposition's leaders looking at each other uneasily. The five men were interspersed amongst their own men, but Leofwine knew who they were. It was easy to catch sight of the men who claimed the most armbands from their king as they flashed in the bright summer sunshine.

When Leofwine's men didn't move even a step closer, but stayed silent and still behind their shields, a ripple of derision shot through the assembled enemy. First one man and then another, unable to contain their battle joy, rushed forward before the orders were given by their superiors. Leofwine knew he had them as soon as they broke ranks.

Leofwine watched with satisfaction from atop his horse as one section of the advancing force broke off from their untidy line of defence. They rushed toward what now looked like an insignificant amount of men marooned in the middle of the summer-ripened crop, a smudge of aged brown wood in a field of summer gold.

There were uneasy looks between the rest of the attackers, unsure how they should proceed, and suddenly all the men were rushing across the empty space, furious cries of rage floating through the air, and Leofwine gave his next order.

In a prearranged line, his handful of archers advanced from below the small hillock they'd been hiding beneath, where Leofwine could easily see them but the opposition couldn't. In perfect unison, they let loose with their deadly arrows and the cries of battle from the advancing Raiders, who'd sensed an easy victory, turned to cries of fear at the rain of death that descended from the cloudless sky.

Wave after wave of arrows flew almost silently through the air, and Leofwine watched as men stumbled where they stood, many admittedly almost upon Horic and the men, but only a handful managing to escape the deadly shower.

When the first man met the shield wall, he momentarily stopped, wondering where his comrades had fallen. Leofwine watched him pause and look behind. What the man saw must have filled him with fear.

Leofwine could clearly see crumpled bodies curled in pain or in death, and the uncertainty of the leaders was evident in the milling around of the rest of the fighting force. Like Leofwine's small force of archers, they'd been hidden from plain sight. Leofwine, however, had known they were there. It was evident, though, that Swein's men had not known about Leofwine's archers.

The lone warrior at the shield wall, having weighed up his odds of leaving the battlefield alive, raised his war axe above his head and with an elongated war cry, rushed towards the spot that Leofwine knew Horic would be occupying.

With an efficiency Leofwine admired every time he saw it, Horic stepped from his place in the shield wall and dispatched the man's head from his shoulders with his war axe as if it were a head of corn. The momentarily stunned body stopped where it stood and slowly collapsed to the floor, while Horic roared his own battle cry and re-joined the shield wall.

A shout of approval greeted Horic's actions while a rumble of anger erupted from the opposing side. Any confusion at the strange battle tactics dissolved and suddenly, as a man, the Raiders were running and screaming, seaxs and war axes raised in a ready position to batter against the shield wall.

Leofwine counted in his head, measuring the steps the men took, and then he too signalled his reserve collection of archers and they, combined with the men who'd already loosed half of their arrows at the enemy, let their arrows fly.

This time, the men fought through the hail of arrows to reach the shield wall. When the archers had exhausted as many arrows as Leofwine had prescribed, they dove back behind the advancing shield wall that Leofwine had allowed Athelstan to command and lead.

This shield wall stretched twice as long as Oscetel's own, but it was not as deep. Jumping from his horse and passing the reins to the boy who was serving as his squire, Leofwine rushed to join Athelstan's forces. There was no possibility that he was going to allow the men to have all the glory. When he informed the king of his victory, he wanted it to be a triumph that he'd taken part in.

Above the din of battle, Athelstan shouted encouragement to the men, which Leofwine echoed down the line of his own warriors, personally chosen by Horic to see to his lord's protection.

The crops before them tumbled under the weight of the combined feet of the mass of men, and Leofwine laughed joyously at the similarity of the crops' fate to the Raiders he now faced.

The sounds of the battle were intensifying, and Leofwine grabbed a firm hold of his sword and his shield. In a carefully practised manoeuvre, Athelstan's force split neatly in two when it reached the smaller force, and Leofwine advanced, pleased when he felt more than heard the two forces join.

Faced with such a long shield wall, the Raiders, as Leofwine had hoped, split their offensive hastily. There was a scrum as some of the Raiders rushed to do their commanders bidding while others remained to batter against the might of Oscetel's and Horic's original shield wall.

This was the moment when care needed to be taken. Leofwine didn't want the additional shield wall to push further forward than the original one. He didn't want his men to wrap themselves around those of the attacking force who'd managed to survive the rain of arrows.

He'd spoken abruptly to Athelstan on this point, and he only hoped that the king's son heeded his advice in the heat of battle.

And then a loud thunk on his shield distracted him from his thoughts as he felt the arrival of the enemy; blow after blow landed on his shield, but he held firm, the man behind him covering his head with his own shield and the two men to either side holding firmly to their shields.

A brief cry of strangled pain and the hammering ceased as the man to his right, Wighard, struck below his shield and hamstrung the attacker. Neatly, Leofwine made a small step forward and stabbed the man with his own seax. A gurgle of blood from the cut across his throat and Leofwine was back within the safety of the overlapping shield wall.

Leofwine could feel the reverberation of more war axes and seaxs on the toughened wooden shields that lined the shield wall, but for now, he had no one attacking him.

He took a moment to breathe deeply, feeling the tension of the last few months ease through his shoulders, and then he felt another thump on his shield. Employing the same tactics as before, he and Wighard dealt with the Raider as a further whoosh of arrows flew through the air. Never raising his head from below his shield, he listened with delight as the man behind him, Leofgar, recounted what he could see of the battle.

Methodically, Leofwine and his men stayed firmly in place as wave after wave of Raiders attacked their shield wall. Each time Leofwine dispatched the man who sought his death, and each time his hope increased that this time a host of men would lie dead at battle's end and that this battle would put paid to Swein of Denmark's intentions towards England.

When Leofwine finally lifted his head, to assess the damage his force had inflicted, a snarl of delight bubbled from his chest. The field of crops was destroyed, and in the distance, he could see a remnant of the original force either running from the battle or chasing a horse so it could carry them away. Swein's commanders were long since gone, and in their stead, they left only the dead and dying.

From his place amongst his shield wall, Leofwine heard a massive sneer of approval from Horic join his own laughter, and suddenly all the men were cheering and shouting, calling to friends and family they'd worried they'd not see again.

Hastily, Leofwine called his household troops together,

exhausted or not, and ordered them to follow the withdrawing forces. Athelstan shouted to him, desperate to offer further assistance, and with the joy of winning encircling him, Leofwine agreed, leaving the leader of the archers to deal with the aftermath of the battle while they hunted down any who were trying to escape toward the southern coast.

With his horse beneath him and Hammer at his side, Leofwine raced forward, noting with a detachment he was proud of the injuries his side had inflicted on their enemy.

Men wore grisly cuts across their faces, the stark red of their lost blood making their pale, dead faces even more frightful to look upon. Arrows protruded from the faces of other men as well as from their stomachs and backs. With compassion, Leofwine hastily killed a man staggering blindly around the scene of devastation, an arrow clean through his unprotected stomach and a massive gaping wound running the length of his face.

Beside him, Horic and Oscetel and the rest of the household troops raced to keep up with Leofwine's horse as it ate up the distance between them and the retreating warriors.

Leofwine tried to count how many still lived but found it impossible. However, many men they'd killed and left to the ravens and crows, there were many more attempting to make their escape. Most of them had found horses from behind their battle line, and as Leofwine raced through the sea of abandoned tents and still smouldering campfires, a sobering thought pressed down on him: this force was tremendous; it was no wonder they'd caused so much damage and had sent Ealdorman Ælfric hurrying to his king in desperation.

Leofwine resolved that he wanted as many of the men as possible dead, but even more importantly, he wanted them gone from his land. With a restraint that surprised him, he pulled back his horse's wild ride and allowed Athelstan and his own men to catch him.

"We should let them get ahead of us," he shouted breathlessly.

"It's better that they leave with tales of their defeat than we kill them now. I don't want another set-piece battle, not when we've left so many of our warriors behind them."

Athelstan glanced at the retreating shapes before them and quickly nodded in agreement.

"I think we should split up, though; the men are scattering all over the place, and I want to herd as many of them as possible."

Leofwine himself nodded.

"Agreed; we'll follow that group over there," and he pointed to where the retreating backs of the men could be seen racing through a small stream. "And you travel that way. And don't forget to light the beacons if you reach the coast. If we can arrange for the ship army to chase them far out to sea, that's even better."

With nothing more to say, Leofwine encouraged his horse back to a slower gallop and steered him towards a stream. He was going to enjoy this, and when he spoke to his king, he was damn well going to get an apology for his years of neglect he'd endured since the death of Lady Elfrida.

31
AD1006

EADRIC EYED HIM WITH OBVIOUS AMUSEMENT FROM HIS PLACE NEXT TO THE king while Leofwine openly returned his stare. For whatever reason, Eadric had decided that Leofwine was, if not his enemy, then certainly not his friend.

It was an irrational hatred that Leofwine could only understand in a similar context to Swein of Denmark's enmity. Eadric seemed to hold Leofwine in contempt for his position as ealdorman, claiming loudly and to any who would listen that it should be his command, not Leofwine's, although his reasoning was never fully explained, and none could find a trace of Eadric's link to the ancient Mercian nobility.

The king, starting to show his age with grey streaking his hair and tidy beard and moustache, glanced knowingly between Eadric and Leofwine before fixing Leofwine with a stony stare. Leofwine nodded to recognise his king's scrutiny, if not his hard stare. He'd not seen his king throughout the long summer's campaigning, and he could already tell that in his absence Eadric had become the king's firm favourite.

Leofwine cursed his king for a fool, again. Finally, he'd accepted that he'd never understand his king and his need for sycophants and liars, but he didn't like it. Without them all, the king would have been a far superior figure.

Leofwine was also unhappy to find himself dependent on Eadric's hospitality, within his home near the border with the kingdom of Powys. It was an elegant home, well built and constructed against the harsh winter storm that blew fiercely outside, but the very king's presence within it marked Eadric with far more favour than Leofwine thought he deserved.

Eadric had done nothing all summer long but stayed safe beside the king and cast doubt on the actions of those who'd mounted an attack against Swein of Denmark.

Athelstan had greeted Leofwine on his arrival at the house and had confided in him that after their stunning defeat of the Raiders, Eadric had gone out of his way to find fault with the battle tactics Leofwine had employed.

Leofwine had not been surprised, and neither was he alarmed that the very aged Ealdorman Ælfric had added his own voice to Eadric's. Uhtred and Ulfcytel had not been as vocal in their denouncement of the battle, but then they were firmly in the king's favour already and didn't need to rely on underhand techniques as Eadric did.

Leofwine's victory had been stunning, driving Swein's men back to their ships. It was not his lack that had brought the Raiders back amongst the devastated remains of the ship army, but rather a sudden and unexpected summer storm that had struck out at sea and forced them to come ashore again near Canterbury.

It was unfortunate that Leofwine had dispersed his fyrd back to Mercia happy that the Raiders had gone. His reasoning had been sound. It had been harvest time, and the fields were full of crops, which after last year's famine needed to be carefully reaped.

And he'd personally seen the vast fleet set out to sea, and he'd seen to the lighting of the beacons along the coast. The king's ship army had arrived with all haste, and they'd followed the path of the retreating Raiders.

Leofwine couldn't have known that the Raiders would sneak back onto English land like rats from a sinking ship. But Æthelred didn't see it that way. All he saw was the reversal of what he'd been told: one day the menace was banished; the next day it was back. The king blamed Leofwine, not Swein, no matter how unjust his anger was.

Swein of Denmark was again raiding in the old Wessex lands, and that was why the king and his family had retreated to Eadric's 'safe area'. The irony that the lands of Eadric were only safe because of Leofwine's efforts and agreement with the king of Powys was not lost on Leofwine.

With bitterness, he'd realised that the king hadn't yet made the connection. He'd been heard to praise Eadric for actions that he'd played no part in.

Before he'd left home, Æthelflæd and Wulfstan had both spoken angrily to him about the king's irrational response to the success and failure of the summer season. Leofwine had attempted to calm them, but it had been hard when he'd agreed with every word they'd spoken.

Æthelflæd's anger had been magnificent to watch as she'd angrily marched from one side of their home in Lichfield to another. All the servants and children had fled at her ire, only Wulfstan, Oscetel and Horic staying in place as she'd vented her anger and frustration.

Leofwine had worried that her words would be overheard, but then he'd realised it mattered little. The king had made his decisions, and no matter what Leofwine now did, he would continue to be used as a weapon, while Eadric became his blunt tool.

Even now he could hear the murmur of the voices of others around him – a loud humming noise where the only word he could pick out was his own name or that of Eadric's before the haze of noise descended again. He'd braced himself for this, but it was not a pleasant experience.

Leofwine purposely only arrived today, under the impression that the witan would convene that day, but for some reason, the king had delayed. Leofwine had wanted to spend as little time as possible socialising with the king and his cronies. Now he had no choice.

Beside him Hammer stirred, sharing his master's restlessness, and Leofwine offered some words of comfort that fell unheard to his own ears, although Hammer stilled. His back was so rigid that a spark of pain shot down it every so often and he'd spoken little and taken less from the table before him piled high with food.

Beside him, Oscetel shared his alertness while Horic, seemingly impervious to their perilous position, laughed and joked with all who came near.

A loud bark of laughter from Horic and his words finally penetrated Leofwine's disturbing thoughts, the use of the word 'Swein' rousing him from his self-imposed introspection.

"You ask me if I can believe that of Swein of Denmark? Of course, I do. Swein is capable of anything. Surely you should know that by now."

Turning to Oscetel, Leofwine raised questioning eyebrows to see if he was aware of what Horic spoke about.

"There are tales of Swein's barbaric treatment of those who go against his wishes. He, like our own king, has little problem with blinding and killing men who displease him, or of getting others to do his bidding and then denying his own involvement."

Oscetel glanced unconsciously at his king as he spoke, and Leofwine laid a calming hand on his arm. He didn't want his men to get involved in his power struggle. Regardless, they would remain his men, loyal to him through their oaths of commendation as well as through their land ties. It was only he who was at risk, and yet he knew the men spoke amongst themselves in concern. He appreciated their outrage but cautioned them all against speaking openly of it; he didn't want his men to suffer in his wake.

A hand on his shoulder and he turned in confusion to find bishop Wulfstan beside him. He settled himself beside him on the wooden bench, although he faced outwards, studying the king.

"You're well Leofwine?" bishop Wulfstan queried quietly.

"As can be expected," Leofwine muttered as respectfully as he could.

"Unease runs through the church at the king's intended actions. You're a good man, loyal without the requisite need to gain from your association with the king. You're an ealdorman alone with your morals and your beliefs, but don't think the church doesn't notice your good ways."

Leofwine turned to stare openly at bishop Wulfstan, not so much shocked at the words as pleased to hear them from the great bishop.

"We live in difficult times. We may have survived the millennium since our Saviour's birth, but still, we're tested almost every day ... some more than others," bishop Wulfstan added as an afterthought.

"The king is a man wise in how to govern, but he lacks skills in his interactions with people. He was king from a young age. He's grown to love those who don't question him, little understanding that by taking advice from others he'll grow in stature."

"You've made a study of the king?" Leofwine queried, intrigued to hear another voice his own thoughts so eloquently.

"Of course, my lord; it's always best to know your friends and your enemies in equal measure."

"And what would you suggest I do?"

"Little or nothing – you must ride this out as best you can. The king is angry. Swein of Denmark is a menace, but so too is Eadric. But my lord, a spy here and there would do you no harm."

"A spy ...?"

"Your son – send him to Eadric's household as he offered earlier in the year. If you inspire the same loyalty in your children as you do your household troops, he'll work for you."

Leofwine shook his head, vigorously in denial, "He's but a boy?"

"Indeed, my lord, but at his age, Æthelred was near enough a king. The path should not be too tricky for a bright lad like Northman. He knows his place well, and Eadric will do nothing to harm or injure him. It's you that Eadric despises, and once he's ealdorman of the Mercians, he'll think he has all he wants. Your son will not even factor into his day-to-day thinking."

Leofwine shuffled uncomfortably on the bench, accidentally kicking Hammer in the process, eliciting a reproachful whine from his dog.

"I'd not want to send my dog to him, let alone my son," Leofwine spoke angrily, the confirmation of his fears of Eadric's intended advance bitter for all that he'd been expecting them.

"Hush, my lord. You mustn't speak so, not here. Eadric inspires either great loyalty or great hatred, but either retainer or enemy would benefit from hearing your words."

Leofwine took a calming breath. The bishop was wise in his words. Leofwine sucked in a breath to ask the bishop what he planned to advise the king, but before he could a commotion at the main door distracted everyone within the hall. Angry cries and the shouts of men could be heard. Instantly, Leofwine felt Horic and Oscetel at his back, and Hammer stood alert, growling low in his throat.

Leofwine quickly realised that this was not to be another of Eadric's underhand techniques to rid himself or the king of any who stood in their way. Instead, a windblown and sodden individual made his way hastily towards where the king had stood.

"My lord king," the man gasped, water pooling on the wooden floor he stood upon, "I bring grave news."

"What is it, man, speak up and speak clearly. And someone bring him warmed clothes, food and drink."

"It's the Raiders, my lord king. They're attacking even now. They've barrelled through the southern lands and are making their way further north. When I came upon them, they were nearly at Oxford."

Æthelred's face twisted angrily at the words, and he looked

about, almost helplessly. Leofwine stood abruptly and bowed to his king.

"My lord king, my men are here with me. I'll mount an expedition and banish them back to their ships."

Eadric stared open-mouthed at Leofwine, but Leofwine ignored him as he did the gasps from Horic and Oscetel. A winter campaign was unheard of.

"We can't let them harry our people further." He could feel his voice becoming angry at the inactivity surrounding him.

Beside the king, Athelstan too jumped to his feet, "I'll accompany him. We'll make a small force, but fleet-footed for all that."

Without waiting for his father's agreement, Athelstan strode from the room, signalling for his followers as he went, and his brother, Edmund also hastened to follow. As the king had still not spoken, either in agreement or denial, Leofwine merely followed suit. Oxford was a part of Mercia after all.

Stepping outside into the dismal storm was a stark reminder of how difficult it would be to mount their attack. Still, Leofwine had spoken, and there was no chance that he was going to go back on his word just because it was cold, dark and wet.

Oscetel and Horic were busily giving orders to the men who'd accompanied them. They'd rushed from the hall in the footsteps of their lord without a word or shout of a complaint. Leofwine knew he was lucky to have such loyal men.

As the wind howled and the rain drenched them immediately, Leofwine gave hasty orders to both his men and to Athelstan and his. He hesitated to order the king's son around, but as Athelstan had made no move to organise his men, Leofwine assumed that he was happy to let the older man arrange their expedition.

There was little daylight left in the short winter day, but he deemed it best to make a start. If they could make it to Deerhurst tonight, they'd make quick work of a journey to Oxford tomorrow and would, hopefully, be able to engage with Swein and his men.

He called for lanterns to be lit and leapt into his saddle, Hammer attentive at his side. He paused for a heartbeat, looking back toward the closed and barred doorway of Eadric's hall, but the king didn't venture outside or wish his own sons well. With a snort of disgust, Leofwine called his force to attention.

THE JOURNEY TO DEERHURST WAS UNCOMFORTABLE AND DANGEROUS, MORE an endurance test than any other expedition to war he'd taken. All fifty of the men arrived drenched and drained. Their faces were frozen into a grimace of determination.

With barely a raised eyebrow, Horic's wife settled to her task of supplying bedding and food for an unlooked-for war band. Leofwine had always known she was a capable woman, but his estimation of her increased a hundred-fold that night. She didn't even miss a footstep when Horic jovially introduced her to the king's sons. They swept her deep bows, but she shooed them towards the fire as if they were her errant children.

Early the next morning, before the sun had risen, all of the warriors were heading for Oxford. Horic's four oldest sons and his household troops had swelled their numbers to sixty-five, and five of the men shot onwards as scouts to track the Raiders down.

The rain had eased during the night, but the ground was sodden and the rivers and streams they came across swollen so much that passing them was a hazardous experience.

Around midday, calls from in front alerted them to a sighting of Swein and his men, and they turned further south. They finally came across the raiding force at an old earthwork, Cuckhamsley Hill. The reports from the scouts counted a slightly larger force than their own and Leofwine felt a moment of panic. He'd not had time to call on any of the men of the fyrd or any of his reeves, intent only on reaching the Raiders and stopping their advance any further north. Hastily he called his commanders and the king's sons together.

"My lord Athelstan, how many archers do you have amongst your men?"

Athelstan pinched from the cold, looked questioningly at his men. "Five of the men are proficient with their arrows. Why do you ask my lord?"

"I normally have a larger contingent of archers, but in my haste, I've only just realised that I have a mere handful. With your own, we should have enough."

"You've decided on a plan of attack already?" Athelstan queried.

"Yes, but first, we'll offer Swein the opportunity of leaving quietly, and then if not, we'll use the same tactic as in the summer only on a much smaller scale. Horic will lead forward with a shield wall of ten men, two deep. The ten archers will then mount an attack and the remaining men will join them when the time is right."

"But Swein will have heard of your ploy?"

"I'm counting on it. I hope he'll try to rush the shield wall before the archers can attack, and as soon as he does the shield wall will attack as the arrows fall, and the rest will hurry forward to extend the shield wall. Even if he's heard of my previous tactics, the familiarity of the attack will lull him into thinking that we, or more specifically I, am too stupid to have changed my methods."

Leofwine knew that his voice was steely with resolve, with no opportunity for arguing. Still, the ætheling thought about arguing, and Leofwine admired him afresh.

"Do you want to approach Swein of Denmark?"

Athelstan, shutting his mouth suddenly on whatever comment he'd been about to make, shook his head. "I would happily, but we both know that the king would not approve."

Athelstan sounded unhappy at the words, but Horic offered him words of comfort. "The king can, on occasion be wise."

Athelstan quirked an eyebrow at the huge man and a faint smile spread across his mud-streaked face. "I suggest we remember that," Athelstan muttered darkly, before stepping away to ready his men.

Leofwine looked to Horic, "Would you like to do the honours?"

"Of course, my lord, I'd love nothing better than to face the treasonous bastard again, but Athelstan has the right of it. It's your place to offer him a bargain."

Leofwine stared grimly towards the small hostile force massing around the earthwork.

"Do the Danes not say something about this place?" Leofwine asked, a spark of memory that had been annoying him all day finding its way to the forefront of his mind.

"Aye, my lord. Well, in my day they did. At some point, someone has told them of this sacred site, deep within the king's Wessex territory and it's become a source of honour to reach it."

"And why is that?"

Horic tried to shrug the question aside, but Oscetel spoke quietly into the silence.

"They believe that if they reach this hill, they'll hold England and will never be forced to leave."

Turning sharply to Oscetel, Leofwine spoke to Horic, "Is this right?"

"Yes, my lord, it's true. For many, many years the Raiders have seen this small hill as an emblem. These men here, they'll return home rich with tales. That's if they return home at all."

Leofwine took a moment longer to consider. "Tell the men this, ensure Athelstan and his brother are aware: this battle, for that's what it'll be, will be a test of more than our resolve; we must beat them back to their ships or kill them and ourselves in the process."

"News of their advance must not be spread further than it needs to. The bloody Danes already think they can take England whenever they want to. I'll not allow their foolhardy prophecy to gain any more weight."

Horic grunted to show his understanding of his lord's words and sauntered off to speak to the rest of the men.

"You'll accompany me, Oscetel?"

"Of course, my lord, but are we to go alone?"

"I think it best. Now come. We must hurry. I want to fight him in the light."

Leaving his horse behind, Leofwine instructed Hammer to walk before him. The dog whined a little at the smell of campfires and blood that filled the air but was finally convinced to walk towards the ancient mound.

They'd taken less than ten steps forward when a similar party of two began to walk towards them from the opposition's side.

"Is that Swein?" Leofwine inquired, his eyesight being next to useless in the dull day.

"Yes, my lord, although I don't know who accompanies him; he's young, though, perhaps one of his sons."

As they walked closer, even Leofwine was able to see Swein's self-satisfied swagger, and his resolve intensified.

"Well met, my lord Leofwine," Swein shouted within spitting distance.

"I can't say the same for you, king Swein."

"Well, that's a shame, to come to your death with such bad humour," was the insolent reply, "but I suppose I can't blame you."

"Why are you here?"

"I came to see if I could reach this excellent place, and now that I'm here I intend to stay, for rumour has it that once this place is mine, it shall remain mine. I'm quite looking forward to being the king of this land." As he spoke, Swein lifted a hand, indicating the area around them.

"You think you can take my king's land with only a handful of men?"

"I think I've done very well so far, with just my few men and that pitiful excuse of an ealdorman, Leofsige. You can tell your king that the man is dead. He had no taste for battle. Where have you been my lord? I'd been expecting you much sooner, but I'm happy that you took so long to find me."

Leofwine barely contained his anger.

"Now that I'm here, you can leave."

"Oh, I don't think so. I'm quite content here. The Isle of Wight is a grim place. The land around here seems well stocked with warm houses and hotter beds."

"None of those houses are yours, and so I must insist you leave, or we'll be forced to chase you from the land."

"Like last time?" Swein countered, disrespectfully.

"Like last time," Leofwine replied, not allowing his purpose to falter in the face of Swein's scorn.

"In that case, I think I must let you do so. Oh, and one more thing Leofwine," Swein stopped his advance back toward his men, his back already turned on Leofwine.

"I've decided that my desire to see you dead was a little foolish. I'd rather you lived so that I can beat you in battle, time after time. It's more enjoyable this way. If you survive here, which you won't, you can take our feud as finished. If you don't survive, I'll ensure your wife knows that you died at the hands of an enemy who no longer wished your death."

Leofwine held his gaze on Swein, feeling the blood in his veins boil and his heart pulse dangerously fast before calmness took him, and he too turned away. He walked a few paces and stopped, noting that Swein was watching him with an enormous contemptuous smile across his bland face.

"If you're too scared to face me, king Swein, you need only say."

Swein's smile fell from his face instantly, but Leofwine had turned aside, a smile now on his face. He'd have the last word.

Signalling for Oscetel to jog beside him, he raced back to his men and had Horic advancing into the centre of the space between him and the enemy before Swein was even halfway back to his force.

Shouts of derision greeted Horic's actions, but Leofwine was deaf to them as he watched with fascination to see if the men would fall for his trap.

When Horic and the shield wall formed up, Swein signalled for his men to attack, wasting no time. With a swiftly caught breath, Leofwine ordered his archers to start shooting and the remainder of his shield wall to rush forward. The shouts of ridicule from Swein's men quickly turned to cries of anger. The arrows and the shield wall advanced with dizzying speed.

Before Leofwine had even managed to catch Horic and the men up, the pile of Danish bodies was impressive. It took only moments longer for Swein's force to be beaten. Looking up from his spot in the shield wall Leofwine noted with detachment that Swein had abandoned the battle almost as soon as it had begun. He was fleeing the place on a horse, surrounded only by about twenty men.

Taking the time to ensure that all those who'd fallen were indeed dead, Leofwine took a moment to savour the victory. He'd not even had the opportunity to fell one of the enemies.

Calling for his horse, Leofwine mounted hastily. They'd chase Swein back to the Isle of Wight, even if it took days to do so. He doubted that Swein would risk a long sea voyage in the winter storms, but at least he could be contained on the island, and then it would be for the king's ship-army to prevent Swein from returning to the mainland.

32
AD1006

Almost a week had passed since they'd precipitously left Eadric's hall. Although Leofwine had ensured word was sent back to the king of their victory, no messenger had yet arrived from the king, and it was galling.

This time they'd chased Swein of Denmark all the way to the coastline, where a ship had been lying in wait for him and had then roused the local reeve to inform him that Swein was again contained.

Athelstan and Edmund had agreed to overwinter near Winchester where they and their men would be within easy distance to counter any more attacks. Leofwine had harboured hopes that his king would be happy with him, but his doubts were starting to set in.

Arriving back at Deerhurst, he was chilled to the bone and almost frozen in position atop his horse. Hammer had been sending him looks of disgust for much of the last two days, and finally, he'd taken pity on the poor dog and heaved him up beside him on the horse. The horse had approved even less than Hammer.

Horic's wife, Agata, greeted them as coolly as she had on their earlier arrival, all efficiency and few words. But the messenger who sat at his table did not go unnoticed, and Leofwine finally called him over.

"You have news for me?"

"I do, my lord, but Agata said it should wait."

"Is it from the king?"

"No, my lord: the bishop."

"What does he say?"

"I hardly like to say, my lord, but he bid me to tell you that Eadric is now ealdorman of the Mercians and that you remain only as ealdorman of the Hwicce."

Leofwine nodded to show he understood.

"And was this decision taken before or after the king heard of my victory over Swein of Denmark?"

The youth looked wretched as he tried to speak, and Leofwine took pity on him.

"Apologies, I guess I already know the answer to that. Would you please thank the bishop for thinking to inform me?"

"Of course, my lord ... and, my lord ..."

"Yes?"

"He ensured that your wife knew as well. I understand that he was to advise her to travel here."

"It would appear I'm even further in the bishop's debt. Thank him most carefully for me, and now please stay as long as you need to recover. The weather is rough today, and I'd not recommend travelling in it. As we rode in, snow was falling."

"With thanks, my lord. I think I'll stay a day or two longer. The bishop said I was to journey to Worcester. It'll be a trip of one or two days?"

"Yes, provided the snow goes. Have no fear. You can stay as long as you need to. I'll not cast you out, and now, if you'll excuse me."

"Of course, my lord, and ... thank you for taking the news so well, I was worried you would be angry with me."

Leofwine thumped the youth on the back, gently.

"It's never the fault of the messenger. Remember that."

“Oh, and one more thing, my lord.”

“Yes?”

“The king has announced that we’ll make peace with Swein of Denmark.”

Leofwine cushioned his head in his hands as he slumped forward on the table, the irony that he was now being told not lost on him.

“Of course he has,” Leofwine muttered darkly, closing his eyes. Again, he couldn’t blame the messenger.

CAST OF CHARACTERS

LEOFWINE'S FAMILY

Leofwine, Ealdorman of the Hwicce and occasionally Mercia

Æthelflæd, his wife

Northman, his oldest son born 996

Leofric, his son born 998

Ealdgyth, his daughter born 1000

Godwine, his son born 1002

Eadwine, his son born 1006

IN THE NORTH

Gita, northern woman

Osbert, Gita's husband

Ragnor, Osbert's father

Eadrid, reeve of Lichfield

Brunhild, Eadrid's wife (reeve of Lichfield)

Ragnor, king's high reeve from Canterbury, Kent

Æthelweard; Leofwine, High Reeve of Hampshire; Leofric of Whitchurch; Godwine of Worthy – all killed in battle in 1001

Kola and Eadsige, killed at the Battle of Pinhoe

Aldric, Uhtred's messenger

Eadnoth, reeve

Morcar and Sigeforth, allies of Prince Athelstan

MEN OF THE MERCIAN FYRD

Eadnoth

Godwine

Brithwold

KING

Æthelred II

THE COURT

Elfrida (king's mother – died c.1001)

Ælfgifu (Æthelred's wife – never queen dies c.1000)

Athelstan (the king's son b.c 986

Ecgberht (the king's son b.c. 987 – died c.1005)

Edmund (the king's son b.c 990)

Wulfhilda (king's daughter b.c. 992 marries Ulfcytel of East Anglia)

Emma (king's second wife, renamed from Ælfgifu – mother of

Edward born 1003

Goda born 1005

Alfred

EALDORMEN

Ælfric (of Hampshire – Kent, Sussex, Surrey, Berkshire and Wiltshire)

Ælfhelm (of Northumbria – his sons, Wulfheah and Ufegat)

Leofsige (of the East Saxons – East Anglia and Essex)

Leofwine (of the Hwicce – whole of Mercia on occasion)

Eadric (of the Mercians)

Wulfric (Eadric's commended man)

Ulfcytel of the East Angles (from 1004 marries Wulfhilda – king's daughter)

Uhtred (of Northumbria)

Æthelmaer, son of Ealdorman Æthelweard of the Western Provinces – not made an ealdorman on his father's death

Pallig of Denmark

HOLY MEN

Archbishop Ælfric of Canterbury

Bishop Wulfstan of York, London and Worcester

Godwine, Bishop of Lichfield

Bishop Ælfheah of Winchester

LEOFWINE'S HOUSEHOLD

Wulfstan (commended man and war leader)

Horic (commended man and second in command); his wife, Agata

Oscetel (part of the warband/household troop)

Brithelm (part of the warband/household troop) (dead at the Battle of Strathclyde)

Wulfsige (part of the warband/household troop)

Lyfing (part of the warband/household troop)

Ælfhun (part of the warband/household troop)

Wighard (part of the warband/household troop)

Leofgar (part of the warband/household troop)

Ælfric (captain of his ship)

Finn (Olaf's former scribe, now a member of Leofwine's household)

Hunter (Leofwine's hound – female – dies AD1003)

Hammer (Leofwine's hound – male)

RAIDERS AND KINGS

Olaf Tryggvason of Norway (King of Norway dies c.999 at The Battle of Svoldor)

Swein of Denmark (King of Denmark and Norway)

Jarl Erik (his commander/ally)

Thorkell the Tall (his commander/ally)

Duke Richard II of Normandy (Emma's brother)

Sigurd (Jarl of Orkney, Shetlands and Manx)

Llewelyn (King of Powys)

Ulf (Swein's man and leader of the force that attacks Queen Emma)

HISTORICAL NOTES

Leofwine is not mentioned in the Anglo-Saxon Chronicle (ASC) for the period of this novel – an absence I find very interesting. This could simply be that he 'fits' none of the required traits in Æthelred's unruly ealdormen to require a mention in the ASC – unlike Eadric he doesn't carry the blame for many of the king's actions; unlike Ælfric he's not incapable of defeating the Raiders; unlike Leofsige he doesn't partake in murder; nor is he murdered as Ælfhelm is – and yet as the charter evidence attests he was a powerful figure at the king's witan, and perhaps, one who simply did as he was told to keep his nose clean.

I've suggested tentatively, and to arouse some debate, that I think the ASC may have undergone some revision at a later date – with the bias of future events and kings affecting what is and what isn't known about this specific period of the early eleventh century. While this is playing devil's advocate it may account for Leofwine's exclusion for a number of reasons – both negative and positive – but I'll elaborate further along in Leofwine's story.

Due to the murky nature of the titles ascribed to Leofwine and to Eadric it's almost impossible to decipher what happened in Mercia and the lands of the Hwicce (a part of Mercia based around Gloucestershire) during this period of time. Ealdormen, unlike the later earls of the medieval period, were not synonymous with the areas they 'ruled' for their king – they were ealdormen for the respective 'people' or 'ancient tribes' of an area, not the area itself (although Kent does buck this trend). This is not an easy concept to understand, and as it has an implication for land holdings it becomes more difficult as well – the ealdormen may have held land on their own in the areas they 'ruled', but much of it was in the gift of the king and he would reclaim it as part of the ealdordom as soon as there were changes in whoever held the position.

In this novel, Leofwine's presence must be an inferred one at the king's court rather than a known fact, and much is highly fictional, as are the characters and attributes of the men and women in these pages.

Later novels in the series are based more on the 'accepted' facts of Æthelred II's reign but even these are still subject to constant revision. The history of Anglo-Saxon England is no more set in stone than the majority of buildings they erected in wood, wattle and daub, and even some of those 'facts' can be interpreted in a variety of ways.

This novel has been extensively edited to fit with the series of novels I've written about Lady Elfrida, the king's mother. (The First Queen of England Trilogy and The King's Mother Trilogy). While the essence of the story hasn't changed, a few events have been added to ensure that the relationship between Leofwine and Lady Elfrida (as far as I know, an entirely factious one) gains the prominence that has previously been inferred.

ABOUT THE AUTHOR

I'M AN AUTHOR OF HISTORICAL FICTION (EARLY ENGLISH, Vikings and the British Isles as a whole before the Norman Conquest) and fantasy (Viking age/dragon-themed), born in the old Mercian kingdom at some point since AD1066.

I like to write. You've been warned!

Find me at mjporterauthor.com. mjporterauthor.blog and @coloursofunison on twitter.

I have a monthly newsletter, which can be joined via my website. Once signed up, readers can opt into a weekly email reminder containing special offers.

facebook.com/mjporterauthor
twitter.com/coloursofunison
instagram.com/m_j_porter
patreon.com/MJPorter
bookbub.com/authors/mj-porter
tiktok.com/@mjporterauthor

BOOKS BY M J PORTER (IN CHRONOLOGICAL, NOT PUBLISHING ORDER)

Gods and Kings Series (seventh century Britain)

Pagan Warrior

Pagan King

Warrior King

The Eagle of Mercia Chronicles

Son of Mercia

Wolf of Mercia

Warrior of Mercia

Eagle of Mercia

Protector of Mercia

The Mercian Ninth Century

Coelwulf's Company, stories from before The Last King

The Last King

The Last Warrior

The Last Horse

The Last Enemy

The Last Sword

The Last Shield

The Last Seven

The Tenth Century

The Lady of Mercia's Daughter

A Conspiracy of Kings (the sequel to The Lady of Mercia's Daughter)

Kingmaker

The King's Daughter

The Brunanburh Series

King of Kings

Kings of War

The Mercian Brexit (can be read as a prequel to The First Queen of England)

The First Queen of England (The story of Lady Elfrida) (tenth century England)

The First Queen of England Part 2

The First Queen of England Part 3

The King's Mother (The continuing story of Lady Elfrida)

The Queen Dowager

Once A Queen

The Earls of Mercia

The Earl of Mercia's Father

The Danish King's Enemy

Swein: The Danish King (side story)

Northman Part 1

Northman Part 2

Cnut: The Conqueror (full-length side story)

Wulfstan: An Anglo-Saxon Thegn (side story)

The King's Earl

The Earl of Mercia

The English Earl

The Earl's King

Viking King

The English King

The King's Brother

Lady Estrid (a novel of eleventh-century Denmark) Can be read as a side to The Earls of Mercia series

Fantasy

The Dragon of Unison

Hidden Dragon

Dragon Gone

Dragon Alone

Dragon Ally

Dragon Lost

Dragon Bond

As JE Porter

The Innkeeper (standalone)

20th Century Mysteries

The Erdington Mysteries

The Custard Corpses – a delicious 1940s mystery (audio book now available)

The Automobile Assassination (sequel to The Custard Corpses)

Cragside – a 1930s murder mystery (standalone)

Made in United States
North Haven, CT
23 August 2023